Lost Prince

Gregory Gourlay

Dedication

To the people who live in the land above the clouds.

Chapter One
Afghanistan

The four men in U.S. Army combat uniforms stumbled out of the ravine, and trundled through the orderly rows of pomegranate trees at a tired run. Two of them supported a wounded man between them. They halted at the edge of the orchard to quickly scan the stretch of open ground just ahead. Beyond was the extraction place, behind a tumbled down mud brick wall. Camel dung fouled the ground amidst a scattering of aromatic rosemary bushes.

"Go! Go!" panted one of them, a short, black man with sweat rolling down his face in little rivers. "I'll hang on here. Just get on that radio."

He slipped a few yards to one side and sank down onto his belly behind a fruit tree.

Garrick Connolly nodded gratefully in the black man's direction, relief evident on his square, sub-nosed features that someone had taken charge and was making decisions now that the officer was dead. He moved onward without speaking, carrying the wounded man with his remaining comrade.

The wounded man's right leg dangled horribly. A piece of bone, jagged and gleaming white in the hot sunlight, had erupted through the skin of his thigh. A gobbet of flesh appeared set to fall off.

He was unconscious, but when they fell sprawling on a patch of slippery camel dung, a horrible, bubbling scream issued from his throat.

"Ahhh!"

The other man, Robert Maguire, a tall, weedy youth from South Carolina known simply as "Molly," scrabbled backwards in quick revulsion.

His eyes looked as agitated and unpredictable as storm scud. His big, under-slung jaw quivered like a baby's set to cry."Sheeeit!" he spewed, despising his wounded friend for his suffering, and for adding to their danger.

Garrick Connolly eyed him disgustedly. "Go ahead," he growled. "Get that radio working. I'll carry him."

"Yeah, man. Shore." Molly licked his lips appreciatively at the offer. He darted a glance at the pomegranate orchard to the rear, then left, his skinny body gliding across the dry Afghan ground as quick and as noiseless as a snake.

Grunting softly, Garrick got the injured man up onto his back. In his early twenties, slim-hipped and wide-shouldered, Garrick carried the load easily. With slow, careful movements to ease the wounded man's injuries, he worked his way along the path Molly had taken.

Molly's voice on the radio drifted in, giving their situation, the words tumbling out. "We got mortared," Molly babbled, "got our shit scattered, only four of us left–one hurt bad. Hajis coming up fast. Require extraction soonest! Repeat, soonest!" He gave their position. "Do you read that? Ovah."

"That's a Roger, good buddy. Ten minutes."

Molly threw himself to the ground, flinging sweat from his face. A soft noise sounded and Garrick appeared. He lowered the wounded man gently to the ground.

"Choppah's comin'," Molly blurted.

"I heard. Thank Christ!"

Molly kept staring at him. "What'cha think?" he shrilled.

Garrick's soft hazel eyes, his one truly beautiful feature, narrowed into anxious slits at these signs of panic, and they tightened further when he looked to the wounded man painting crimson patterns on a patch of sparse grass with blood from his smashed leg. It was their responsibility to get him out, and if Molly didn't keep his head....

"You all right?"

"Shore," Molly shot back. But the telltale tremor in his lantern jaw was back, so Garrick knew he was lying.

Nothing in boot camp, or in advanced individual training, could possibly prepare a soldier for the shock of his first firefight. The realization that enemy soldiers were actually intent on killing you. *Killing you!* He winced, hearing again the evil sound mortar rounds make leaving the firing tubes–*phafft, phafft*–and the shattering *karrumpp* as the shells sent shrapnel and stones and dirt winging in all directions.

A spine of rock slanted down, providing a narrow place for them to shelter behind, the broken mud-brick wall offered some small protection also. Garrick squatted in the meager shelter and waited. He placed a smoke grenade close at hand, and removed the safety clip from a fragmentation grenade. Then, he fell to checking his rifle with nervous fingers for something to do. Long minutes went by. A soft breeze arrived, fanning his cheek and teasing his nostrils with the combined scent of camel dung and rosemary.

"When's Simpson coming?" he wondered aloud, referring to the black soldier at the pomegranate orchard. "He should pull back. We're gonna be outta here soon."

As if in answer to his question, a lone rifle shot cracked, sounding like one of the World War Two vintage .303s the Taliban sometimes used for longer range work. Garrick's stomach jumped ever so gently. An eternity dragged by, then a recognizable three round burst from a M4 carbine erupted. That would be Simpson.

Garrick crept forward to peer over the ruined wall. Deadly sparkles of light twinkled and buzzed through the orchard. Kalashnikov 47s...the Taliban confirming their arrival. Further bursts and a few bright red pomegranate flowers drifted to the ground.

The M4 abruptly ceased chattering. Five endless minutes of silence passed.

"Gawd! Simpson must be hit," Garrick rasped, unsure what to do. "Whadd'ya think?" he fired helplessly at Molly. "Should we go back and check it out?"

But one sideways glance at Molly and he knew the South Carolinian wasn't going anywhere–his jaw wobbled, his eyes were jammed shut as if trying to keep out what was happening. He looked as unstable as the desert wind.

His face tight, Garrick scanned the horizon. Finally...there...one...no two dots in the hot, blue sky. He set off the smoke grenade to guide them in, bilious green smoke adding a surreal aspect to the chaos. The radio crackled as the pilot demanded confirmation of the smoke color. Garrick grabbed the radio and gave the confirmation.

Chump-chump-chump!

The helicopter, a Chinook, loomed larger, escorted by an Apache attack helicopter.

Chump-chump-chump!

A burst of gunfire erupted from the ravine. The Apache swung its belly and, opening up its 30mm guns, it poured round after round into the gullies and rocks. The bite of "the mosquito," the Taliban's name for the Apache, is lethal.

The noise became deafening.

"Something's happened to Simpson," Garrick shouted above the din. "We gotta go see."

"Shut the fuck up, Connolly." Molly's eyes were open now, staring wildly about. "The choppah's heah–I'm gittin' out."

A deadly stream parted the air, buzzing past just above their heads and flattening them to the ground. They lay there face to face, like lovers a little apart after love-making. The backs and armpits and crotches of both men were soggy with dirt-sweat, but as Garrick watched, a fresh wet stain spread over the other man's crotch.

Jesus! He's pissed his pants, he realized in horror.

Guilt flooded into him for witnessing this. He blinked his eyes slowly once or twice in confusion, hating Molly for doing this in front of him.

He forced his mind back to Simpson. Was it worth going back?

Fire from the gullies sliced up the very air and Simpson had been quiet a long time.

"Here the choppah," Molly babbled.

Garrick didn't look up. He was still trying to decide what to do about Simpson.

The big Chinook swept in low, AK-47 rounds from the Taliban rattling the ship's sides. It halted by them, not quite touching the ground.

A teen-age private manning one of the mini-guns showed his pimpled face in the open crew door on the starboard side. "C'mon. C'mon," he screamed. "They're shooting hell out of us." Bringing his gun to bear, he fired burst after burst. "Tango bastards! Bastards!"

4

Molly bolted for the chopper. Garrick stooped to help the man on the ground, then sat back, stunned, as the man's head exploded. Popped like a ripe grape. Evil-looking matter spattered Garrick's front and slimed his arms.

For a moment he remained stuck on his haunches, gaping at the thing on the ground with a smashed pumpkin for a head.

"C'mon," screamed the gunner.

Garrick sprinted through the green smoke in a crouching run.

"Let's go," the gunner yelled into his mike to the pilot. Bits and pieces from the hatchway pinged off his helmet. Through the crew door, Garrick saw the Apache slide over the orchard seeking the fourth soldier, Simpson. They began to lift off. "Let's go," the gunner yelled again. He swung his machine gun around. "Bastards! Bastards!"

Not ten seconds later, the roar of his mini-gun crashed into stillness. Garrick glanced over quickly. The gunner with the acne problem was slumped over in the ship, a red, dripping hole where his eye used to be.

Molly began to retch, the yellow jet spilling onto his lap.

They left the rocky, broken slopes behind them and swung out over the desert, then over a huge opium field. Beneath them, like a boundless and richly textured carpet, lay a multicolored sea of green and purple and red-white poppies, impossibly beautiful and shining in the sunlight.

A-Stan. Ambush country.

Chapter Two
Coming Home

Garrick saw them as soon as he entered the lobby of the airport in New York City. A group of war protesters holding up signs behind a row of empty boots which, Garrick supposed, represented dead American soldiers. "Christ!" he muttered.

Casting about, he saw a tall, curvaceous woman waving to him. Aunt Diane.

Three boys in their early teens were ogling her, nudging each other and grinning. His aunt, even in middle age, had always provoked this sort of response from the male half of the population, and it still embarrassed Garrick. For the umpteenth time in his life, he wished she wouldn't dress the way she did.

One didn't tell Diane Lofton anything, though. If she chose to wear those skimpy skirts and revealing tops, there wasn't a single thing anyone could do to change her.

A man of Mediterranean appearance, slightly shorter than Diane and with a noticeable paunch, was with her, and also waving. Good, thought Garrick. She'd brought her boyfriend, Harry Alexander, along. He liked Harry.

Diane surged toward him, heavy yet shapely legs showing gaudy expanses of thigh as her skirt rode up. She had a provocative way of walking, as well. It was a progression. Diane Lofton *progressed*, she didn't walk.

One of the three young boys made a remark to his friends that brought a burst of laughter. With a sigh of resignation, Garrick started forward.

A young, bearded war protester with a pock-marked face spotted

Garrick's uniform and edged over to block his path, waving a sign. "Stop this useless war," was splashed on it in blood-red paint.

The protester looked vaguely familiar, swarthy complexion and thin, slightly hooked nose. Like an Afghan or Pakistani thought Garrick. He stood briefly and stared at the man, then shook himself and tried to walk on. Some of the other protesters moved up. One middle-aged woman shouted something about her dead son.

The young, bearded man pulled at Garrick's arm, thrusting his head in.

Nose-to-nose, perhaps fifteen seconds passed. The corners of Garrick's mouth whitened, a tic began to pulse in his forehead.

Feeling lonely all of a sudden, the protester attempted to withdraw. But people were pushing from the rear. He bumped against Garrick's chest.

Garrick drove a fist into his face, smashing cartilage in his nose and sending blood spurting. The man went down, and tried to scuttle clear. Grabbing a handful of long hair, Garrick hauled his head back onto his shoulders. He hit him again, and again, his fist rising and falling, rising and falling.

Hands pulled at him. "Garrick, stop!" Diane screamed. "Harry, make him stop!"

~ * ~

Harry Alexander was waiting outside the apartment when Garrick climbed the stairs with a case of beer under one arm. Wind gusted along the street rattling signs and windows, and tossing Garrick's dark blond hair to give him a fresh, terribly juvenile look.

"Hi, Harry. Slumming it this afternoon?" Harry and Diane lived outside New York, moved away from the dirt and crime of the city center like everyone else who could afford it.

Harry surveyed him shrewdly. "How's it goin', kid?"

Garrick unlocked his door with a noncommittal grunt. Leaving Harry in the front room, he carried the beer to the tiny, cluttered kitchenette.

"I don't know how you can live like this," Harry complained.

"Don't start again, Harry. Goddammit!"

"This place is a hovel, for Chrissake! You had a good stash of money when you left the Army. You can't be broke. Find another place...live like a normal human being." He paused a moment before adding cautiously: "Why not stay at Diane's until you finish college? Drive in each day."

"Diane sent you, didn't she?" Garrick accused swiftly, storming in from the kitchen, a bottle of beer in his hand.

"No, she didn't. But she does worry, you know."

"Then tell her I finished college two weeks ago."

Harry glanced over in surprise. Then, it dawned on him. "So, you quit school again."

Garrick shrugged and said nothing. Opening his bottle, he sat down and dangled a leg over one arm of his chair.

Harry leaned forward, a concerned expression on his face. "What happened? At one time, it seemed you were dying to become a journalist...a writer. And you have the talent for it. The attention span of a grasshopper, maybe, but talented nevertheless. Diane says you have talent. You sure as hell won enough of those short story competitions."

Garrick picked at the label on his bottle.

"You quit school the first time because you decided to go into the Army. What's gone wrong now?"

Garrick took a long swig of beer.

"Don't tell me. Lemme guess. Everyone at the college was an asshole. Right? Everyone but you."

"Bingo. You're a clever sonuvabitch, Harry." Garrick grinned at him. "Calm down–have a bottle of beer."

"No, thanks," Harry muttered, flushing a little as Garrick's grin broadened.

Harry Alexander had given up a lot of things to please Garrick's aunt– beer was one of the things he now professed not to like.

Harry was a business and financial consultant, an effective problem-solver from all accounts. He travelled quite a bit, trouble-shooting for clients in different parts of the world. Diane was a magazine editor and writer. The two had been friends for years, and had even worked together on a project or two.

Along with respect, Garrick felt a sort of kindred feeling toward the man. All through his youthful years, in upstate New York first and later when they moved to the city, he had battled to protect his fledgling manhood from his aunt's overweening femininity. She'd proved a handful for Harry as well.

Let it be said, however, that Garrick Wilson Connolly owed a huge debt to Diane Margaret Lofton.

Despite the years of low-intensity warfare between nephew and aunt, she had done for him, by God. With his father gone–only the devil knew where–and his mother dead at the incredibly young age of thirty-two from a car accident, unruly, tousle-headed Garrick would've had no boyhood at all except for her.

Because she'd done for him, and because she was the only family he'd ever really known, he loved her in the way any boy loves his mother.

He'd never told her so, though. Not in those words. She made it too difficult to get them out. And also, Garrick had always been an introspective type, boy and man. So tight-lipped he hadn't even told her he was joining the Army. He'd just left her with Harry and run off to war.

Under cover of guzzling his beer, he cast the paunchy man opposite a covert glance. Harry Alexander was Greek-American, his name Anglicized from the impossible-to-pronounce original, your archetypal, short Mediterranean type. A bit greasy-looking, too, it had to be admitted. And Diane Lofton was...well...Diane Lofton.

Somewhat guiltily, for Garrick liked Harry, he wondered what his aunt saw in him.

Leaning forward, he asked: "Why haven't you and Diane married by now?" When Harry shifted uncomfortably, he chuckled. "I don't blame you for taking your time. Marriage is a big decision. And frankly, as a wife she'd scare the hell out of me."

Harry managed a brief smile.

"I'll tell you something else. She's a helluva woman, but I sure wouldn't marry her if I had to give up drinking beer."

"Stow the comedy routine," Harry growled. "Look here. What're you going to do now? You don't have exactly the right qualities to make a good insurance salesman, or stockbroker...or...." His expression softened then, and his voice dropped off in a kindly way. "I know the war was tough–"

"Stop, Harry! Don't get into that shit."

9

Harry shook his head stubbornly. "On 9/11, this city...country...was attacked by terrorists, so you figured you had to sign up. Okay, I can get that...you weren't the only one who felt that way. But you had some crazy, fool notion it was gonna be like cowboys and Indians...or like jumping on a horse and going off on the Crusades. Well, it was never going to be that way. Not at all."

Garrick fixed on the wall above the older man's head. The wind outside had picked up, clearly heard inside the apartment; the window made little, nervous sounds.

Harry was silent a moment, thinking, then said, "I'm going to South America in a few days. Business trip. A couple of weeks probably...straightening out some problems for a few clients. I can use an assistant, someone to write things up, do background stuff...reports. How 'bout it? Wanna come with me?"

"I'm not a kid anymore. Don't offer me handouts."

"You sure act like a kid at times. Look, you'd probably get your travel expenses and that's all–"

"Did Diane put you up to this?"

"She doesn't even know about it. What do you say?"

Garrick was fixed on the wall again. The wind tore at the window, trying to get in, like storms on the Afghan desert do. It carried pictures and sounds with it. Disturbing pictures and sounds that mounted his shoulder and sat there, unbidden and unwanted.

"Harry?" he murmured.

"Yeah, kid?"

"God screwed up, man."

Harry said nothing, just waited.

"Know what pissed me off 'bout 'Stan? Really pissed me off?"

"What's that, kid?" Harry said gently.

"We never got to really win the war."

Chapter Three
Slade

Two men crouched in a patch of thorny, green tola bushes, in the midst of a bulbous, spiny forest. Giant cactuses, like heavy-branched trees, littered the bleak Andean plain in every direction. Under the glimmer of a cold half-moon, they loomed even larger; blurred images from another world.

A faint noise sounded when the shorter, stouter man shifted slightly to rearrange cramped limbs. He stopped when his companion seized his arm in a steely grip of warning.

A murmur of voices floated across to them. Two other men stood by an automobile some fifty yards off. The automobile's headlights bouncing along the dirt track, followed by the purr of its engine, had invaded the utter stillness of this Bolivian plateau about an hour earlier. Until then, the watcher with the iron grip, a tall, lean, youthful man, had almost come to believe there were no other living things on the planet. So perfect had been the hush.

Cold, shivering minutes stretched. The moon left the sky, the eastern horizon gradually greyed and displayed the first timid smear of color. Birdsong was heard. A chinchilla, shy and furry as a rabbit kitten, headed home to a rocky ravine after a night of foraging. Around the spectacular forty foot flower spike of an ancient giant puya, a bromeliad plant, a number of finches fluttered.

The coming of the sun had once again coaxed life into the harsh highlands.

Now the car was clearly seen–a grey Mercedes–as were the two men standing by it. The car was parked facing a gravelled, private airstrip.

The tall watcher's flat, metal-grey eyes widened in pleasure–the posture of the men by the car was so relaxed as to be casual. A walk-in job, he congratulated himself, running fingers through his short, black hair in satisfaction. Thin lips parted in a fleeting grin that bared square, very white teeth.

One of the men by the car, a burly, bearded fellow with the lumbering gait of a bear, had stepped off to one side to relieve himself when the airplane was heard, the sound travelling an incredible distance through the clean, thin atmosphere. A speck in the sky grew steadily larger.

As the big, silver bird hurtled closer, the tall watcher placed a finger on one wrist, timing his pulse rate. He paused for a moment of concentration, and listened intently as a series of precisely-spaced sounds began inside his head.

Tick-tick-tick....

It was a trick on himself he employed at will. And as always, the perfect rhythm calmed him. In mere seconds, his pulse rate slowed to normal and he could have been simply anticipating a stroll in the countryside.

The aircraft touched down in a whirlwind of dust and taxied swiftly forward.

It was time! The watcher searched the face of his friend, a Bolivian in his early thirties named Oscar Blacut, and saw that his dough-boy, ivory-skinned features were tense, but not fearful. Good! He was a tough, steady man, in spite of his bland exterior.

Donning masks of the sort seen at Andean fiestas and religious festivals, they crept forward. Now, while everyone concentrated on the landing.

Near the edge of the landing strip, the watcher paused for another second or two of concentration.

Tick-tick-tick....

The pilot shut off the plane and got out.

"Listo—ready?" the watcher asked Blacut.

At Blacut's nod, they parted the last of the bushes and launched a sprint.

Blacut ran heavily, putting big feet down hard. His taller, leaner companion went on the balls of his feet, in a curious dancing motion that covered the ground with deceptive speed.

A pistol in his fist, he was on the three men at the plane before they knew what was happening.

"Suave–softly," he warned.

They gaped, like open-mouthed goldfish, at the creature in a devil's mask who seemed to have dropped from the clouds.

Blacut rumbled up, brandishing a shotgun. Those twin black circles, held in steady hands, had tremendous powers of intimidation. Seeing the stunned expressions on the faces of the others, the man with the pistol almost burst out laughing.

"On the ground. On the ground. Now! Now!" Blacut roared in guttural Spanish.

The man in the devil's mask searched them for guns and threw the weapons he found across the strip into the bushes. Then, he clambered inside the plane.

He came back out immediately and went to the pilot. "The keys, man," he demanded in Spanish. "I'm taking the plane."

But the pilot had recovered his composure. "Show me how good you are," he said, a sneer splitting his round, fat face. "Take her without the keys. Hot wire her."

"Don't think I couldn't. I hate wasting time, though. Gimme the keys."

The pilot was either amazingly brave or a fool. He affected not to have heard.

"You have two choices! You can live or die! The keys!"

The pilot remained mute and motionless.

"Deme–gimme," the man rapped at Blacut. They traded weapons. He slammed the heavy butt of the shotgun down on the inside of the pilot's fleshy thigh, and jammed the barrels under his nose. "You want to die for someone else's money?"

His face twisted in pain, the pilot slowly moved his hand to his pants' pocket.

Burr-r-r

A car was coming. The pilot stayed his hand. It was clear now why he had stalled.

"Slade! Car's coming!" Blacut burst out.

At the sound of his name, the man in the devil's mask whirled on his

13

partner. "Shut up, fool," he hissed.

The mechanical burr became a double sound. Two cars! Jesus!

Slade snapped his fingers at the pilot. "The keys."

"Too late, amigo," the pilot grinned from behind the gun barrels. "You'd never get her turned around and up in time."

"Vamonos. Vamonos," Blacut shouted hoarsely.

Two big, late model cars closed in. One of them skidded out across the long, spiky ichu grass of the plain, greasy with dew. It dodged a huge cactus, straightened, and shot in from the side.

Blacut blazed away briefly at the car, then bolted for the far side of the strip. The men on the ground stirred. "Suave," Slade warned, sweeping the shotgun in a menacing arc.

The pilot laughed at him. "You screwed up, amigo."

Slade drove the gun butt into his face, punching out teeth and smashing lips. A bubbling sound replaced the pilot's laughter. Then, before the others could move, he was gone, racing after Blacut's rapidly disappearing figure.

He'd waited almost too long. An automatic pistol stitched holes in the dirt at his heels. Ahead, Blacut lunged into the bushes and vanished.

With a last burst, Slade made it also, ditching his mask and shotgun and veering off on an angle as soon as he was inside cover. The automatic pistol carved a path along his original route, cutting twisted branches from the tola bushes, and sending tiny, green leaves floating into the air. A cactus was reduced to a pulp.

Running parallel to the airstrip, bent over, chest heaving, Slade drew away from the barrage. Then, he turned at right angles to the strip and ran. He kept running long after the sounds of pursuit died away behind him.

Blacut was at their meeting place ahead of him; a secluded, rocky defile in a jumble of swelling hills. The Bolivian lay slumped against a rock, his smooth, round face red with exertion and dripping with sweat.

Slade stalked forward, quivering with fury. "You used my name, fool! Now they know who we are!"

~ * ~

The whore waited patiently while Slade dressed, her short, blocky, naked body gone slack, like a work animal at rest. He counted out her money on the table beside the rumpled bed, but when she reached for it his hand closed over the notes.

"Bring my jacket," he told her.

The whore nodded dully, and stumped across the room to where his coat hung over a chair. She didn't want to anger him. This man had been here for two days and owed, what was to her, a great deal of money. Besides, she was a little afraid of him.

Slade rubbed his jaw in irritation. He was short of money, and now that he was finished with the whore he was reluctant to pay her. He'd come here only because he needed a safe place to stay and this was the safest place he could think of.

For a moment, he considered stiffing her. The dingy room was poorly lit. A single, naked bulb of low wattage dangling from the ceiling kept the room in perpetual twilight. He could palm some of the money, he thought, and then deal with any arguments later. The bouncer-pimp who slept in a dirty cubbyhole of a room next door did not concern him.

"Señor."

Too late. She was back with his jacket. She'd had a Caesarean section once, and in the soft light, the wide, zipper-like scar stretching toward her belly button faded into a configuration of blurred, black lines. A hint of her pissy, musky woman smell hung about. On impulse, he leaned closer to her scarred crotch, and then sat back laughing softly.

"Bien," he said, handing her the money.

She counted it swiftly, holding it up to the naked bulb, before shrugging into her own clothes. Funnily enough, Slade felt a little sense of satisfaction as she tucked the money into her brassiere and left the room.

There are some things a man just does not do, he mused. *Cheating a whore is one of them.*

Also, the trouble he would have caused himself was not worth the money. He prided himself on self-discipline, and his restraint on this occasion pleased him.

Removing his pistol from an inside pocket of the jacket, he tucked it into his belt behind his back, slipped the jacket on and followed her from the room.

Outside the door, he stood quietly for a minute or two, listening. The whore had disappeared. A low murmur of voices came from the room where the pimp stayed. She must be in there with him.

A door slammed on the floor above. Someone began walking toward the stairs. Slade strode quickly down the short hall and out the door. He went five paces to the corner of the building and entered the shadows there.

Seconds later, a man, probably a customer, left the house and crossed the street to a car. He started it up, switched the lights on, and made his careful way around the worst of the mud holes that made this street, and others like it in La Paz, a nightmare to drive on. At the nearest corner, he turned and drove away.

He left behind a darkened, quiet street in Bolivia's main city, the chaotic and over-crowded urban center that filled the bowl and climbed the slopes of the spectacular ravine two miles above sea level. At this hour, few people were about.

Slade moved off, zipping his coat up against the chill.

He climbed steadily up and down the narrow, hilly streets, past a series of long, low buildings and dark-walled tenements, his lungs sucking greedily on the thin air. After fifteen minutes or so, he came abreast of a bar on the opposite side of the street with a mud-spattered sign hanging out over the sidewalk, and stopped and waited. After watching the place for several minutes and seeing nothing amiss, he crossed the street and went inside.

This bar was not likely to be frequented by the people he wished to avoid, but he stayed out of the light by the door just the same while his small, grey eyes swept the noisy room, crowded with Indians and Mestizos drinking, and chewing the ever-present coca leaves. A careful man, he left little to chance.

A faintly unclean odor permeated the room. His mouth puckered briefly in distaste. He was a clean man, without being fastidious about it, and the lack of hygiene in the Andean cities constantly annoyed him.

He spotted Oscar Blacut at a rear table talking to a hook-nosed Indian dressed in a bright-red, not-too-clean shirt. That Indian would be Paco, the man he and Blacut were here to meet. Slade headed for their table, working his way, loose-limbed and graceful, through the crowd.

As he approached, Blacut gestured in his direction. "Amigo mio," he explained. "The one I told you about."

"Gringo," Paco stated in instant hostility, his voice jerky and nasal. He was a short, wiry man maybe forty years of age.

Slade smiled coldly. He seated himself where he could face the door and held out his hand. "My name is Slade," he offered in Spanish, adding, "Yes, I'm Gringo, American."

There was no point in pretending otherwise. Whether this man disliked Americans or not, Blacut would've told the fellow at least that much about him. Besides, he *looked* American and, while his Spanish was fluent, his accent clearly announced his nationality.

"Slade what?" Paco demanded.

Slade merely smiled thinly again, and shook his head.

Paco's own head moved about continually, spasmodically. His sloe-black eyes darted back and forth between the two men opposite him. The movements seemed more than signals of distrust, however, at times appearing poorly coordinated. Slade wondered what sort of disorder he suffered from.

"Do you want to drink something?" Blacut asked him.

"Claro--ron, sure–rum," Paco answered. His head twitched left, his eyes shot right.

With drinks in front of them, Blacut opened discussion. "Paco has a car and wants to go to Peru to do some business," he told Slade. "But he's broke right now, so I suggested we go together. We use his car, and in return we give him some money." He gave a Latin shrug of his meaty shoulders. "Eso es. We help each other."

Blacut had told Slade already about this man–a small time thief, an occasional worker in the mines, and a brawler of note. He had an affinity for the blade, which had caused him to flee Peru a couple of months back, after stabbing a fellow worker in a fight at a mine where he was working.

According to Blacut, Paco was *poco loco*, a little crazy. He was eager to get back to Peru, however, and he'd an old car to take them to the border. For a small payment they could accompany him. *And no questions asked.*

Slade's mouth puckered irritably. It annoyed him beyond measure to have to rely on someone like Paco. And all because things had gone so stupidly wrong at the airstrip a week ago. For a man like Slade, who organized and planned his way through life, it was almost too much to bear.

"Why're you going to Peru?" he challenged, letting go of his self-control for once. "I heard you had problems there a while back. You had to run back here to Bolivia, no?"

A fire flared up in Paco's black eyes. "First you tell me something," he flung back. "What's a puto Gringo doing in La Paz?" He delivered a high-pitched giggle. Twitch. Twitch. A second giggle, and one of his hands vanished under the table.

Slade saw the hand go. He has a knife there, he decided at once. A fight was the last thing the American wanted, so he widened his slash of a mouth into a level smile and drawled, "I'm trying to make a living, Paco. Just like everyone else."

"Suave, Paco," Blacut intervened. "Softly, softly. My friend meant no offense."

"I don't trust Gringos," Paco insisted stubbornly, his voice surly. "Tell me more of this one."

The Bolivian hesitated. This was awkward. He was unsure how much the Indian already knew and the fewer people aware of his and Slade's situation the better. They needed his help, however, so he leaned across the table and spoke to him in a lowered voice. "My friend and I worked for the same...er...employers, off and on, for about a year. He is a good pilot. I organized shipments...various cargoes, which he flew to the United States and to other countries."

"Then a week ago you became greedy," Paco giggled. "And now your *employers* are angry. You hide like *zorros*, foxes, and you ask my help because you're desperate."

Blacut's round, smooth face flushed angrily. Paco gave a foxy grin, pleased with himself. His mood had changed, quickly and easily.

"Where'd you hear this?" Blacut hissed.

"Oh, here and there. When you were so eager to leave the country, I naturally wondered why. And when you insisted I say nothing to anyone, I made inquiries around. Discreet inquiries, you understand."

18

His pleased grin broadened. "Paco can find out anything."

The Bolivian leaned closer, inches from the Indian's big, hooked nose. "Listen to me, Indio. If you have spoken to *anyone* regarding our whereabouts, I'll...."

This left Paco unperturbed. He shrugged in a deprecating manner. "I've spoken to no one. I listened. I did not speak."

Blacut slumped back in his chair, a sour expression twisting his face. "Beautiful!" he spat petulantly. "Just beautiful! I suppose all La Paz knows of us by now."

"If all La Paz knows, it's because a fool blurted out my name," Slade snapped. "Of course they know who we are. How in hell can they not know?"

Blacut fidgeted uncomfortably, falling finally into a glum silence. He formed wet rings on the table with his liquor glass and ventured nothing more.

Slade sat back in his chair. "Now that we've all been fully introduced, maybe we can make some plans."

"Is it true you're a pilot?" Paco asked him.

"Yes, it is."

Paco's hidden hand appeared back on the table. He thought for a moment, then said, "The mine I worked at in Peru used a plane to fly in their payroll every month. A big mine, very rich–copper mainly, and some silver. The silver is flown out by the same plane." He glanced speculatively at Slade. "An inviting prospect, Señor. A big payroll, a cargo of silver, and a plane to fly away in. Like winning the lottery, eh?"

"Not interested. My friend and I wish your assistance in leaving Bolivia. That is all. We'll pay you for this, of course–as Blacut has promised. I've no interest in robbing mines or mine payrolls."

The Indian would not give up easily, however, and went into details of the mine's layout in a way that showed he'd pondered the situation a great deal.

Idly, Slade wondered if the man intended to try to rob the mine on his own. It seemed so. He found that amusing. The clownish fellow was bound to bungle it, and wind up twitching and giggling in a Peruvian jail for his efforts.

"You have friends in Peru?" he asked, not really caring. "Try that job

19

alone and you'll get caught."

Paco twitched furiously, so Slade again spoke soothingly to him: "I merely caution you. It sounds a difficult job for one man, and I've heard that Peruvian jails are most unpleasant. I wouldn't like to see you get caught, my friend."

"We must leave La Paz immediately," Blacut broke in impatiently, with a nervous glance toward the door. "Quietly. By a back route." He twirled the last of the liquor in his glass and drained it.

"Claro," agreed Slade. He pushed his own glass to one side. It had remained untouched all this time.

Paco nodded assent, then motioned toward the full glass of rum. "Finish your drink, Piloto. Then we'll go."

Slade stood up. "I never drink when I'm working," he said.

Chapter Four
Puno

A cold wind, with an edge like a flint-bladed knife, furrowed the leaden waters of Lake Titicaca, the legendary birthplace of the Incas. Titicaca means "rock of lead" in one native language, Quechua, and "rock of the puma" in another, Aymara.

Slade leaned an elbow on the rail of the steamer in a tourist's pose. With a peaked cap shielding his upper face, he gazed at the snowy spine of mountains, the *Cordillera Real*, shimmering above the high, blue plateau they had just left. When the steamer twisted in the chop, he heaved himself upright, hand on the rail to steady himself, and drew in long drafts of the rarefied air.

A manic laugh erupted beside him. "You are not a man like I am," Paco sneered.

Slade made no comment. Paco was an Aymara, a race well adapted to the lofty, wind-swept *altiplano.* If he considered that made him superior in some way to the American, Slade didn't care enough to argue. Instead, he looked around for Blacut, and found him in a relaxed stance among a crowd of people on the other side of the vessel. Good. *He attracts no attention. Unlike this fool, Paco.*

The Aymara was upset the two men still showed no interest in his various schemes, the robbing of the copper-silver mine being his pet project.

It was obvious by now he'd helped them leave Bolivia on the expectation they would eventually change their minds and join him. So, with their continued refusal, his sulkiness increased accordingly. In particular, he resented Slade.

"I can *run* on the *puna*,"–the high plateau, he crowed. "On the *puna*, a Gringo finds it difficult even to walk." He ended with a falsetto giggle and a marionette-like twitch.

While conceding he'd handled the Indian poorly, Slade wasted no time on regrets. It was necessary to tolerate him only until they reached the city of Arequipa, in Peru. There, he could separate himself from both of the other two men and fly on to Lima. He must lay his hands on some money soon, and he'd decided that was best accomplished alone.

"We'll be landing soon," he said. "It's better not to be seen together."

Moving away, he resumed his masquerade of tourist by pretending interest in a floating island at the edge of a dense reed brake. The island, constructed of layers of totora reeds, undulated gently on the surface of the wind-roughened lake. A family of Uros Indians–the lake's ancient, original inhabitants–lived there, as their ancestors had for centuries. Outside a reed hut, an elderly man in an old fedora hat played a flute, his music swallowed up by the pounding of the steamer's engines.

A whistle blew, and the incessant hammering lessened. A diesel locomotive hooted piercingly from the shore. They were nearing Puno, the metropolis of the lake, on the Peruvian shore. As the ancient, white vessel headed for her moorings, Slade made his way forward to go through customs alone. If his companions ran into trouble, he wanted no part of it.

A rambling, grey shed served as the immigration and customs office. The official stamped his passport without so much as a glance at him. Slade jammed his cap back onto his head, and walked out the door into brilliant sunshine. Ahead of him, several passengers picked their way through the train yard that lay alongside the wharf. Slade ambled along behind them.

Sprawled half-way up the slopes of the round-topped, treeless hills overlooking the lake, metal roofs sparkling in the sun, lay Puno. This was near the end of the rains and fresh green painted the hills.

In a grassy field one hundred yards from the wharf, by the esplanade that led to town, a small flock of sheep competed for forage with a half-dozen pigs and several Andean seagulls. On the far side of the esplanade, small boats loaded with colorfully-dressed people plied the waters of a green-scummed bay. Local residents being ferried out to the floating islands.

Slade paused here to look back toward the ship. Blacut and Paco approached. The Bolivian strode up, grinning. "No problems with the authorities, eh companero. Hah! These montoneros can barely read and write. They waved us right through."

Slade consulted his watch. It was just past 4:00 P.M. "Take us to the hotel," he directed Paco. "That quiet hotel you spoke of, where you say no one asks questions. Get one room for the three of us. Blacut and I will pay for it. For the next day or two we all stay together."

They went down the esplanade to the football stadium, then turned through the market. It teemed with brown-faced, black-haired people of small stature, many of them barefooted, almost all garbed in colorful woolens and wearing hats. At the stalls, a wide array of articles was on display, everything from kitchen utensils, clothing, writing paper and umbrellas to books and locally grown agricultural produce.

As they pushed through the crowd, the sky darkened and the fluffy clouds took on an ominous tinge. In minutes, the brilliant sunshine disappeared entirely and hail half the size of moth balls bounced off the ground.

Vendors rushed to secure flimsy plastic awnings. People cowered in doorways, watching resignedly as the hail changed to torrential rain. In an instant, the streets became rivers.

The three men huddled in the entrance of a dilapidated restaurant. The rain formed a solid sheet, with no apparent intention of ever stopping. Finally, Blacut suggested running for it–the hotel lay a short block away.

They arrived drenched and cursing.

"Mucha lluvia"–much rain, the emaciated, young man in T-shirt and sneakers observed from the receptionist's table at the end of the gloomy hallway. He gave them a fool's grin.

Slade pulled his hat down nearly to his eyes and waited off to one side as Paco argued with the receptionist. It took a little convincing before he agreed to allow the three men to share two beds in one room.

After a brief haggle over price, he showed them to a room with yellow paint peeling from the walls. He switched the light on, gave the room key to Blacut, and left.

Slade went to the window. It overlooked a solid row of dingy, run-down buildings lining a cobbled street. "Good enough," he said. He removed a change of dry clothing from his bag, shivering as he peeled off wet socks—with the sun somewhere above the clouds, the temperature had fallen off dramatically. "Goddamn country."

~ * ~

After prowling the hotel room for an hour, Paco declared he was going out for a drink. An argument started between him and Blacut.

After observing them for a while, Slade finally announced in his thin-lipped way: "It's nearly dark and the rain has stopped. We may as well go eat."

Paco headed to the door. "Indio," Slade said flatly. "I said eat, not drink. For the next couple of days, we stay together, we stay quiet, and we stay sober. Me entiende?"—understand me.

Laughing loosely, Paco led the way down the hall, yet he avoided Slade's eyes and the icy warning they contained.

They wandered along the narrow, cobbled streets until they found a place to Slade's liking; small and quiet. The local populace who patronized it, concerned with little other than ordinary affairs of life on the harsh altiplano, would forget the three visitors minutes after they'd gone.

Paco insisted on a bottle of liquor. He swigged at it aggressively, straight from the bottle, in deliberate defiance of Slade. Eventually, the effects of the liquor began to show; marionette jerks and sudden hyena laughs followed one another in rapid succession.

When they finished eating and went outside, Paco disappeared. One instant he accompanied them, the next he was gone. Vanished.

It was completely dark by now, with a bite to the thin air. The rain had returned as drizzle. Slade and Blacut hurried here and there searching, breath jetting out in little clouds. They split up to comb the nearby streets. After a half-hour of fruitless searching, Slade tramped back to the hotel in a foul mood.

Blacut sat on one of the beds. He avoided Slade's savage glare.

"Why didn't you say that twitching, brain-damaged bastard was completely goddam crazy?"

"I told you he was loco."

"Poco loco, you said. Poco loco! The sonuvabitch should be in an institution!"

Slade was nearly screaming, his customary coolness lost.

"It was necessary we get out of Bolivia, remember. Who else could I ask?"

Slade pinned him with an unwavering stare, his neat, almost-too-perfect features beaked and cruel.

"What do you want to do?" Blacut asked meekly.

A sudden commotion erupted in the hall, the door sprang open and Paco entered the room, his mouth open in a great, leering grin. Shoving a fresh bottle of liquor under Slade's nose, he shook it defiantly.

"Puto!" snarled Blacut, hurling the all-purpose South American insult.

Paco flung the bottle at him, and leaped across the room.

Taller and considerably heavier than the Indian, Blacut handled him without difficulty, throwing him onto a bed the way one would a child.

Trembling with fury now, as well as drunk, Paco's hand was still quick. A knife appeared as if by magic.

Slade made no move to interfere. He saw the steel flash in the light. And he watched the blade curve in a graceful upward arc.

With a soft sigh–"Ooohh."–the Bolivian sagged to the floor, utter disbelief twisting his features at the knife protruding from his stomach. "Slade," he got out weakly.

Paco's hand darted to the bloodied blade. To pull it free. Quick! Quick!

Slade's foot lashed out. Two well-placed kicks dropped the Indian, writhing, to the floor. Then, searching out pressure points about his head, Slade methodically kicked him to death.

"Gracias a Dios," gasped Blacut. "Good! Good! That loco was going to kill me."

Slade studied the knife plunged to the hilt in Blacut's upper abdomen. A most serious wound. Too serious. Even with medical help he might not make it. The question was academic in any case; calling the authorities was impossible.

He nodded reassuringly to him, however, with a finger to his lips to signal silence. Drawing his pistol from his pocket, he stepped softly to the door and peered out. The hall yawned back emptily at him. He waited a moment longer, listening. Nothing. Fixing the "no molestar" sign on the outside door knob, he closed and locked the door.

"Slade!" Flecks of blood spotted Blacut's lips.

Picking up a pillow and going over to him, Slade thought, *what a great pity.*

"I'm sorry," he said.

In the last seconds before the pillow smothered the life from him, Blacut understood what was about to happen. In that instant, his face registered both terror and astonishment.

"I *am* sorry," Slade whispered to the struggling man beneath the pillow. "I really am. But you see, I have no choice."

His face was a mask revealing neither sorrow nor pleasure. A studied concentration showed, as if he strove to complete an unpleasant task as expeditiously as possible. He continued the pressure for several minutes after Blacut's body went limp, then stood up. He listened carefully once more. Again, no sounds came from the hall.

Closing his eyes to concentrate and placing a finger over a wrist, he sought out a reassuring sound.

Tick-tick-tick....

Perfectly calm now, he sat on the bed to think. Perhaps three or four minutes passed before he rose to his feet, a plan formulated.

He unlocked the window, opened and closed it several times to test the mechanism, and leaned out to examine the ground below. What he found pleased him, for with a grunt of satisfaction he returned to the two dead men and emptied their pockets and bags. He kept the small amount of money he found and burned all identifying papers, bit by bit, with his cigarette lighter. That done, he repacked his own bag, adding a few things of Blacut's he could use.

With his own bag by the window ready to go, his preparations were completed. A long wait stretched ahead of him. He shut off the light and shifted the chair over by the window.

For the next several hours, he sat quietly. Once, he lit a cigarette, but stubbed it out when it left him gasping. Oxygen was too scarce at this altitude to permit smoking.

Below him, up and down the street, the drinking establishments were doing a good trade. Music blared until well after midnight.

Toward morning, a fight exploded on the street. A dozen young Indians, too drunk to do serious damage, flailed away briefly at each other before giving up and departing in different directions. One youth with a bleeding head passed under a street light beneath Slade's window, a friend supporting him. Arm in arm, they slipped their way out of sight, leaving behind a deserted street.

With the arrival of the false dawn near 5:00 A.M., Slade got to his feet and opened the window.

His room was on the second floor–an advantage; windows on the ground floor were barred. Leaning down as far as possible, he dropped his bag. It hit the ground with a soft plop. Easing himself over the sill, he dangled loosely, clinging with one hand while he worked the window closed with the other. Then, hitting the ground on all fours to lessen the shock, he was off into the half-light.

Full dawn found him shivering behind the wall of an unfinished house, one block uphill and in view of the train station on Avenida La Torre. Last evening's precipitation had ended in the form of snow. Slush lay underfoot.

Below, glassy to the horizon, Lake Titicaca shimmered in the sunshine. After the dark, cold night, the morning light was welcome and pleasant, lighting up the hillsides quite prettily, bouncing off house windows and causing them to glisten like diamond shards.

When the ticket office opened, he walked casually down the hill to the grey stone railway station and bought a ticket. Departure time was not for a few hours yet. He must find a safe place to wait until then.

Up the street he saw a crowd moving toward the market. A man went by dressed in a festive costume and wearing a mask with a false beard and moustache. A parade of some kind appeared to be in progress. Excellent!

Slade tagged along with the growing number of colorful, gyrating revellers.

A round-faced Aymara girl, dressed in layers of short, flaring skirts, whirled about swinging a tin fish. She noticed Slade walking nearby and, shy but flirtatious, snatched off her bowler hat to play peekaboo with him.

He forced a pleasant smile onto his slash of a mouth, and even winked at her. Giggling, she ran off to join her friends, long, twin braids of hair bouncing on her back, sliding barefooted through the slush. As she ran, she twirled her tin fish.

Amid the drabness of this lakeside town, the paint-box bright colors of her clothing flashed like the plumage of an exotic bird.

A boy peddling a three-wheeled pedi-cab, a passenger squatting in the cab's big front box, rang a bell to demand passage. Slade moved aside for him. Like everybody else, they were heading toward the *Plaza de Armas*, the town square.

Slade joined the throng, through the open air stalls of Puno's market, smiling friendlily at the people he passed.

At the plaza, swarms of people danced in front of the cathedral, creating a cheery, noisy scene, with a riot of colors competing for attention.

Keeping his peaked cap down low on his face, Slade pretended to enjoy the antics, laughing at the ribald shouts flung into the cold air.

It was perfect cover for him.

Just before train time, he strolled back through the market, walking casually as tourists do. He showed his ticket to the guard at the gate, passed through without incident, crossed the concrete platform, and mounted the steps to "Pullman Car M." Although dingy, the brown and yellow Pullman car was the best accommodation the train offered.

As usual, the train left late, forty-five minutes behind schedule. Gaining speed gradually on the brown-green flat lands outside town, it headed for the valleys that led to the cloud-high puna.

Once away, Slade felt confident enough to visit the buffet car. He sat down at a table and ordered a beer. He'd made it! Exultation welled up inside him.

Slade stayed on a high for hours, enjoying the spectacular vistas as they rattled on to the west. When they stopped at Crucero Alto, half way to Arequipa and five hours along on their journey, a thought struck him. Check-out time at the hotel was 12:00 P.M.

By now, the maid would have tried to enter the room, after wondering why no one responded to her knocks. And any time now, the young receptionist in the T-shirt and sneakers would get inside with the passkey and see the surprise left for him. Enjoying himself hugely, Slade pictured their reaction to what they would find. And...what on earth would they tell the authorities?

A third man had accompanied the two dead men.

"What did he look like?"

"Well...he stayed in the background wearing a hat pulled down low. I couldn't see him very clearly."

"What else can you tell us?"

Just imagining their hapless expressions, he snorted in amusement.

A dark-skinned Puno merchant, going to Arequipa on business with his plump wife and two young, excited daughters, glanced at the man seated opposite and wondered at the self-congratulatory smile on his face.

Chapter Five
The White City

Garrick Connolly looked out over the Plaza de Armas—occupying a full block in the city of Arequipa—as the tour guide, the slender, tallish girl with the startlingly-clear, sea green eyes went through some of the history of "the white city," this urban center of white volcanic stone buildings seven thousand five hundred feet up in the Andean foothills. It was a breezy, sunny day and forty to fifty people, mostly of Indian or Mestizo blood, gathered around the plaza's fountain or sat on the public benches.

"There's a legend," she explained, tossing shoulder-length, black hair, "that the fourth Inca, Mayta Capac, arrived here in the thirteenth century, and that some of his captains, taken with the beauty and mild climate, asked permission to stay. He exclaimed to them, 'Ari quepay,' yes, remain, and hence the city's name, Arequipa."

Her eyebrows arched as she spoke, however, giving the impression she herself did not believe this story. Her face was slightly concave in shape and the disdainful arching of her eyebrows served somehow to soften the hooded profile, reshaping her whole facial structure for an amazing second or two.

"You don't believe the legend?" Harry Alexander asked, standing beside Garrick. As he talked, his pudgy fingers fiddled with his camera.

She flipped a hand. "The great expansion of the Inca Empire didn't begin until two hundred years after Mayta Capac's time. Mayta Capac never left the Cuzco Valley." She spoke in a cool, clipped manner, throwing her head back and squaring her shoulders occasionally.

Her ice maiden style intrigued Garrick. Either she's a cold bitch, he thought, or she's shy and is trying to hide it. He studied her more closely trying to decide which.

"So, what's the real story then? The agency said you're a student of archaeology, an expert on this stuff," Harry persisted.

Garrick smiled. Harry could be a stickler for details.

"It's a charming legend, and people want to believe it...but the fellow was simply a member of the royal clan of Mayta Capac, sent here by a different Supreme Inca in the fifteenth century."

Positioned as she was, head tossed and raven tresses flying in the breeze, she was quite striking. That's the word, Garrick decided, *striking*, not pretty in the usual sense. He struggled to recall her name...Roxana something-or-other...Roxana Carpio. Yes, that was it.

Two elderly British couples on holiday filled out the little group. One of the men asked a question and the history lesson continued.

"Ever notice how stolid the locals are?" Garrick commented to Harry, gesturing toward the Indians on the nearest benches. "Everyone just sits and stares straight ahead in silence."

"Yeah, I noticed that. Their home environment in the mountains is pretty harsh...it leads to a certain stoicism, I guess." He swung his camera about, snapping.

A hand tugged at Garrick's elbow. Glancing down, he saw a ragged boy of about ten.

"Por favor, Señor." The boy held out a grubby hand. Garrick dropped a coin into the opened palm and, when the boy made to leave, he stopped him and added several more. "Gracias, Señor." The boy left wearing a surprised grin.

"He'll be back in a minute with his friends," Harry warned, regarding the younger man with a wry expression.

"So what?"

"But the little urchin was dirty...and his friends will hound you."

"The little bugger looked as though he could use the money," Garrick drawled. "Besides, the coins had germs on them. Bet you never thought of that Harry. I gave the kid germ-laden coins."

"Young Garrick," Harry guffawed. "I swear, I think there's hope for you yet. You show signs of actual maturity." He swung his camera, *click-*

click, aiming at a lean, tough-faced man by the tiered fountain in the center of the plaza.

Garrick glanced in the same direction, gave the fellow a cursory look, and said immediately to himself, *he looks American. An ex-military man, too, by God!* he thought, seeing something in the stranger's bearing that reminded him of the Army.

The fellow swivelled his head slowly around, metal-grey eyes quartering the plaza as if in search of something. He stopped abruptly when he saw the camera, an expression of extreme annoyance flooding his face.

Click-click. Harry snapped him again. The man stepped swiftly behind the fountain. Now, there's a guy who doesn't like being photographed, mused Garrick.

The plaza's pigeons took sudden flight in a whir of grey and white, wheeling and diving in the sunlight, turning as one in the cool air. When they settled again, the man was gone.

Two policemen in green uniforms had just arrived, and were standing idly, surveying the activity in the square with bored expressions. The taller of the two caught sight of Roxana, and his attention lingered. She was stretched upwards, buttocks twitching invitingly, as she pointed out something of interest on the towering, two-steepled cathedral that occupied one entire side of the square.

Then: "Nothing more to see here," she announced shortly. And with that, she struck out across the plaza in a free-swinging, no-nonsense stride, leaving the rest of them to tag along behind.

Her severe demeanor was still in place as she drove the tour van to their hotel an hour later. Garrick waited to catch her eye and, to see what she would do, slipped her a broad wink. Her deep set, sea green eyes widened momentarily in surprise, then flashed angrily. The now-familiar toss of the head followed.

At the hotel, Garrick allowed the others to exit the van ahead of him, then said to her in a lowered voice, "Thanks for the tour. Frankly, though, I found you the most interesting part of the whole day."

Not deigning to reply, she gunned the engine. He barely got the door closed before she took off down the street.

"Sheath your sword, slugger," Harry laughed behind him. "You struck out."

"Stick to taking pictures, Harry. I was just trying to find out if there's really a female under all that ice."

The gardener had just finished raking dead grass from the lawn in front of the hotel and a dozen or so pretty grey doves had their yellow and blacks beaks industriously at work in the aerated soil. Harry unslung his camera. *Click-click.*

"You resembled the Pied Piper at the end there," he said from behind the camera.

"Don't speak in riddles, Harry."

"You had so many kids tagging along after you, at times we couldn't hear what your girlfriend was saying."

"It was a boring tour. At least the kids got something out of it."

A twinkle entered Harry's brown eyes. "That's why you kept giving the coins...and trying out your lousy Spanish on them? Because you were bored? That right?"

"Sure," Garrick drawled. "Why else?"

Chuckling, Harry re-slung his camera. "C'mon, I'll buy you a drink," he said good-naturedly. This brief side trip to Arequipa for some sight-seeing was the last leg of their trip. They were going home in the morning and Harry was looking forward to it.

They crossed the veranda and entered the bar. Inside, they ordered "pisco sours." Garrick sipped his slowly, savoring the sweet-biting flavor of the Peruvian cocktail, and gazed out the window at the late afternoon shadows creeping across the volcanoes that towered over the city. According to Indian legend, they were brothers: Volcan Misti, said to represent the wrath of God, and his two brothers flanking him on either side, Chachani and Pichu-Pichu. At this time of day they changed color, streaks of deep purple painting the spectacular slopes.

Those images married easily with the peacefulness of his immediate surroundings. He stretched his legs out comfortably, glad Harry had brought him along. He'd found South America fascinating.

The trip had been good for him.

Then Harry began to chatter about their return to the States and, without warning, the jaws of a vise reached around him and started to squeeze. A bit desperately, Garrick groped about, trying to analyze the abrupt change of mood.

The war. It always went back to the war. The Army, the war, the 'Stan, the unit. It seemed nothing could adequately replace those reference points in his life.

The war, the 'Stan, the Army, the unit!

Murderous pinpoints of light from mountain passes. Pretty patterns in the clear, dry air.

A family of Afghans trudging along a road with salvaged belongings from a bombed-out village.

Taliban country.

Aw, hell!

"...Lima, tomorrow," Harry was saying. "Then back to the grind Monday. Well, there's worse places than New York..."

At that moment, gazing across the table at the other man's comfortable expression, Garrick Connolly would have given almost anything to be like him. The middle-aged, pot-bellied Greek-American was a man at ease with himself. Not bullied by his feelings as Garrick was.

"...Diane's having a party next week-end," Harry continued. "You should come along. The crowd'll be a bit older than you, but–"

"I've always loved Diane, you know."

Caught completely off guard by Garrick's statement, Harry just stared at him.

Garrick shrugged his shoulders. "The sort of love a boy has for a mother who has always been good to him. Tell her for me, Harry. I've never been able to get the words out."

"Sure, Garry," Harry finally answered.

"She does make some things damn near impossible, you know."

At that, Harry broke out laughing. "You're not telling me anything I didn't figure out a long time ago."

"Harry," Garrick said quickly. "What would you say if I stayed on for a couple of days? By myself, I mean. You don't need for me to go back with you, do you? I mean *need* me.... Christ, you didn't need me in the first place–"

"Cut it out, kid. I'd have been snowed under trying to write up all that

34

stuff."

Garrick smiled wanly. "Thanks, man...and look, umm...I appreciate what you've done for me. I'd just like to stay on a while, that's all.... Do a little thinking. Okay?"

The older man was quiet. Garrick knew what he was thinking–how would Diane react?

"I've really enjoyed myself on this trip. My head's better. Still screwed up, I know. But that's the whole point. I wanna hang on alone...see if I can unscrew it."

Harry fiddled with his glass.

"I'll be along in a week or so."

"Sure, kid," Harry rumbled finally in defeat. On his face were signs of relief, however. This wasn't as bad as some other craziness Garrick might've come up with.

"Everything's gonna be all right. Don't worry. Tell Diane not to worry."

Chapter Six
The Meeting

An ancient taxi wheezed to a stop in front of the hotel. "That'll be my taxi," Harry declared from the veranda. Garrick helped him carry his camera gear and luggage.

"Play it cool, pal," he said, winking cheerfully as they shook hands. But he couldn't hide the concern on his face as the taxi door closed behind him.

Garrick went back to the veranda and ordered a beer. He sipped at it while trying to decide what to do with the day. This was Sunday and Arequipa was abominably quiet on Sundays. The bull fights were on today, though, he recalled, so he finished his beer and struck out down the street.

At one of the few busy corners, he found a battered, multicolored taxi whose driver actually managed to understand his mangled Spanish.

~ * ~

Tents and small trailers sprawled across the flat, sandy fair ground of Cerro July. Makeshift stalls had sprouted here and there, the week-end entrepreneurs at them busily hawking beer and sweetmeats. A man at one stall, bent over a brazier of grilling meat, glanced up expectantly as Garrick approached—one eye was cloudy-blue and sightless, the other lustrous and obsidian.

A tent moved up ahead. Garrick kept his eyes on it and eventually saw that the big, white rectangle was a bull. The size of the animal left him gaping.

At Arequipa's bull fights, bulls fought bulls not matadors. As with boxers, there were different weight categories; this one was definitely *peso pesado*, a heavy-weight.

Surrounded by admirers, yet heedless of the stir he caused, the bull blinked drowsily in the sunshine.

"The bull's name is Misti, this year's champion," a familiar, feminine voice explained in English.

Looking over, Garrick saw the tour guide, Roxana Carpio. Same curved-in face, same measured manner. She accompanied the two elderly British couples who'd been on yesterday's tour. One of the men noticed Garrick and nodded to him.

Roxana turned, offered him the briefest of nods, and then ushered her group inside. Garrick trailed after them to stand close by, in the mass of spectators lining the perimeter of the field.

Casually dressed and wearing wide-brimmed hats, people laughed and chatted. Men swilled beer and walked casually off to urinate against a fence whenever they felt the need. Khaki-shirted, mounted police, long sabers dangling from the saddles, trotted their horses back and forth, keeping spectators in line.

A medium sized, piebald bull appeared, followed soon after by another *mediano*, a brown bull. The brown bull bawled loudly at the sight of the piebald bull, broke free from his handlers, and rumbled across the field with lead ropes trailing from his horns.

Both were named after famous boxers: the piebald bull, Marciano, and the brown bull, Louis. They locked horns with a clash, and heaved back and forth. After five minutes of fierce struggle, Louis began to retreat. After being pushed backwards the entire width of the field, he broke and ran. Ropes still trailing from his horns, he charged directly at the spectators at the far end, scattering them like chaff.

The audience roared approval.

Several more bouts followed before the champion bull, Misti, put in an appearance. A murmur went up as the giant, white beast was led, blinking, to the center of the field.

His opponent, a bull every bit as huge named Tornado, lumbered in, head down, tongue out, heavy feet kicking up dust.

Both bulls stood quietly near to each other, however, showing no desire to fight. A cow in heat was led slowly between them. Another moment or two passed before, as though upon a pre-arranged signal, they swung simultaneously on each other. You heard the *thwack*.

Heads almost brushing the ground, horns locked, mighty neck muscles bulging, for a brief period they seemed perfectly matched. Then Tornado took one small step back, another and another. He was not lacking in bravery, however, and had to be tango-danced, backwards, around the field several times before he finally gave up and lunged for the sidelines.

Throwing his head up in a satisfied bawl, Misti resumed blinking unconcernedly in the sunshine.

Tornado rumbled toward Garrick's section of the crowd.

With people diving wildly for cover, Roxana was jostled, lost her footing and fell. She was up again immediately, but hesitated, unsure in which direction to run.

"Quick," Garrick barked, throwing an arm around her. She began an irritated protest. "Oh, for God's sake," he snapped. Gathering her unceremoniously under his arm, he leapt aside.

Nostrils dripping, eyes rolling, Tornado thundered past.

"Ohhh!" she cried.

Although clearly shaken, she attacked him angrily when he released her. "That wasn't necessary. I was quite able to take care of myself."

"Oh, I see," Garrick drawled sarcastically. "Well, pardon me all over the place, lady."

Her back rigid as a steel bar, she marched over to where the four retired Britons were reassembling, laughing nervously over the scare they'd just had.

Back on the field, Misti's handlers sprayed beer over him, rubbing him down with the cool liquid. Completely content, the bull paid no attention as his happy owner mounted the grandstand to receive the winner's trophy.

Everybody now shuffled for the exit. Roxana and her group had already disappeared. Outside the gate, Garrick made a dive for one of the few taxis available, but lost out in the scramble.

"Hey, there," a voice called above the hubbub. Roxana's slender arm waved from a battered Land Rover. "I can give you a lift to town."

He loped over and got in. "I thought you were mad at me?"

"I can give you a lift," she repeated with a shrug.

"What happened to the tourists?"

"Rich tourists. They went home in a hired car." She ventured a brief smile, the first time he'd seen her do so.

They threaded their way through the confusion of people and vehicles. Bovine warriors plodded toward a neighboring field. Some were already being loaded onto trucks.

Garrick attempted a banal conversation: "Quite a spectacle, two bulls fighting each other like that."

"I like the fact the bulls don't get killed...like in fights with matadors."

"Uhh...I've been wanting to ask. Where'd you learn English? Your accent even sounds American."

"It should. I lived in California until I was thirteen." She gave another smile. A fleeting, teaser of a smile, but a smile nonetheless.

"You're a very good tour guide, you know. Umm...very efficient."

"Very efficient, am I?" An actual laugh sounded. "I do it only occasionally, and just when I visit Arequipa. To help my uncle, and to earn a bit of money."

"To help your uncle?"

"He owns a part interest in the travel agency. Uncle Hernan does not speak English, though, and the usual guide is in Trujillo. I know Arequipa well enough to fill in. I lived here with my uncle and aunt before I went to Lima, to study at the university."

"Where are your parents?" He blurted the question without thinking, and immediately wished he hadn't. Pain pulled at the angles of her face. "Oh! I'm sorry," he said quickly. "It's none of my business. I didn't mean to pry."

"My father died in the States. My mother died in Lima a little over a year later." Her voice was in control, brisk.

"Sorry."

"Forget it. It was years ago. An old story."

An awkwardness followed. Garrick tried to speak lightly: "The similarity between us lasts only up to a point," he laughed. "I was raised by an aunt, too, and also went to college...although I left before I graduated. I joined the Army instead, and went to Afghanistan."

39

She scowled her disapproval. "Oh, that war is terrible. We saw pictures here in Peru of the poor villagers, the refugees...the children especially. You will be glad when the Americans leave, no?"

"Aw...shit!"

"What did you say?"

"I said, shit."

"That's not a very intelligent comment."

"Did you see the pictures of all those Americans with arms and legs missing?" he demanded. "No? Well, I saw them. Many of them friends of mine. Too many. And those bastards killed a whole lot of innocent people in my own home town!"

Taken aback by his bitterness, she sat silently.

"I just killed one guy I'm sure of," Garrick blurted.

"Oh," she mouthed.

"A kid in his late teens," Garrick went on, the words coming out on their own. "He drove his motorcycle up to a checkpoint we were at...left the bike and took off running. Seconds later, the bomb went off. It killed a buddy of mine and damn near blew the arm off another."

"You killed a young boy!"

"In a hut in a nearby village. We went looking for him. I ducked inside a hut and there he was."

They were into the city now, slowed for the traffic. Garrick closed his eyes, journeyed back to the dirty, nondescript village, and the hut with the kid.

Everything slowed down, like a dream scene in a movie. But the edges were hard and clear...the gloom of the hut notwithstanding. At that moment, that precise point in time, the entire world consisted of him, his gun, and the scrawny young man in the baggy clothing squatting on the dirt floor.

The kid knew what was coming. He had to know. He didn't move, though. Not a muscle.... Why in hell not? Why didn't he do something...stand up...try to run away...shout?

Anything?

He just squatted on his haunches, bareheaded, a mop of hair hanging down over his forehead, and looked up at him with those big, almond eyes so many Afghans had.

Garrick opened his eyes again. They were halted at a corner waiting for a car ahead of them to move. Roxana eyed him curiously, a probing look with unasked questions behind it.

He couldn't think of what to say. In his confusion, he wound up angry at himself for blurting out the story. And, once again, he suffered the hot flush of conflicting emotions over what had happened in the hut.

"It's my turn to apologize," Roxana offered, looking as though she meant it.

"I pulled the trigger," he finished, spitting the words out. "There was a splat. A hole appeared in his forehead, just above the eyes. He jerked backward, and sagged to the floor. Then, I walked back outside. And I didn't puke, or piss my pants, or any of that bullshit stuff either.... Wanna know something else–I haven't been scared of anything since."

He fell silent then, suddenly and acutely embarrassed.

The car in front pulled away. Meshing the gears, she followed. "Where can I drop you off?"

"Sorry," Garrick said.

"For what?"

"The story I just threw at you. I've never done that before."

"Was it true?"

"Sure."

"Do you regret that it happened?"

"Now I do. At the time, I didn't."

They entered the Plaza de Armas.

"Anywhere around here," Garrick told her.

She stopped at the steps by the white stone portals.

He started to get out, then hesitated. "I'm going to be here for another week or so," he ventured, a bit desperately. "What do people do to entertain themselves around here?"

"Same things they do in any town."

On impulse, he asked, "What're you doing tonight? I don't know a soul in town. Let me take you to dinner."

She shook her head. "No, I can't. I'm busy."

"Tomorrow, then?"

"I'm going up to the Colca Valley tomorrow, very early."

Garrick grinned thinly. "Right. I get the picture." He opened the door and got out.

"I've been planning to visit the Colca Valley for weeks," she put in hurriedly. "I'm going to do some work up there. Honestly!"

"You're taking a tour to the mountains?"

"I'm an archaeology student, remember. I want to do some field work. A friend of my uncle's is the manager of a big copper-silver mine up there. I stay at the mine and do field work up and down the valley."

"Oh. Well, then, maybe I'll see you when you get back."

"The people at the airlines office know where to find me when I'm in town." With a quick wave, she ground the gears into position and eased her way back into traffic.

Mounting the steps by the movie theater, Garrick started along the portalled gallery.

A lean, muscular man with short, dark hair eyed him. Something about the fellow struck Garrick as familiar. Then...of course. The man who had disappeared yesterday after Harry Alexander took his picture by the fountain.

A squat, incredibly dirty woman in an orange sweater sat on the pavement, staring ahead through sightless eyes and holding a plastic begging cup in her lap.

When Garrick slowed to drop a coin in her cup, the man said, "Hi, buddy."

Garrick nodded to him. "How'd you know I speak English?"

The man grinned. "I heard you talking to the girl who just left. You sound American. Is she American, too?"

"No, Peruvian, although she lived in the States for some time."

The fellow made no reply, just bobbed his head in a friendly way.

Garrick did a quick appraisal. He was in his late twenties or early thirties, and obviously American. "You here on holiday?" he asked him politely.

"You could say that." He held out his hand. "My name's Slade."

Garrick shook hands, and introduced himself. "Uh...I was just going up the street for a beer. Wanna come along?"

"Okay," came the casual reply. Slade picked up a valise from between his feet and fell into step beside Garrick.

Along Calle Mercederes, they found a small bar-restaurant and went inside. Tables lined one wall, while a bar occupied most of the opposite wall. At the rear was a kitchen that would never pass health inspection in the U.S.

A short, thick-chested waiter hurried over.

His eyes were startling, liquid and black beyond all possibility, and set in a smooth, coppery-brown face. A big nose centered his face above a wide mouth. A thick shock of straight, black hair covered his head. Pure Indian.

The bulk of the town's population was made up of Indians and people of mixed blood. To Garrick, they all looked vaguely similar.

"The waiter says they have fresh lomo today," Slade translated. "That's beef. It's not always available, but he says today they have steak if you want it. You hungry?" When Garrick shook his head, Slade ordered two beers and the waiter left.

"You handle the lingo pretty good."

"I get by. If you live in South America long enough, you learn."

Slade's gaze was restless, roaming the room as he talked. Once, when he moved his head to one side, light from an overhead lamp caught his pale eyes in such a way that, for a moment, they looked as dead as those of the blinded beggar woman in the plaza. He was a good-looking man, managing to be delicately-featured and strong-faced at the same time.

"You live in South America, then. I thought you were here on holiday?"

"A bit of holiday, a bit of business." He made an attempt at a smile, then asked. "Are you and that girl I saw you with good friends?"

"You mean Roxana? No, we just met yesterday. She was the guide on a city tour I took. We happened to meet at the bull fights this afternoon."

Slade chuckled. "You seemed pretty deep in conversation when I saw you."

Garrick gave a self-deprecating laugh. "If the truth be known, I was asking her to go out with me and she was refusing. She's busy...going to visit a friend who works at a mine up in the mountains."

"Oh...a mine?"

"A big copper-silver mine. It's in a valley...I think she said the Colca

Valley. She's actually interested in archaeology. She wants to do some field trips, and she sleeps at the mine."

Slade seemed to drop into thought and Garrick had temporarily run out of things to say, so he sat quietly studying the man across the table. Slade's face was expressionless, giving away absolutely nothing. *This guy's murder in a poker game, I'll bet.*

He sensed a certain toughness about this lithe man with the machine gunner's eyes. Not the type you got close to very easily. Still, he'd known men like him in Afghanistan and had always been pleased to soldier alongside them–when shooting started, they could be relied upon.

Slade had military stamped all over him.

Garrick tried a ruse. "Damned if I don't think I've seen you before," he exclaimed. "I've been trying to place you ever since we met. Lemme see...." He snapped his fingers. "Kandahar, that's it. A year or two back." He made a *dap*–forming a fist and lying the thumb flat above the knuckles–to point at Slade.

Slade made a similar fist, tapped knuckles with Garrick and let go with a barracks room laugh. "I'll be damned. Well, you're almost right. I was in Iraq."

Garrick regarded him with new interest.

Speaking slowly, Slade began to recount a fire fight he'd been involved in.

When he finished, Garrick felt as though he had come home. *This man knew. He actually knew.*

He began to speak in turn, sentences and pictures slowly forming.

They remained there, deep in conversation, until the sun went down and the air grew chill.

"Goddammit, man," Garrick exclaimed. "It sure feels good to talk like this." He laughed in slight embarrassment. "There's never anyone to talk to. Know what I mean?" He fumbled for the words to express himself.

"No need to explain to me, Garry. I know *exactly* what you mean."

Garrick beamed at him. "I feel as hungry as a lion. Whadd'ya say we have a couple of those steaks the waiter was talking about?"

"Ah...I think I'll pass."

"Not hungry?" Garrick was a bit surprised. It was getting late.

Slade appeared embarrassed. "Nope. No money. Or not much. I have enough to pay for my beer, but that's about all. Lost my passport, most of my money, and all but one small bag two days back. Stolen as slick as a whistle."

"Hell, man! Say, I don't mind helping."

"Thanks, but I should be all right. I've sent to the States for some money. It'll be here in two, three days. Meanwhile, I'll just hang tough." Grinning weakly, he picked up his beer.

"Nope!" Garrick stated firmly. "Where're you staying?"

"Last night, I stayed in a hostel by the train station. I checked out this morning."

"Then, you're coming with me."

"Hey, Garry, I appreciate the offer and all...but look, man–"

"Stop, for Chrissake! We're both at loose ends here for the next few days. Just before I met you, I was wondering how I'd get through the next week without dying of boredom. When your money comes through, you can pay me back. So, where's the problem?"

"Sure you don't mind?"

"'Course I don't."

"Right, soldier," Slade said, obviously relieved. He snapped a mock salute. "What's the program? Get laid? Beat the hell out of a cop? What?"

"We'll figure out something," Garrick laughed.

"Y'know," Slade offered slowly, "I've heard of this Colca Valley. Supposed to be spectacularly beautiful. When'd you say she was going up there?"

"Tomorrow morning."

"Maybe she'd take us? You're in charge, soldier, but it's an idea. Might make for an interestin' few days."

His desire to go sight-seeing surprised Garrick slightly–he didn't seem the type–and Garrick was reluctant to ask Roxana the favor. "Jeez, I dunno," he hedged.

"Offer her a coupla' bucks. She might welcome the chance to earn a little money. I'll split it with you later."

Garrick slapped the table in decision. "Okay. Why not? I'll try to get in touch with her through the hotel." He waved a hand at the waiter. "Now, order us two of those steaks he was trying to sell earlier. I haven't been this hungry in a long time."

Chapter Seven
The Valley

The voice on the line hesitated. "This is a little awkward. I don't quite know what to say."

"I realize it's an imposition," Garrick replied, already regretting he'd let Slade talk him into this, "and I wouldn't ask, except that I've met a guy from the States who wants to see the Colca Valley...says he's heard a lot about it." He paused for a reply, but was met by silence. "Okay, sorry to have bothered you," he said shortly. "I shouldn't have asked."

"No, no, don't get me wrong," Roxana broke in hurriedly. "I don't mind your coming. Really. It's just the practical problems I'm concerned about."

"Practical problems?"

"Yes. Where you and your friend would sleep, mainly. I'll stay at the mine, but I'm not so sure you'd be able to. Mmm...all right, then. If you're willing to take a chance on accommodation?"

Her conciliatory tone made Garrick feel child-like for snapping at her. "That's terrific," he hastened to say. "I appreciate this."

Her voice changed, became businesslike. Brisk phrases crackled over the wire. "I always get an early start. It's a long drive, and I want to get as much done as possible. Be outside the hotel at 4:30 tomorrow morning and I'll pick you up. Be on time," she admonished. "I won't wait." With that, the telephone line went dead.

At least she was consistent, Garrick mused, dead telephone in hand. Or perhaps, consistently unpredictable was more apt—warm and helpful one minute, brusque the next.

~ * ~

A vehicle swung off the main road toward the hotel, headlights slicing through the darkness.

"Here she comes," Garrick commented to Slade. "Wait'll you meet her."

"How's that?"

Garrick laughed. "Roxana comes on pretty strong at times. She's overly defensive, I guess you'd say. Pity. She'd be damned attractive if she'd just loosen up a bit."

Her battered Land Rover skidded to a stop. "Get in," she called out above the sound of the motor, and gunned the engine as they climbed aboard.

They sped through the darkened Yanahuara suburbs to where the climb between Misti and Chachani commenced, their snowy caps luminous in a grey-black sky.

Daylight was spreading, but the day not quite arrived, when they reached the *puna*, the high, arid tableland of the Andes. The sun lifted higher and light suddenly flooded in. Garrick stared in silence, a wondering, man-caught-in-a-storm look on his face. Viewing the puna for the first time at cold dawn was no small thing.

The plain stretched endlessly, silent and lonely. Trees didn't exist here, just occasional stunted shrubs shiny with hoar frost, and clumps of spiky, green and yellow ichu grass. With the rainy season just ending, bright green fuzz carpeted the stony ground.

They bumped along, the world empty except for a lone partridge, and once, on a jumble of rocks, a viscacha–grey, long tailed, rabbit-like rodent.

Snowy peaks, rosy with the early sun, edged over the horizon offering spectacular relief from the barrenness of this great, high, empty place. Above it all, the sky vaulted huge, blue and overarching.

"The high pampa," Roxana stated simply, waving a hand in a futile, encompassing gesture.

A stone-walled corral heaved into sight. A flock of about fifty llamas and their look-alike cousins, alpacas, some wearing identifying ribbons in their ears, milled around inside the grey walls. A tan-colored pig wandered loose between the corral and a circular stone hut. A leathery-faced gnome of a man headed for the pig with a rope in his hand. He had a withered leg and leaned to starboard, dipping as he walked.

They passed suddenly into cloud cover and everything vanished. Roxana switched on the windshield wipers.

When they emerged they saw a bus ahead, halted on the rutted, dirt road to allow the passengers to get off to relieve themselves. The driver lifted a hand in greeting as they went by.

Three hours from Arequipa, Roxana slowed. "There," she said, "that's your first glimpse of Chivay."

In a verdant valley far below, a toy village was on display, tiny metal roofs twinkling in the distance. The road descended to it in a succession of hair pin curves. At this season, the valley was at its most lush. Terraced gardens bloomed everywhere. Fields of yellow and orange-red, ripening *quinua* grain inched up the slopes, layer upon layer. Barley fields danced like green water under the stroking of the wind.

The lower they went, the taller and thicker and greener were the shrubs and ichu grass. Purple lupins put in an appearance, dotting the roadside, and pretty yellow flowers, like buttercups, flourished at each tiny brook.

Roxana stopped in the town square. "I have to speak to someone in the church," she said, pointing to the romantic style building with the two bell towers beside the plaza. "I'll not be long." She went off in her free-swinging style.

The two men got out, squinting against the fierce sunlight. After a perfunctory survey of the surroundings, Slade strolled over and sat down on one of the benches on the tree-shaded plaza. Garrick, though, fascinated by this close up view of Quechua Indian life, peered eagerly in every direction.

To the west, the icy crests of mighty Hualca-Hualca and Sabancaya shone in the sun, in the pristine, rain-washed atmosphere appearing almost close enough to touch.

Undersized people in bright, multicolored clothing moved about, scuffing up the dust of the streets in open-toed sandals.

Slade ignored the goings on, sitting quietly on the bench, head drooped in concentration.

For a man who'd suggested the trip up here in order to enjoy the scenery, he showed scant interest in it. He was certainly a strange fellow. Garrick couldn't recall ever meeting anyone quite like him. He thought he understood what was going on, though, and felt a wave of sympathy for the man.

Purposeful distantiation the head doctors called it. Slade had built a wall around himself higher than Garrick's was, even refusing to give out his first name. Garrick understood that shyness, the utter intent on privacy...keep people out...let only a few in on your own terms...reduce the pressure.

The wars had done that to many men.

A blast of Latin music filled the air, coming from a big, concrete building just off the corner of the plaza. Garrick drifted over.

The building housed the market, with a mix of manufactured products and various services offered for sale. Lining the walls outside, wrapped in blankets, dozens of Quechuas, mainly women, squatted before goods of every description heaped on blankets and plastic sheets.

Sharing a common wall with the market was a restaurant of similar size, painted in the same pastel blue-green so often seen in Andean towns. Dogs of dubious pedigrees roamed beneath the long, wooden tables searching for scraps.

A woman cooking meat over an electric hot plate noticed Garrick and made a gesture for him to sit and eat. Her smile of encouragement displayed blackened stumps where teeth should have been. With a shake of his head, Garrick walked on through the restaurant to the street at the rear.

A bus turned the corner and trundled past, horn blaring. Garrick recognized it as the bus they had passed on the puna. It pulled to a stop in a cloud of dust at the end of the street. Passengers piled out. Shouting began as the luggage was handed down from the rack on the roof. Two of the men working on top were barefoot.

It was damn cold nights and early mornings to go without footwear, yet it seemed quite common. Poverty was a fact too obvious to be ignored in this exquisite valley. In the faces of the people around him, though, there appeared no overt signs of bitterness or desperation.

Not like in parts of Afghanistan, for example.

The color and exotic nature of this mountain town reminded him somewhat of that unfortunate country. "Shit!" he muttered.

A horn blew once, and then again. Garrick glanced up and saw Roxana signalling to him. He side-stepped a pedi-cab, and got into the Land Rover.

"For a minute there, I thought you were communing with *Collaguata,* the sacred volcano of the Collaguas," she said, her wit tinged with sarcasm.

"I was thinking of something...wool gathering you might say."

They crossed the Colca River and swung downstream, bouncing on a dirt road better suited to burros than vehicles. From a rise a little further on, the full glory of snow-capped Hualca-Hualca and Sabancaya exploded into view. Cone-shaped Sabancaya, on the left, was smoking. A grey puffball cloud spewed from its summit, rose above the cumulus and continued to climb, changing shape as it went into a woolly animal–a dog or llama. High-riding wind currents finally shredded it.

"That's quite a sight," Garrick mouthed, fascinated.

"How much farther is it to the mine?" Slade broke in.

"We're stopping at Coporaque first," Roxana replied tartly. It was clear she didn't like Slade.

"Coporaque?"

"Yes. I want to speak to Mother Catarina. The priest at Chivay told me she's there today."

~ * ~

"Say hello to sacred Umachiri." Roxana halted at the bottom of Coporaque's central square, and pointed with her chin toward a rounded mountain behind the village.

"The Collaguas, the ancestors of these people, regarded certain mountains as sacred. This mountain, Umachiri, was the special deity of Coporaque. Its protector."

"It has a kind of sheltering, protective appearance to it, all right," Garrick offered.

"That's it." She drove up the square to the big, stone church with the gleaming, white-washed front.

"Who's Mother Catarina?"

"A valley legend. She's lived here for years. She divides her time between Coporaque and Yanque over there."

Across the river, terraced wheat fields mounted a hillside, stacked one above the other like pale golden layers on a wedding cake. At the foot of the terraces, a collection of houses could be plainly made out in the distance.

"It's on the far side of the river. That's what I wanted to find out in Chivay. We'd have wasted time driving along the other bank. Yanque was an important town during the days of the Incas, rivalling and eventually eclipsing even Coporaque in importance. In those days, it was in a different location, though...probably with a different name." She shook her head. "It can be rather confusing."

"It's a magnificent location. I've never seen anything to match that view over there."

The river had dropped out of sight below a bluff, but on its far side the valley bulged, becoming bowl shaped. Tier upon tier of terraced gardens and flowering fields stretched up the mountain slopes. Colors ran riot.

"This view is called the 'Anfiteatro,'" Roxana said quietly. "That's amphitheater in English...because of the resemblance to the ancient Greek and Roman amphitheaters. It has changed little over the centuries. Before the Spanish arrived...long before even the Incas arrived, those stone-walled terraces were what we're seeing today."

"Amazing. Amazingly beautiful."

"The Andes got their name from a Spanish word for terraces. You can see why. Under the Incas, no one in Peru went hungry."

"This still looks like the Garden of Eden. There can't be too many people going hungry in these parts."

"Oh, in bad years some do. Although I don't suppose things have changed all that much in the countryside. In the cities, people suffer. Parts of Lima are terrible." Her expression softened. "Coporaque is my favorite place in all the world. There's a lot of history connected to it, too. I'd hate to think that I'd never see it again."

With that, she abruptly turned on her heel, mounted the stone steps, and strode inside the church.

Garrick sat down on the steps. Slade stood over by the Land Rover, a blank expression on his face.

The church overlooked the town and some of the surrounding fields. Two Indian women, at this distance tiny polychrome figures, picked beans in a dark-green field between town and river bank. A pair of ragged children played on the steep, dirt streets running into the square. Not another person was in sight. The ancient village appeared nearly deserted.

A lean, brown pig fought a furry, black dog over a piece of offal at the bottom of the square. The pig won, wrenched the tidbit free, and raced through the stone arch at a corner of the square with the dog in pursuit.

Then, the village went back to sleep.

"Hell of a view, eh," Garrick called to Slade.

"Yeah."

"What's got into you? You were the one who wanted to come sightseeing."

"I think the view is magnificent. How's that?"

Garrick left him, and strolled over to the arched entrance of the church. Roxana, another woman, and three men were gathered about a large statue of Christ, affixing it to a vehicle of some kind.

The other woman, a slight figure dressed in trousers and shirt, offered a smile of welcome when she saw him, and returned to what she was doing. The lowered conversation between her and the workmen gave off muted echoes in the cavernous chamber.

Displayed on one wall was a relief of a woman being crowned. As Garrick bent closer to study it, a firm, calm voice said, "That's the Coronation of the Virgin." Although accented, the English was excellent.

The slim woman in the trousers offered her hand, a polite smile creasing warm, brown eyes. She appeared about sixty and had a weathered face. Her hand, when he shook it, was roughened and calloused.

"It's beautiful," he said, referring to the relief. "And the church, too."

"Sometimes age simply equates with beauty. Coporaque is the oldest town in the Colca Valley, and this is the oldest church...built in 1569."

Roxana joined them, and the conversation veered to some valley legends she was interested in.

The trousered lady, Mother Catarina, seemed to have an inexhaustible store of local knowledge. She addressed Roxana's questions easily, in the same calm manner she'd used with Garrick.

A plump, middle-aged Indian woman entered the church from its side door and spoke rapidly to the nun in Quechua.

Mother Catarina questioned her in the same language, directed a few swift phrases to Roxana in Spanish, then turned to Garrick. "Excuse me, but I must go. It's been pleasant talking to you, however briefly."

She hurried out the side door with the Indian woman.

Garrick and Roxana left the church and stood on the steps outside, blinking in the sunshine.

A flock of a dozen sheep passed by, heads down, an old ewe with a red bell about her neck leading the way. A full-breasted young woman with a single, long pigtail hanging down her back walked behind them spinning as she went–down whirled the wooden spindle, spinning like a top as she fed out another length of alpaca wool.

Her face was a blank. One got the impression nothing was happening behind it and that, like the sheep, she merely followed the ewe. Her spinning movements appeared purely mechanical, long-practiced and accomplished without thought.

The ewe knew where to go, for she turned left at the lower end of the square without instruction from the woman, passed through the archway and, with a clear tinkle of her bell, led her flock down the rutted road out of sight.

"Mother Catarina's quite a person," Garrick commented. "That was Quechua, the language of the Incas, she was speaking, wasn't it?"

"Yes. She speaks fluent Quechua as well as Spanish and English."

"Quite a lady," Garrick repeated. "What was the emergency that caused her to rush off, anyhow?"

"A child fell off a horse and hit his head. He's been unconscious for hours, apparently. His father just now thought to bring him here."

"There's a medical center here?"

"Not a medical center. An infirmary, sort of. People with nowhere else to go always come here. She will turn away no one who asks for help. And she feeds people every day with the food she raises herself. She's really rather wonderful."

Garrick grinned at her. "She wouldn't even turn you away, who came here only to pick her brain."

"Mother Catarina hears a lot from the people around here. The old folks especially. She's a good source." She shot him a glance. "I was asking her about some old legends. What's wrong with that?"

"Hey," he laughed, "don't go so defensive on me all of a sudden. Nothing wrong with it at all."

A moment's pause and, with an actual smile, she asked: "You don't believe in ghosts, do you?"

"Ghosts?"

"See that memorial over there with the sculptured bust on top of it...inside the fountain? Well, that's a tribute to Inca Mayta Capac. One of the Coporaque legends is that a copper palace stood in this very spot we're standing on, before the Spaniards destroyed it back in the sixteenth century. A century earlier, a general of the *Royal Clan Mayta Capac*, appointed by the supreme Inca, established his headquarters in Coporaque, and from it conquered all the lands to the sea. And that he fell in love with and married Mama Tancaray Yacchi, the daughter of a Coporaque chief. So, the local people built a huge house of copper for him and his bride."

"Copper palace...myth or fact?"

"A large house with copper walls did exist here. Gonzalo Pizarro, Francisco Pizarro's half-brother, passed through here in 1547 with his army. He had the palace torn down."

"He tore down this splendid building? Why?"

"Because mighty Gonzalo needed the copper to make horseshoes and harness parts for his cavalry. And while he was at it, he put a senior chief to the torture, trying to get information about hidden gold and silver, and the location of the copper mines. The old chief refused, and was burned to death." She grimaced, shaking her shoulders in anger. "They were always doing things like that to these helpless people. Anyhow, a friar called de Ore came along a few years later and used the remaining copper to make church bells." She pointed upward. "Look."

From inside the towers above their heads, bells glinted coppery-gold in the sunshine.

"I'll be damned...the same bells!" Garrick said slowly.

"What a charming legend," came a flat voice behind them. Slade had come up noiselessly. "We've wasted enough time here," he put in. "Let's get the show on the road."

Caught up in the old tales, Garrick had completely forgotten about him. *The man moves as quietly as a cat*, was his immediate thought.

"Yes, it *is* a charming legend," Roxana sniffed, her distaste for the man showing. "This valley abounds in legends of all kinds." She slowed her speech and filled out her syllables, as though explaining something difficult to a slow child. "There's been very little archaeological work done here, so far. So, you see...there's a chance for an important find." She finished talking to smile patronizingly at him.

She'd made him appear childish and you could tell he didn't like it. He didn't know what to do about it, though, and finally wound up sneering at her. "And you're the brilliant archaeologist who's going to make that find, huh?"

"Look, buddy," Garrick snapped, tired of his moodiness. "If we're having a good time and that upsets you for some reason, try not to let it show. I only came because of you. Remember?"

A storm blew up behind Slade's eyes, hardening them into round, metal points. But then he turned away for a fraction of a second, and when he turned back he wore a crooked grin.

"Thanks, soldier," he said, sounding sheepish. "You're right. I guess I haven't been very good company. I'm in a lousy mood today." Looking directly at Garrick, he added earnestly: "You know how it is."

"Aw, forget it," Garrick rushed to say.

"No. No. And you're right about this place, too. The whole valley is simply gorgeous."

Garrick grinned in relief at his friend's change of attitude.

Roxana was less impressed. "A scenery lover, eh." Her tone was dry. "Then you're going to love the drive to the mine. There's lovely scenery all the way to Mina Madrugada."

The expression on her face belied those casual words. It was clear she now regretted having brought these men along. "Let's go," she said shortly, and marched, straight-backed, down the steps to the Land Rover.

Slade clapped Garrick on the back, laughing. "Hear that, Garry. Marching orders. I swear...she's exactly like some of the *top kicks* I knew in Iraq."

Chapter Eight
Huaracu-1530

The condor extended its wings to their full ten-foot span, spreading the feathery tips like fingers, and hopped from the cave to the edge of the cliff.

This was an old male bird of fifty, and he had not fed in weeks. Hunger stirred within him now, and it caused his pale-brown eyes to scan the valley below in a manner more searching than usual.

A scrabbling noise sounded behind him and the female appeared. Contracting her white ruff to warm her neck, she settled beside her mate.

Fifteen minutes of patient waiting went by.

The heat of the sun on the thin air eventually gave them what they wanted. Wind currents began to ripple the sky. The great birds left the perch on an updraft, riding it in circles, planing like gigantic, black, predator moths.

At the town of Coporaque, a huge mass of people had assembled, and outside town the condors found a heap of offal with two foxes feeding on it. A flock of llamas had been slaughtered to provide meat for a feast.

The foxes moved off warily as the scavengers fell from the sky. Nearing the ground, the condors lowered their legs and flexed wings for a final spilling of air. With a flash of white wing patches, they were down, twisting naked heads to peer about. Then, they hopped forward to dip hooked beaks into the stinking repast.

For several minutes the foxes crouched, ears pointed forward. But with the giant birds settled down to feed, they finally trotted to the far side of the gory pile and began to help themselves.

amed Ollanta by one of his uncles. He gave a toothy grin at the
ne–Ollanta, from a warrior hero of ancient legend, was the name
e chosen himself.

n-chested coughing caused him to look toward the edge of the
rin vanished and a scowl appeared. Yahuar Huaccac, his half-
n years his junior, was doubled over with a small hand pressed
His thick shock of straight, black hair quivered to the racking

oughing died away. The boy wiped his mouth, and then
hand. No red stain, he saw with relief. He'd not coughed up
two months now, but he worried that it might start again.

nother stroked his thin, freckled cheeks. "How are you,
ama Ocllo whispered. She was Changa's second wife, the slim,
of a royal concubine.

from his father's generous nose, the child most resembled his
oned and soft-featured, with long, black eyelashes and a full,
lso like her, his head was round. She had refused to allow him

ept deep-set, black eyes upward to the anxious, youthful
ng over him, gave her a reassuring nod, and then turned back to
dn't want to miss anything.

solemnly adjusted his striped red and white shirt and white
minute now, he would join his peers in bowing before the
ledging homage to the Inca.

urn, he went forward, knelt before the small nobleman seated
and had his ears pierced with a golden bodkin, so as to
the cylindrical pendants which were worn by men of the

aracu, the entry of youths into manhood at the time of the
e, as it was practiced here in this small province was not to be
the glorious festival carried out before the Supreme Inca
zco. However less splendid and less lavish, the ceremony
his high valley was still of immense importance to those who
t.

t act, the young men were presented with crowns of feathers

~ * ~

The muscular young man with the elongated, shorn head grunted with
effort and lengthened his stride when he passed the stunted, lone quenua tree
on the Inca Road. The tree, so gnarled and wind-whipped it grew horizontally
out of the hillside, meant the exhausting race, from its start on the mountain
top to the town ahead, was nearing its end.

The strain of the ordeal showed plainly on his hawk-like features.
Behind him, a few youths lay sprawled, exhausted, beside the stone-lined
road, although the rest of the young men, teen-aged sons of important
families, struggled manfully to catch the long-legged runner in the lead.

This same brawny youth, a head taller than his contemporaries, had
excelled similarly in the earlier physical contests: wrestling, boxing, mimic
combats.

He rounded a bend and towering, white-fanged Hualca-Hualca sprang
into view, joined soon after by her slimmer, cone-shaped sister, Sabancaya.
Sabancaya's top was hidden under a canopy of smoke and debris from a
recent eruption.

As he ran, he regularly passed cultivated fields, hummingbirds in
them darting and hovering among the early flowering plants. It was the time
of the summer solstice in the southern hemisphere. The season of the rains
had begun, hurrying crops planted months earlier to maturity. Potatoes,
"quinua" grain, sweet potatoes, varieties of beans, and the millet-like
"canahua" occupied every square foot of tillable land. Maize was found at
lower elevations a little farther downstream.

As he raced past a stretch of rocky, sterile ground, a mountain
caracara, a type of hawk, dropped screaming from the sky onto the ground by
a huge pile of offal two condors and two foxes were feeding on.

The young man saw none of these things, however. Coporaque had
appeared, winking at him in the distance, its flowering fields and orchards
spread out lushly before it like the extended skirts of a seated woman.

His thoughts were for the crowd gathered in the great square below
the palace of copper. And, when he eventually made out the palace, all
agleam in the sunlight, a smile of triumph crept onto his face. He increased

his pace, testing his strength to the limit, ignoring the stabs of pain shooting up his side, glorying in his sure knowledge that he possessed the fortitude to set the added hurt aside.

The final ten minutes were brutal, all uphill, between mud-plastered stone walls and outlying houses, along manure-strewn streets.

Bursting onto the square and hearing the cheers, he yearned, in that moment, to be in mighty Cuzco, navel of the world and seat of empire.

Mayta Yupanqui, cousin of the Inca, sat on a stool on a platform before the shining, red-gold bulk of a massive, high-peaked copper house, surrounded by noblemen and *curacas*, chieftains.

A man past middle age and conscious of his authority and lineage, Mayta Yupanqui presented a dignified mien, in spite of ordinary features and small stature. His hair was cut short in the style favored by Cuzco, with bangs in front and a bob at back, and his brightly-decorated tunic and cloak were of the finest weave. On each arm flashed bracelets of both gold and silver. His earlobes, weighed down by heavy gold pendants, sagged almost to his shoulders.

It was the curaca nearest him, however, who seized and held the attention of the young man with the flying feet. Towering over the others on the platform, the powerful, hook-nosed chief displayed rare signs of pleasure on his axe blade visage. Seeing this, the runner leaped within—his father, Changa, was pleased with his son's performance.

The young man commenced to prance, lifting his knees high, so all could see that ample strength remained.

Changa's dark, heavy eyebrows rose and almost met in a straight line above his beak of a nose. It was a curious way he had of expressing approval, and it appeared to lift his whole facial structure, further emphasizing the tapered, elongated shape of his big head. The curaca's misshapen head told a story. He belonged to the Collagua people, his head bound as an infant to resemble Collaguata, sacred volcano of his people's distant homeland.

With the straggle of exhausted youths drawing nearer, a group of young girls standing at the finish line broke into excited laughter. "Come quickly, young men," they exhorted. "We are waiting for you."

Brandishing jars of chicha, the fermented maize brew of the Andes, they urged the competitors to greater efforts.

58

The runner preened himself, bouncing father's falcon's beak of a nose and his big he hair for this occasion. Swivelling the oversized pronking along, he looked like some fantastic from a habitual bloodshot condition, brought a and nights spent in smoky dwellings.

The combination of condor's head a impression of such intensity that it bordered or Several of the girls stared at him in fascination

A child, diminutive and doll-like, ho the runner as he flew by. This was Yahuar blood, younger half-brother to the speedster. to calm him.

At the finish line, the victorious runne the governor, and then stalked off to bathe ir Later, when the other runners had arrived and to the ceremonial center on the nearby hill of

The masses of people, in clothing dec and triangles, created a shifting, singir overflowed the road and covered the steep most part, they were Collaguas with elongat the people of Cuzco were well represented a here and there, square-headed Cabanas—and down valley—were easily identified.

Overawed by the magnificence of Cc in such a multitude, the Cabanas stayed tog to each other's tunics so as not to become sep

On the sacred mountain of Yura governor addressed the runners, praising th affectionately.

"You have done well, Children of th in a clear, piping voice. "You are worthy to the season of manhood, be reminded of tl accept, for the empire and for the Inca."

At this time, also, the young mer

59

runner was choice of nar he would hav

A thi crowd. His g brother, seve to his mouth sound.

The examined his blood in over

His Huaccac?" M tiny daughter

Aside mother—fine-b wide mouth. to be bound.

He sw woman hoveri Ollanta. He di

Ollanta mantle. Any governor and

In his on the stool, accommodate highest order.

The hu summer solsti confused with himself in Cu carried out in participated in

As a la

and symbolic breech cloths. Then, everybody returned to town.

The thousands of people gathered here from various parts of the province spilled from the great square of Coporaque onto the streets and alleys which led into it. It was as if a vast quilt of many hues had been flung over the city.

The sun disappeared behind dark clouds, and a spatter of rain began to fall, washing the smooth stone flagging of the square. The temperature plunged instantly. Of hardy upland stock, clad in warm woolen clothing, and well fortified with alcohol by this time, everyone simply ignored the chill.

Drums sounded and the light, airy lilting of flutes floated over the square. All Coporaque began to dance.

As the beat quickened, the married women stamped the ground in their untanned sandals and revolved before their husbands. Emboldened by the swirling mass of humanity, the young, unmarried girls ventured also to dance. Immediately, they were complimented by the young men and offered invitations to make love.

Ollanta leered at one of the few Cabana girls present. "I have a woolen sandal in which to put your foot," he rasped in slightly-accented Quechua, using the expression for deflowering a virgin on the wedding night.

Ollanta's friend, Yeure, a youth with a twisted jaw, laughed. "Use a boot of ichu," he suggested, referring to the sandal of grass used by women who were not virgins on their wedding night.

The people nearby shouted laughter. The girl fingered the necklace of seashells about her neck, and dipped her square head in embarrassment.

A man from her village, with a head as flat as a cliff top, drunken and a little resentful of Coporaque's size and magnificence, glowered in Ollanta's direction. "Toad's stomach," he sneered in carefully enunciated Quechua.

The enmity between Collagua and Cabana was of long standing. Among several reasons for this was one of language; Cabanas spoke Quechua, the language of the Incas, as their lingua franca; Collaguas commonly used Aymara. The stranger's pointed use of enunciated Quechua was a deliberate insult.

As the son of an important chief, Ollanta had attended school in Cuzco and spoke fluent Quechua. Allowing a grin to spread across his face, he spent a second or two taking in the fellow's ugly box of a head. Then, boring right in with his blood-flecked eyes, he spoke slowly in clear Quechua: "How are the children I gave your wife?"

The Cabana's rush was drunken and clumsy. Ollanta threw him heavily to the ground, and pranced up to the Cabana girl, looming over her. "I am stronger than other men," he announced, a laugh rumbling up from his belly.

She fluttered at the power of him.

Two other men from her village were unwise enough to try to assist their neighbor. They were likewise harshly dealt with. Laughing hugely, Ollanta subdued one. His friend, whopper-jawed, thick-chested Yeure, handled the other.

Watching Yeure pummel the stranger, Ollanta scowled in irritation. He had required no assistance and resented the implication it was necessary. A woman's coarse laugh sounded behind him. Turning, he saw Cora, which meant weed, one of Coporaque's two prostitutes, enjoying the impromptu entertainment.

Young, full-hipped Cora had a pair of drunken admirers lurching beside her. She returned Ollanta's gaze boldly, invitation in her round, coppery features. Like a small, pink animal, her tongue slipped into view and slowly wet the edges of her mouth.

Pushing her suitors brusquely to one side, Ollanta signalled to her with a curt jerk of his head. With a knowing smile, Cora sauntered from the square, hatchet-faced Ollanta stalking stiff-leggedly behind.

~ * ~

Tasque, the long-haired serving girl, stumbled against the low clay stove in Changa's house, burning her hand. Muffling a cry, she stuck her fingers in her mouth.

Mama Ocllo began a reprimand, then checked herself. The girl was upset at having had to leave the celebrations to cook a meal for her and Yahuar Huaccac. So, when the food was readied, Mama Ocllo told the girl with a laugh: "Return to the square if you wish. Perhaps a young man awaits you."

Tasque left hurriedly. Ocllo served Huaccac, adding pepper to his maize and potato stew to flavor it, and giving him a lump of rock salt to lick as he chose. She then watched anxiously as he merely toyed with his meal, moodily pushing it about with his wooden spoon, feeding most of it to the domesticated guinea pigs that came to beg at his feet.

Kneeling behind him, she searched his hair for lice, crushing the insects between her small, square teeth when she found them.

A small, brown dog with a pointed face and curled tail, hairless except for a mop of hair between his ears, whined for scraps. Huaccac brightened immediately, and placed a morsel on the dog's nose. After waiting a moment, he said, "All right, Piqui Chaqui–flea foot–now eat." The dog licked the food from his nose and begged for more. It was an old game the two played, one Huaccac had taught him. A gentle lad, he had a way with animals.

As usual, the stove smoked badly from its fire of dried quinua stalks. Some of the fumes drifted out the high, narrow door, but most of the smoke remained inside to mix with other unpleasant household odors, adding to Huaccac's sour mood. Angry with his mother for making him come home early, he purposefully dredged a cough up from his throat to get back at her. As he'd known would happen, Ocllo was instantly solicitous, keeping a worried arm around him long after the cough had subsided.

Mama Ocllo-Lady Pure-was the daughter of a concubine of a Prince of Cuzco, her father one of the innumerable brothers of the late Inca Huayna Capac. The plurality of wives and concubines allowed the royal male offspring ensured a vast, extended imperial family. Notwithstanding this, and in spite of the fact that her own mother was a commoner, Ocllo's bloodline carried enormous significance. It elevated her far above the common people of the valley, as did Huaccac's smaller portion of royal blood.

She was an attractive woman, neat about her person, rouging her face and plucking her eyebrows regularly. Awarding the petite princess in marriage to a delighted Changa, shortly after his first wife had died, had been designed to cement the curaca's loyalty.

Mama Ocllo had never regretted leaving Cuzco and the cloistered life allowed her there. She enjoyed the valley's greater freedom and her elevated status among its people. And, of course, she had Huaccac.

Yahuar Huaccac had been born prematurely, a bad omen. And he proved a weak and sickly child, on one occasion hovering near death. The entire family fasted. They prayed to the sacred mountains and made sacrifices at the Sun Temple on Yurac-Qaqa. None of this had helped, however.

It was only when Ocllo thought to give the baby his own umbilical cord to suckle–she had preserved it for this very reason–that any gain in health was noted. Staying close to his cradle day and night, she alternated the umbilical cord with her own breast. It worked. Gradually, Huaccac sucked the illness from his body through the cord, and began, bit by bit, to gain a measure of strength.

But Mama Ocllo still refused to leave him for even a moment.

Children normally received very little pampering. Further, the rules absolutely forbade anyone to pick up a new-born infant. For a mother to give suck, she merely leaned over the cradle to offer the breast, three times daily.

Not so with Huaccac. Not only did Ocllo carry him around almost constantly, she also nursed him for over three years, much longer than normal.

Changa viewed her behavior as obsessive and unhealthy. She resisted any attempt at restraint, however, with the spitting fury of a mother puma, so that Changa, mindful of her imperial blood, at last accepted it.

The boy remained very close to his mother, although he was inclined to chafe at her constant nearness sometimes.

"Eat your food," she urged him. "Shall I fill your bowl again?"

He shook his head firmly, bothered by her fussing. Tossing aside his wooden bowl, he announced: "I'm tired now." Ducking under her arm, he climbed the ladder to the floor above where the entire household slept. When she insisted on following him, he drew his cover up quickly to avoid her doing it for him, and turned on his side to face the yellow, mud-plastered wall.

The sounds of revelry from the square came to him clearly through the wall; along with most of Coporaque's elite, Changa's compound was very near the center of town. Lying damp from the rain that worked through the thatch, Huaccac pretended sleep. The noises gradually died away. The house filled as people stumbled in. Well into the night, he drifted off.

~ * ~

At first full light, Huaccac awoke to find the room quiet, filled with sleeping people. On ordinary days, by dawn the house would already be abuzz.

When he glanced over to where his brother usually slept, Piqui Chaqui wiggled his nose at him instead. Against all orders, the dog had come upstairs and, finding the bed unused, had burrowed into it for warmth. Ollanta must have stayed out all night, thought Huaccac, blinking sleepily.

Seeing his young master awake, Piqui Chaqui commenced wriggling so excitedly, Changa showed signs of stirring. Fearing his father would banish the dog from the house entirely, Huaccac crept over and dragged the reluctant animal down the ladder and outside to the courtyard.

There he left him, tied to a rock and whining so piteously you would have thought he was being roasted alive over one of Mama Ocllo's cooking fires.

Chapter Nine
The Water Bird

With a practiced jerk of his hand, Huaccac set his top spinning. Piqui Chaqui watched until the toy stopped whirling, then raced off to inspect a flock of llamas and alpacas striding past.

Ollanta was supervising the animals, along with four other young men. He aimed a heavy kick at the dog, which Piqui Chaqui dodged nimbly. Ollanta's eyes were even more bloodshot than usual, and his head hurt from too much alcohol and too little sleep. "Yeure," he croaked to his friend, "take these accursed creatures to the high pasture."

Yeure's crooked jaw dropped a fraction. All of them bore equal responsibility for the flock. "Since you will be with us, you can show us the pasture you mean," he replied sarcastically.

Turning his bloodied eyes on him, Ollanta invited a staring match. For a moment Yeure met the challenge, but his resolve soon wavered. He muttered something unintelligible, and shuffled awkwardly on his feet.

Ollanta savored his victory a few seconds longer before allowing him a way out. "It's that I have important business I must attend to," he said, understanding full well that all of them knew it for a lie. "I'll join you later."

Yeure accepted the pretence immediately as a way to retain a measure of dignity. "Yes, yes," he said, a little too quickly. "In that case...."

Smirks appeared on faces in the group, although no one was inclined to argue with Ollanta. They hissed to the flock instead, and began the trudge to the high pastures.

Ollanta relaxed, leaning against a wall as they passed out of sight. Huaccac stroked his dog. He'd seen his brother's attempt to kick the animal and gave him an accusatory look.

Ollanta's heavy mouth curved sullenly. A bully's expression of contempt settled lazily about his eyes.

He wondered, yet again, at how fate had intervened. Why had the gods decreed his widowed father be given a woman of royal blood for a wife? And that a brother like Yahuar Huaccac would result? The boy would never be his equal in strength and force of character, yet he was obliged to pay him deference because of his small amount of imperial blood.

The boy's eyes observed him steadily. Black and lustrous, they were made to seem impossibly huge because of the hollowness of his face.

"How are you feeling this morning?" Ollanta asked him. The boy blinked his fine lashes and smiled. He was forgiving by nature. Releasing the dog with a final pat, he replied, "I'm fine. Are you not going with Yeure and the others today?"

"No. I want to spend some time with you." A toothy grin appeared. "Let's walk to the river."

Huaccac's smile broadened. It was rare his brother showed any companionship toward him. Then, he stopped to think. His father had told him to collect cactus fruit. "I must go to pick tuna," he said regretfully.

"Oh, that's all right. We won't be long."

With such assurance, Huaccac readily agreed. They set off beside the main aqueduct that fed Coporaque with water from far upstream.

The stone houses they passed were painted white or grey, were rectangular in shape, and had high pitched roofs of ichu grass. Some abutted each other, although most were found inside spacious, walled compounds used also as corrals for stock. Many homes were two-storied, and as much as a dozen long paces in length and width. Carved into the massive stone lintels above the entrances were the deities of each household–animals, birds, plants, people.

Coporaque boasted a population of almost two thousand. Ullo-Ullo, a town of similar size across the river, and Lare, farther downstream, were the province's other main urban centers. Cabanaconde, the Cabana metropolis, rivalled the big Collagua towns in size and population.

They swung down one of the streets radiating outwards from the town center and came to the great square. While crossing the square, Huaccac aimed a labial click and raised a reverent open hand toward sacred Umachiri, the mountain deity to the rear.

At the top of the square, all gleaming and golden, stood the copper palace, the huge house with the metal-sheeted walls built in the days of Changa's grandfather.

Traversing the square, they were obliged to step around heaps of slumbering humanity.

For many of those sprawled here, a visit from their isolated farms and hamlets to a town the size of Coporaque was a rare occurrence, and a most welcome release from humdrum duties in the fields. Overindulgence inevitably resulted. Before collapsing, most had managed to collect in familiar groupings of relatives and friends.

Huaccac offered friendly greetings to the people he met, the occasional Cabanas included, unlike Ollanta who had lapsed into a brooding silence.

They met the aqueduct again, crossed it by a footbridge, and started down the slope of land upon which Coporaque was situated.

Last night's rain had played itself out, leaving behind an empty bowl of sky. Out of it the sun shone brightly.

They were using a zigzag path Ollanta knew well, dropping down through lush fields. They came eventually to a rocky piece of ground on the bluff above the river.

Two poorly-built houses stood there, encircled by a rude, stone wall. A round female face with full, sensuous lips peered over the wall. "Back so soon," laughed Cora the prostitute. "You're welcome all the same."

Cora, one of the *pampairuna*, women of the field, lived here with another of her profession, a woman called Paya.

Prostitutes were barely tolerated in Inca society, a fact which bothered Cora not in the slightest. It was she who had initiated Ollanta, a few years previously, into the arts of love. She had been quite pretty once and was still not unattractive. "Who's your companion?" she asked Ollanta with one of her bold stares.

"He's my brother."

"Shall I be his teacher, also? As I was yours." She laughed heartily at her own joke.

"Be silent," Ollanta snapped.

Cora obeyed. Despite her mocking manner, she was always careful around this fierce-eyed son of the curaca. He had used her roughly in the past.

Huaccac threw a stone along the bank for Piqui Chaqui.

Watching the dog race off barking, an idea took shape in Ollanta's mind. Entering Cora's yard, he chased out her flock of Muscovy ducks. Protesting noisily, the big, black and white and red birds waddled for the river bluff.

"Hey–" Cora objected.

The birds were her particular pleasure, earned through the use of her body. But when Ollanta pinned her with a glare, she retired sullenly to her hut.

Ollanta called to Huaccac: "Did you see me run yesterday?"

"Of course, I did. You were the fastest." Huaccac smiled happily, pleased at the opportunity to praise his brother.

"Would you like to run as swiftly one day?"

"More than anything."

"Can you catch those ducks then?"

Huaccac eyed the birds a bit doubtfully. Obviously heading for a swim, they were most of the way down the greasy slope that led to the water. He would have to hurry. "Yes," he answered at last. "I can catch the ducks."

"Show me. Catch the ducks and bring them here."

The boy started in pursuit. Ollanta unwrapped a sling he wore about his middle and whirled some pebbles at the ducks, moving them smartly along. A last shrewd throw as his brother reached the edge of the slippery bank and the birds fluttered into the water.

Belly-rumbling with laughter, Ollanta shouted, "Don't let them get away. Catch the ducks."

Little legs churning helplessly, Huaccac skidded over the bluff into the snow-fed river. For several teasing seconds he remained within arms' reach of shore, then, relentlessly, the river tugged at him. He edged into the faster current.

"Ollanta! Ollanta! Help!"

The rushing waters covered the sound of his brother's wild laughter.

Huaccac was dressed in the usual layers of clothing his mother insisted he wear: two knee-length cotton tunics covered a pair of breeches, over which was a tunic of alpaca wool and a vest. Around all this, Ocllo had tightly bound a belt. He'd hit the water upright, trapping a pocket of air underneath the garments.

From upstream, Ollanta could make out only the garish turban-like headgear on his brother's head. Then it too bobbed out of sight.

In a field of maize downstream, a burly, middle-aged farmer sat guarding his half-grown crop against marauding birds. This was the highest point in the valley at which corn could be grown and he valued his crop highly. Wearing a fox skin over his head to frighten the birds, occasionally shaking a staff upon which rattles and tassels were attached, he went over yesterday's festival in his mind. He'd drank too much and suffered for it today, although that was of small importance. It had been exciting...with much to talk about for days to come....

A bleary eye wandered lazily toward the river, and suddenly, he started.

What was this rushing down the current? He blinked slowly, and looked again. It was still there, sweeping closer. It must be a brilliant water bird of a type he'd never seen before.

But when the current curved toward the shore, he made out a pale, little face, stiff with cold, under a bright turban.

With stabs of his staff, the farmer tried to grapple the mid-section of the little-boy-water-bird. One last thrust emptied the pocket of air under the billowing garments, and Huaccac disappeared underwater.

When the farmer hauled him out, he seemed lifeless.

Tiny fists doubled at his sides, his body stiff and still, the farmer was certain he was dead. Laying his head to the boy's chest, though, he discovered a slight heartbeat. Hangover forgotten now, he wrapped his cloak about the child and started for town at a rapid half-walk, half-run. He recognized the child as the curaca's youngest son, the little prince.

At the compound, he found Ocllo grinding maize, crushing it on a flat slab with a semi-circular stone. Coughing to gain her attention, the farmer held forth his burden.

Ocllo's hand darted to her throat. "No! No!"

She rushed him inside, her hands flying at his clothing.

"Bring blankets quickly," she babbled in near hysteria to the other women. "My long, red one, also."

The farmer was left squatting on his heels at the entrance to the compound. Later, when he managed to catch someone's eye, he asked for the return of his cloak. Then, slinging it over a shoulder, he went back to his corn field.

Ocllo ran her hand over Huaccac's forehead and found it hot and moist. He'd broken into a fever. She sent a messenger to inform Changa of the situation, and to urgently request his attendance.

~ * ~

That afternoon, a deeply concerned Changa, summoned the *camasca*, physician. The old man chanted his rituals, administered his herbs and powders, and offered the curaca some advice: "Make sacrifices to both the Sun and Viracocha. Offer coca to the Sun...gold and silver to Viracocha. Make certain you omit no detail," he added. "Observe the ceremony strictly."

Once again, the powers of Viracocha, the creator, and the Sun, the supreme deity, were demonstrated. When Changa returned home the next day, a smiling Mama Ocllo met him with a happy announcement. Huaccac's fever had broken. He'd awakened a short while ago, she told him, and was able to talk and sit up a little.

Changa found him sipping water from a cup held by Tasque, the long-haired serving girl.

Ollanta was there, as well, standing silently off to one side. To disguise his relief at Huaccac's recovery, the curaca gruffly demanded of his eldest son, "Where have you been all day?"

"With the llamas, of course.... How is Huaccac?"

Changa bent over the boy. "How did you fall into the river?"

Huaccac closed his eyes, and he was back in the icy river. Someone laughed at him. It filled him with fear and uncertainty, and he didn't know why.

When his eyes opened again, they sought out Ollanta.

"How was it you fell into the river?" Changa repeated.

Ollanta stared back at Huaccac, unwavering.

A horrible realization gripped Huaccac. *No! It was not possible!* He twisted his head away, unable to look at his brother any longer.

"What happened?"

"I...I was playing with Piqui Chaqui and slipped on the wet grass." His voice fell into a thin cough.

Ocllo elbowed Changa aside. "He must rest now," she shrilled.

Thrown off balance by his wife's temerity, Changa stood quietly while she fussed over the figure on the sleeping mat.

Ollanta snapped his fingers at Tasque. "Bring food," he ordered. "I am hungry."

~ * ~

In the month that followed, Huaccac gained gradually in strength. His mother took him several times to bathe in the thermal hot springs not far from Coporaque. And she insisted on making further sacrifices to the deities, hounding Changa relentlessly until he complied.

To his personal amazement, the curaca did exactly as she demanded. Later, he admitted grudgingly to himself that she'd been right, because when another thirty days had passed, their son had regained all that he'd lost. And by the time of the first crop ripening, he had put flesh on his thin frame. The rosy circle on each coppery-brown cheek deepened in color, as evidence of improving vigor and health.

And not least of all, Mama Ocllo reverted to her gentle ways, smiling often and laughing frequently, so that once more Changa was pleased to enter his house.

Chapter Ten
The Post Runner

In the second year after Yahuar Huaccac's misadventure in the river, near the time of the celebration of the vernal equinox, a *chasqui*, post runner, sped west on the Inca Road toward Coporaque.

Frenzied activity on the road was common nowadays, as runners brought news of the war that raged between the Inca Huascar and his half-brother, Prince Atahualpa of Quito.

The death of Inca Huayna Capac, several years past, had sowed the seeds of civil war.

In his palace in the newly-conquered province of Quito, Huayna Capac had lain dying. Fevered, pustules erupting on his skin from a foreign pestilence, he had desperately sought to arrange his succession. But it had been left too late. Before his heir could be settled upon, the great Inca died.

With that, the chief priest in Cuzco, far to the south, conferred the royal fringe on Prince Huascar, a son of Huayna Capac and his sister-wife Queen.

In Quito, Prince Atahualpa, darling of the huge Northern Army, watched and waited. A favorite son of the late Inca, he nevertheless refused to accompany his father's mummified remains to Cuzco. Nor would he journey there to witness Huascar's coronation.

War eventually erupted between the two, south fighting north, Cuzco pitted against the new province of Quito. The slaughter was unimaginable.

When princes go to war, thousands of lesser men must die.

Now the unthinkable had occurred. Huascar, God King, the Son of the Sun, had been tumbled from his golden litter!

The chasqui entered the outskirts of town, sandalled feet slapping on the hilly road as he made for the great square.

Without breaking stride, he lifted a conch shell from around his neck and trumpeted a blast to announce his coming.

Changa was in discussion with the governor, Mayta Yupanqui, and several other men in the courtyard of the Copper Palace. They broke off when the chasqui entered.

The runner came forward and saluted the governor.

Seated on a stool, Mayta Yupanqui ordered the man to speak. "From your manner I can see you bear important news."

The post runner panted, gulping air before speaking. He was a tallish man and, stripped for running to the chasquis' light tunic, his body was as lithe and lean as a panther's. Running at top speed for short distances, these men could deliver a message from Cuzco to Coporaque in one twenty-four hour period. A man on the march, even a forced march, would take five to six days. When the runner spoke, he used fluent Quechua.

"The Inca Huascar has been defeated in a battle near Cuzco," he announced breathlessly, fingering his *quipu*, a memory aid of knotted strings.

A stunned silence fell over the courtyard.

The governor hunched forward on his stool. "There has been a great killing then?"

The runner fingered his quipu again. "In the battle, many thousands were slain! Cuzco's defenders have fled in terror!"

"And what of the noble Prince Huascar?" the governor asked softly.

"The Inca Huascar has been taken prisoner." The runner hesitated then, licking his lips nervously before adding in halting tones: "It is further said that Atahualpa's generals dressed the Prince in women's clothing...and...forced him to eat excrement from Cuzco's streets."

A collective gasp halted him. He stood quietly, eyes darting about.

The governor held up a hand. "Go on," he told the runner.

"Many of Huascar's family have been killed. Hundreds! And others who supported him in the past, also. Often, he is forced to watch the executions. Some perish by torture–even women and children. Prince Atahualpa has ordered a purge!"

This was terrible news! Terrible! For all Huascar's faults and instability, he remained a man of Cuzco and these men gathered here were his followers. Some were kinsmen to him, including the governor. Each man now wondered which of his friends and relatives he would never see again.

"Where is Atahualpa now?" Changa asked.

"The Prince remained in Quito while his army marched south under his generals. He is expected to travel soon to Cuzco."

Changa stole a look at the governor. For a man whose life was now clearly at risk, Mayta Yupanqui had received the news with surprising equanimity. Already high in Changa's estimation, the old nobleman rose another notch. The governor asked the runner, "Is there aught else you wish to tell us?"

"One thing more," the runner replied, breathing more easily now and speaking in a normal voice. "There have been further stories of the strange bearded men."

Changa started. The bearded men! For several years now, reports had drifted in from the northern coast of strange, white-skinned men with hair on their faces.

"What can you tell us of the bearded men?" he asked.

"Only that they are at Tumbes." Tumbes was a city many days travel to the north.

"What else?"

"Nothing else," the runner said, relaxing completely. He was finished now.

Mayta Yupanqui waved him away. They must hold a council immediately. He issued an order to summon all high ranking officials.

~ * ~

When all had gathered, Changa kept to one side, his face expressionless while Mayta Yupanqui related the news to those who had not yet heard it. The reactions of these men interested the curaca. Until now, they'd not been directly affected by the war between the Princes. Except for occasional recruits demanded by Huascar, this southern valley had been spared the fighting.

"How could the mighty Huascar's army be defeated?" a cousin of the governor demanded in shocked disbelief. "The people of the north could never defeat the true Inca."

The governor's usual reserve snapped. "Huascar has been defeated," he rapped in his clear, piping voice. "Atahualpa is the new *Sapa Inca*, Supreme Inca. It would be better to accept this." He turned to Changa, whose judgement he valued. "What is your counsel? Speak to us."

Changa spoke slowly. "Let us remain patient a few days longer, to await further news. When we're certain of the situation, we can send a delegation to the Inca, be he Atahualpa...or Huascar." It seemed a vain hope, but it might yet be possible for Huascar to regain the upper hand.

Voices exploded before he finished. These followers of Huascar were loath to pay fealty to another. But Changa saw it was more than that. Fear gripped them. Smiling grimly to himself, Changa resumed his position to one side.

"...Maybe the runner was wrong..."

"...No. Huascar has been overthrown. I believe it. There have been many fires in the night sky of late. And the large number of earthquakes that have shaken the land in the past year is most unusual..."

"...Atahualpa is a man of Quito. Perhaps he will remain there, and we can live as always..."

A wiry, dark-skinned curaca called Guanmalla rose to speak. "Listen to the words of Changa," he advised, holding up his hands for quiet. "Let us remain calm and decide what to do when we have further information. Later, if we must journey to Atahualpa to offer fealty, we will do so."

Changa nodded gratefully to him. Guanmalla resumed his seat on the ground.

And so the council proceeded. The sun dipped toward broad Hualca-Hualca. The brief twilight began. When a chill evening wind arose, curling up from the river bottom, everyone simply wrapped themselves more tightly in their wool and continued the palaver.

In the end, nothing was resolved.

What was more, Changa thought sourly as he walked home, dissension had been evident. He'd never witnessed such a thing before. As a man accustomed all his life to strict discipline, this troubled him greatly. The authority of the governor and the curacas had been invested in them by

Huascar and Huascar's father. All that was set aside now. The very pattern of their lives seemed in doubt.

"Order," he rumbled to his household that evening. "If the old order disappears, what can replace it?"

Ollanta was curious about the bearded strangers. "I hear they have hair on their faces... like llamas." He laughed at the idea. "But is it also true they possess miraculous powers?"

Mama Ocllo said, "If they do have white skins and hair the color of gold, maybe they truly are Children of the Sun...sent here to aid us against Atahualpa."

Changa wanted no more of this talk. Huaccac sat at his feet, listening carefully, although not able to fully understand what was happening. His father issued an order to end the chatter and placed a hand on Huaccac's shoulder. All sought out the mats of straw upstairs.

Wrapped in his sleeping robes, Changa felt tired, incredibly tired. Yet a feeling of foreboding caused him to toss restlessly, denying him sleep long after others slumbered around him.

~ * ~

Sitting on the ground inside the compound, Huaccac searched Piqui Chaqui for fleas. As he groomed the dog, he heard incredible sounds coming from the house; his mother was actually arguing with his father. In his short life, he could not recall another such instance. Piqui Chaqui whined, and pawed at his leg. "Shhh," he quieted him, cocking an ear toward the house.

"He's too young," Mama Ocllo insisted, her voice shrill. "Leave him with me."

Huaccac could picture her clenching her skirts, a thing she did when upset.

"He's not too young," came a bass rumble. "At his age, Ollanta attended the *Yacha-huasi*, House of Teaching, in Cuzco. It's time for Huaccac to go also.

"Wait a couple of more months, at least. There's much fighting as yet."

"We must travel to Cuzco without delay–to offer Atahualpa our loyalty. It's best to bring Huaccac with us. Placing him in the *Yacha-huasi* now will demonstrate his own fealty. It will be safer for him than hiding here."

"You're taking Ollanta. Why risk both your sons? You can't be sure what this murderer from Quito will do."

"Enough of this dangerous talk! Atahualpa is carrying out a purge of all whom he believes loyal to Huascar. Have you forgotten what happened to others of your family?"

"Huaccac has a few drops of royal blood and no more."

"Both you and I have been closely connected to the noble Huascar. That in itself is more than enough provocation for Northerners who hate us, and who see enemies behind every rock. Huaccac will accompany us to Cuzco," he roared.

From Mama Ocllo there came bitter silence.

The blanket that hung over the door flew back and Changa strode out. He made off toward the square.

Huaccac screwed his face up in concentration, reflecting upon what he'd just overheard. A journey to Cuzco! Imagine! He'd heard wonderful tales all his life about the marvels outside his home province. He supposed some dangers existed also, but, knowing little of politics and less of war, he decided to trust his father. If Changa had decided to take him, it must be all right.

His rosy cheeks bunched in excitement. Maybe he would even see the incredible bearded men.

Piqui Chaqui barked for attention. Huaccac showed him a knot of alpaca wool tied into a ball. The dog wriggled. Huaccac threw it across the compound. This was a new game he was teaching him. "Run, Piqui Chaqui," he hollered. "Catch the ball and bring it here." The dog bounded off, barking, while Huaccac shouted with laughter.

~ * ~

The fifty men moved up the Inca Road along the river, passing hamlets and farms along the way, and the stone huts where the post runners lived.

They spent the first night in a rest house above the fortressed town on the river bank where the long aqueduct began that carried water all the way to Coporaque. By afternoon of the next day, they had reached the top of the valley, where the silver mines lay, and where the copper for the Copper Palace had come from.

Here, they left the valley behind, and climbed up through the grey mist to the sun-brightened puna above the clouds. On the endless plateau, the broad Inca Road, well marked by stones and wooden markers, pointed north to Cuzco and the farther reaches of the empire.

"*Apachicta muchani*, I worship at this heap," said Ollanta at the summit of the pass, tossing a pellet of coca he'd been chewing onto a pile beside the road.

The other men of high caste likewise tossed pellets of coca, thank offerings for the safe journey thus far. The men of lower caste simply used pebbles.

Yahuar Huaccac had never seen this high, empty land before. He peered around in wonderment. Aside from his friends, not a living thing existed, not a tree, hardly a sound. Stones, large and small, were scattered everywhere, as if flung helter skelter from the hand of mighty Viracocha. A chill wind chased little puffs of grey dust into the air. From off in the lonely distance, a bird trilled: "Puco-puco."

He edged closer to his father's comforting presence. This strange, open place made him uneasy. He had lived within shadows and valleys and sheltering hills all his life. For a moment, he wished his mother and Piqui Chaqui were here.

"Forward," called Mayta Yupanqui.

Changa signalled to Huaccac to crawl onto a litter. The boy did so willingly for the long, arduous ascent had left him tired. They'd started out in the pre-dawn hours, yet would still have to march briskly to reach the nearest rest house before nightfall.

An hour farther on, they passed a trio of geysers spitting boiling water into the air. Beyond them, shimmering in the distance, lay a lagoon with barely made out pink figures prowling its waters. These brackish lagoons, all that remained of once great inland seas, supported the primitive marine life flamingos thrived on.

It was nearing dusk when they came to the long, narrow lake with the boggy shores. It teemed with bird life: gulls, puna ibises, ducks, Andean geese, and giant, black coots.

Huaccac observed this with utter fascination until a litter bearer grunted and gestured toward the far shore.

Six Andean geese stood among the boulders back from the shore, keeping wary eyes on the procession of humans. Initially, Huaccac thought the man was merely pointing out those big, black and white birds, but he gestured again, waving his hand far, far back to where a rise of land broke the horizon. There, Yahuar Huaccac saw the lovely lady of the puna.

It was his first sighting of a vicuna, the creature with the golden fleece.

She was a young, delicate female, made to seem tiny by distance, part of a group of eight, one male and his harem. The little female was making pathetic demonstrations of supplication before the male, bending her knees and arching her long, lovely neck in total submissiveness. Suddenly, the male attacked her, assisted by a large, pregnant female.

The little female was being expelled from the family.

The male attacked again, his tail raised in hostility, his white bib waving from his lower neck. He loped at her, screeching, his neck nearly horizontal, his eyes dead ahead.

She ran to a little hill and halted there to gaze back in bewilderment at her family. They were now placidly grazing.

Huaccac's caravan had reached the far end of the lake before she finally turned and walked away. He watched until she disappeared from sight, but she never looked back again.

The caravan picked up the pace. Jovial banter was tossed back and forth. The rest house had come into view, pebble-sized from here, on the plain in front of a chimney of the Andes, a smoking crater whose lip was as piled with yellow sulphur as any of the gates of hell.

From behind them came a "gronk." The geese had taken flight. Powerful wings beating, they wheeled and swept off to the west, into the diminishing sunlight.

Chapter Eleven
Little Andy

Andrew Slade, Sr. splashed whiskey into his tin cup, settled his lean, muscular back against the maple tree, and stretched his long legs out, comfortably, in front of him. He sighed in pleasure. Andrew Slade waited all year for this–a crisp autumn afternoon in the Green Mountains of Vermont, and the opening of the deer hunting season.

A chipmunk, tail up, scampered through a pile of dead leaves, making an amount of noise all out of proportion to its size.

"That chipmunk sounds louder than a bull moose in those leaves," laughed Andrew, Sr. He cocked an indulgent eye at the sixteen year old boy sitting by the fire, going over his rifle with skilled, sure fingers. "Want a drink of whiskey, Andy?" he offered. "I don't mind you having a drink...long's it's with me."

Andrew Slade, Jr. shook his head. "Nah," he said, and continued with what he was doing. The boy didn't talk much.

"Goddammit," cried a voice from over by the tent. A stocky, balding man clumped over to place a locked gun case on the ground. "Forgot the damn combinations again," Gino de Fazio complained. He emptied his pockets for the paper with the lock combination on it.

Everybody laughed. Gino's son, Michael, a boy a year older than Andy, with a round, happy face and his father's broad, comfortable frame, got the biggest kick out of it, though. His father's terrible memory provided a constant source of humor for the de Fazio family. And now he couldn't open the case of that fancy, imported shotgun he was so proud of.

"Let Andy have a go at it," Andrew, Sr. said, more than half seriously.

"If he can't figure out the combination inside of five minutes, I'll buy you a new gun."

Young Andy smiled knowingly. He had no doubt he could do it, and inside of five minutes, too.

"That's quite a talent he's got," his father went on, chuckling. "I get real nervous, though, thinking about how he'll ever put it to use."

"Got it," Gino announced triumphantly, holding up a piece of paper. A cheer sounded from around the campfire.

Gino fitted the pieces of the shotgun together and threw it to his shoulder. "I'll try it out on partridges tomorrow afternoon." He sighted a last time along the twin, gleaming barrels then held it out to Michael. "Go ahead, Mike. See how smoothly it handles. Those British gun smiths make the best shotguns in the world."

Michael hefted it, following a black squirrel as it ran along the branch of an oak tree. His movements were as ungainly as his father's. He looked awkward with a gun, unlike Andy who was graceful with a firearm.

Andy smirked a little watching the other lad's clumsy efforts. Michael caught the look and handed the gun back to his father. "Yep. She's a real nice gun all right." Sitting down by the fire, he studiously avoided looking in Andy's direction.

There had always been tension between the two boys. The fathers were close friends, and so had brought their sons together. But it proved a poor match. Easy-going, sometimes bumbling Michael, and Andy, an intense, solitary lad, with all of his father's good looks and natural athletic ability, didn't get along too well.

"Little Andy's the very spit of his father," folks said, when the two walked down the street together. "As alike as peas in a pod."

Big Andy and Little Andy they were called.

~ * ~

At dawn, the usual opening day barrage erupted. Gunfire split the quiet in all directions. None of the four even saw a deer, however, so on the way back to camp for lunch, Big Andy suggested they try the cedar swamp near the pond.

"It's along the way," he reasoned to Gino. "A damn good spot for a smart buck to hide in. We'll put the boys on either side, and you and me'll go in and dog the place out."

It worked out as he wanted. A big, mature buck kept his head right up until the last minute, only losing his nerve and running when Gino was almost on top of him.

Whistling in alarm, he bounded right past Michael. Spinning awkwardly, Michael fired at the blur.

"Whoop!" he yelled as the buck went down. "Got 'im!" It was his first buck and the excitement in his voice resonated through the trees.

The buck thrashed feebly as the others hurried up. His back broken, unable to rise, he still pawed the ground, scraping his rack in the humus and leaves littering the forest floor.

Gino beamed at his son. "Nice shootin', Mike. We'll have to bleed him, though. It's your deer, you do it."

The buck picked that moment to turn a tortured eye on Michael. It proved too much for him. Recoiling a step, he glanced sideways at his father, pleading on his face.

"Mike, you gotta bleed him. You know that. It's your deer." When he didn't move, Gino's voice rose a notch. "Get a knife in your hand and cut that buck's throat."

Michael shook his head. "No," he bleated, and dropped his gun in the dirt.

When Gino cut the creature's throat, and then proceeded with the field dressing, pulling the steaming contents from the paunch, Michael vomited his breakfast down the front of his brand new, red-checkered hunting shirt.

No one said a word as they dragged the carcass back to camp, to hang it from the "meat pole."

~ * ~

Three days later, Little Andy shot a deer, a spike buck that plunged into a steep ravine on its death run.

By leaning over, he could see the little buck in a trickle of water at the bottom, twenty to thirty feet down. Initially, looking down made him feel merely uncomfortable, then without warning, his head began to spin. He stepped back a pace, closed his eyes, and thought *tick-tick-tick*.

When Andy was twelve, he and his little sister and his parents had visited his mother's sister. She was a spinster lady who gave piano lessons to neighborhood children in order to supplement a meager income.

Andy hated going there. And he didn't like his aunt either. She was forever fussing over him in her syrupy fashion, hugging him, using pet endearments. All the things he most disliked.

On this occasion, Andy had been forced to sit by while a child received a piano lesson. His parents and sister had gone to the supermarket, so his aunt's home was completely quiet except for the inept playing of the youngster. That and the sound of the metronome on top of the piano...tick-tick-tick.

Its perfect regularity, alike to the rhythmic sounds heard inside the warmth and security of the womb, fascinated him at once. Afterwards, when the child had gone and he was alone, he set the arm moving and sat there listening to that steady beat. He found it comforting. A happy smile appeared. Andy liked regularity. He liked things well organized.

Right then, he decided to try using the metronome as an organizer for himself. A comforting agent. The idea came to him just like that, like a brilliant thought out of the ether. And it worked perfectly.

It had been his valued inner compass ever since.

Tick-tick-tick, went Andy by the ravine. He bent over to look at the buck again. His head spun. He felt slightly queasy.

Tick-tick-tick.

His head spun faster.

Tick-tick-tick.

Panic. A coppery taste filled his mouth.

In a nervous sweat, he slumped to the ground.

Michael walked up. "Heard a shot," he called out. "Hit anything?"

"A spike buck," Andy muttered. "He fell into that hole there."

Mike took a look. "Gawd! How you gonna get him up?"

"Where's the others...my father?"

"I'm not sure. Might be over by the cedar swamp again. I guess they didn't hear the shot."

"Oh!" Andy chewed his lip in indecision.

"We'll have to climb down and get him up ourselves."

"There's some rope at the camp," Andy hedged. "I'll go bring it."

"Waste of time," Mike stated decisively. "He's a real small buck. With the two of us working we can haul him up by hand." This was bold, commanding language for him to use, the sort of thing you would expect more from Andy.

Andy shook his head. "It's pretty steep, almost sheer. It's too dangerous without the rope."

Michael broke into a scathing grin. This was a signal success for him. Although his embarrassment at having thrown up while watching his father gut the deer had dissipated, it still bothered him that Andy regarded his behavior as shameful.

Andy was cornered and he knew it. "All right, then," he stated evenly. "Let's do it without the rope."

Michael grinned again, placed his rifle on the ground, and gingerly eased his body over the edge. Going carefully from ledge to ledge, he commenced working his way to the bottom.

Andy forced himself to follow. He had not gone more than a few yards, however, when his head started spinning again. Desperate to make it stop, he made the mistake of glancing down. The little buck sprang into view, his head at right angles to his body, his neck broken by the fall.

Andy froze.

Tick-tick-tick.

"What's wrong?" Mike shouted from the bottom.

Andy didn't hear him. He had departed to a place over which he had no control. Different colored lights flashed by at horrendous speed.

Tick-tick-tick.

A rushing sound invaded his ears.

Tick-tick-tick-tick-tick-tick...

Michael clambered back up. "You okay?" he asked, concern in his voice.

No response.

"C'mon," he soothed. "Let's go up top. It's not far."

No response.

Michael plucked at one of Andy's feet, and placed it in a foothold six inches up. Prying a hand loose, he fastened it into a grip above Andy's head. "C'mon, for Chrissake," he grunted, and got below with his head in the other boy's crotch. He heaved, and Andy inched nearer to the top and safety.

It took a full half-hour before Michael de Fazio, laboring mightily, pushed him over the edge. Streaming sweat, he collapsed onto the ground and glanced at Andy in amazement. It was simply astonishing; whoever would have dreamed Andy Slade would choke up like that.

Andy didn't stop trembling for a further fifteen minutes. Then, he broke down and cried.

"Forget it ever happened," Mike offered magnanimously. "You're just scared of heights, that's all. A lot of people are." He smiled confidentially. "My problem is looking at blood and all. The smell, too, I guess. Like with the deer I shot. I didn't like watching it die that way."

Andy stopped snuffling. "What're you saying?"

"Everyone's got problems. Certain things they're scared of."

"And that makes you and me more or less the same, does it? Isn't that what you mean?" Andy's grey eyes had steadied. A steely glint appeared.

Mike began to lose his temper. "Hey, you might as well admit it. You lost your cool. You froze on that ledge. I damn well had to carry you up here."

Andy's jaw clenched. His lips straightened into a bloodless line as he searched for words that would hurt. "Never compare yourself with me again," he spat. "You're a slob Italian! A meatball!"

"I fucked Evelyn," Michael struck back, swiftly and cruelly.

Andy's face went white, this time from rage.

Many of the boys at the high school he and Michael attended had made use of dark-haired Evelyn McKnight's soft, willing body. Evelyn enjoyed sex more than the boys did. And more than that, she enjoyed the obvious fact the boys were enjoying themselves. But she was an out-going, jolly girl and Andrew Slade, Jr.'s bloodless personality repelled her.

So, although he was supple and muscular, and far handsomer than Michael de Fazio was, she had rejected his every advance.

He had never gotten over the humiliation.

Mike got to his feet, grinning, seeing he had scored. "Evelyn says

86

your hands were like cold grease. She says she can see why you're always alone. None of her girlfriends want to bother with you either."

Andy rose to his feet, trembling. He stood looking at Michael, unable to think of a reply.

Mike laughed in his face.

Andy's booted foot lashed out, acting on its own, smashing into Michael's right kneecap. He collapsed, gripping the knee with both hands, his round features twisted in pain. Andy's boot flew once more, this time seeking out a place behind the ears, at the stem of the brain. Michael went limp.

Tick-tick-tick.

An incredible calm settled over Andy. He remained for a time simply gazing at the inert form on the ground. Five minutes passed, and a soft smile appeared on his face. He nearly laughed out loud. Of course! That's what to do. Why hadn't he thought of it right away?

Thunk! went his boot. Thunk! again. Then, thunk-thunk. Working around the head, his boot located the vulnerable points, seeming to know them as if by instinct.

In no time at all, Michael de Fazio was dead.

Then, he rolled the body into the rocky ravine and walked back to camp.

"There's been an accident," he announced. "Mike was climbing down a ravine after a dead buck and slipped and fell. I went down after him, but I couldn't get him to move."

~ * ~

Little Andy Slade impatiently cracked his knuckles. This ceremony at the cemetery was a crashing bore. He'd known it would be, and resented having to leave what he'd been doing at home to come. Andy had an interest in airplanes. Just recently, he'd bought a kit to build a model plane operable by remote control. He was good at that sort of thing. In fact, he was working on some modifications he'd thought up himself that he was sure would make the plane fly better.

Around him people wept. Michael de Fazio had been very popular. A large crowd had gathered for the final rites. Little Andy shifted uncomfortably. Gino and his wife sobbed uncontrollably. That was to be expected, of course, but Big Andy looked amazingly disconsolate as well. He stood slouched over by Little Andy's mother and sister. His mother's tall, buxom form appeared hardly less grim than Andrew Slade, Sr.'s was.

Andy moved a little ways off to get away from them.

Chapter Twelve
Mina Madrugada

The mine's airstrip ran at right angles to the road, pointing in the general direction of a cluster of buildings sprawled at the base of a hill a mile off. Mina Madrugada–mine of the dawn.

Parked on the airstrip by a wooden shack was a big-tailed, high-winged aircraft. A bored-looking fellow in a security uniform leaned against the shack.

"That's a 206," Slade said.

"A what?" asked Garrick.

"That plane's a Cessna 206." He sounded very satisfied about something. "She's turbo-charged from the look of that exhaust system, she's got wing fences on her, and I bet she's got a Robertson S.T.O.L. Conversion, too. They got 'er rigged up perfect for this high, rough country. She'll cruise at up to 160 miles an hour, and with those extra wing tanks, she'll fly for a thousand miles without having to refuel."

"I didn't realize you knew so much about aircraft."

"If it has wings, I can fly it. With this plane, I could go anywhere I chose."

His words came out flat, unhurried. A simple statement of fact. And because he, himself, obviously believed what he was saying, Garrick was convinced also.

"Were you a pilot in Iraq?"

Instead of replying, Slade leaned across to speak to Roxana. "That's the mine's plane. Right?"

Her dislike for him still on display, she answered with a curt nod.

Three burros, laden with tola bush for firewood, blocked the road. She blew the horn and attempted to maneuver around them, but one contrary beast edged in front and halted there, feet planted. He was a shaggy creature, badly in need of a haircut. Grey hair hung in untidy patches, and the bangs hanging down over his eyes were so long and thick it must've been difficult for him to see where he was going.

The young Quechua in charge of the burros belabored the stubborn one with a switch torn from its load of tola bush, and the creature moved at last, braying its outrage. When one of the others joined in, their discordant chorus pursued the Land Rover long after they'd left the airstrip behind and had turned for the mine.

The guard at the gate recognized Roxana. After a brief exchange, he opened the gate on hinges that whined softly in protest. She drove to a parking area behind a brick-sided, one story office building.

Two hundred yards to the rear and up a gentle slope lay a little town of workshops and living quarters connected by gravel footpaths.

Ugly mountains of slag scarred the intermediate landscape. Barely made out above one of them, a headframe for a mine shaft, like some giant gallows tree, stabbed the sky.

The mine and its environs would have made a depressing picture in any setting; in this bucolic countryside they were absolute horrors. Grime and soot and used chemicals from the processing plants fouled the windows of the office building. Once-white window frames had become a drab brown-grey.

The two men waited while Roxana went into the building, banging a swinging door behind her. After briefly surveying the immediate surroundings, Garrick gave up in disgust and gazed off into the distance instead, to where mighty Ampato, mountain of the gods, peeked above the rim of the world.

Slade's attention stayed active and close.

Roxana soon came to the door and called them in.

Two youngish women and an older, heavy-set man worked at desks in a large front room. The three visitors walked across the room and down the corridor to the rear, passing offices with people in them. One office at the end was locked shut behind a stout, steel door.

In the room opposite, a tall, skeletal figure sat bent over a desk studying a sheaf of papers. He looked up when they entered.

Roxana introduced him. "This is Domingo Valdivia, the mine manager."

Valdivia unfolded his emaciated frame from a swivel chair, and crossed the floor in one lazy, giant stride. He was an odd looking fellow, his head curiously wedge-shaped with greying hair standing out in great electric tufts all over it. His eyes skipped about, shiny and brown, with tiny veins of yellow road-mapping the whites.

"Bienvenido a Mina Madrugada," he said, a rigid smile of welcome on his face.

His speech came out loud and confident through lips that barely moved; old, shiny scar tissue on his mouth seemed to lock it into a perpetual sneer.

Slade stepped forward. "Pleased to meet you, Señor Valdivia," he said amiably. "Quite an impressive operation you have on the go here."

Valdivia's sneer did not waver, but his gaze lingered approvingly on Slade. "Yes, Mina Madrugada is a thoroughly modernized mine." He spoke very understandable English, and swaggered a bit with his gestures.

His attention wandered to Roxana, and an unmistakable gleam entered his eyes. "Roxana is the niece of an old friend," he boomed. "And more than that. She brings light and color to La Madrugada." He peered at each of them in turn, as if inviting applause for his gallantry, then finished with a shout of laughter.

Garrick laughed along with him, unable to help himself. It seemed that Domingo Valdivia had more than an avuncular interest in Roxana, and any picture he could conjure up of the two of them together struck him as hilarious.

A prissy, pouty twist to Roxana's mouth showed she knew why he was laughing.

"She has charmed myself and my friend also," Garrick assured Valdivia, while giving her a devil's grin.

The mine manager's pie-shaped head bobbed sagely, as though he and the young American had just shared an intimacy. "Listo," he said, beaming. Then, he consulted his watch and announced he had to see to certain matters.

"You are welcome at La Madrugada," he declared before departing. "There's a place for you to sleep–Roxana knows where. I'll join you for dinner." With a last devouring eyeful of Roxana, he bent his angular frame around the door and disappeared.

"If the light and color of La Madrugada will show us where we bunk," Garrick guffawed, "we'd sure as hell appreciate it."

Roxana's bottom twitched angrily all the way back up the corridor.

~ * ~

The long, low mess hall used by the senior staff occupied a little rise overlooking the small, grimy world of Mina Madrugada. Aside from the group at Garrick's table, another fifteen or so people ate there that evening.

Domingo Valdivia planted his elbows on the plastic-covered table while he spooned alpaca stew into his stiffened mouth. "Mina Madrugada is principally a copper mine," he explained between mouthfuls, "although significant amounts of silver are found in the ore, as well."

Slade asked a polite question regarding the recovery and processing of the silver. After the answer, he shook his head admiringly. "Mining's a damn tough life."

"You have worked as a miner yourself?" Valdivia asked.

"Yeah, for one summer," Slade chuckled, holding up a single finger. "In a uranium mine in Arizona–one summer only. Just long enough to learn how tough it is underground, and to decide to do something else with my life. I admire miners, though.... Like I said, it's a tough life."

Valdivia leaned back in his chair, steepled his fingers, and regarded Slade with that look teachers reserve for students who may be worth spending extra time with. "I've heard that uranium mining is very difficult," he said. "It's very hot underground near the uranium, eh? Very hard to breathe. Fortunately, the work we do here is not so exhausting. Tomorrow, if you wish, I could show you around."

"I'd appreciate that."

He turned to Roxana. "What're your plans? How long will you spend here this time?" He leaned forward in anticipation of her answer, and when she replied, "Oh, a few days at least," he sat back, a pleased expression lighting up his face.

One of his hands drifted over to rest beside hers, a bony finger twitched onto her arm. She slid her arm off the table and dropped her hands onto her lap. His hand disappeared also and, seconds later, there was a scraping sound as she shifted her chair away from him and a little closer to Garrick.

"What are you going to do tomorrow?" Garrick asked her.

"Going to Coporaque. To see Mother Catarina again. She mentioned something interesting today. I want to follow up on it."

"Interesting?"

"Catarina mentioned an old man living in the hills who is regarded as extremely knowledgeable about this area. I'd like to talk to him."

"I'll go along then."

"It may involve some climbing," came the brisk warning. "You're not acclimatized to the altitude yet. You may find it too difficult."

To have a woman question his physical prowess in this manner set Garrick sputtering. "Don't waste your time worrying about me," he huffed. "If *you* can climb the hills, I rather think I'll manage somehow." Calling the waiter over, he ordered a drink from the makeshift bar. "Ron con Coca Cola, por favor."

"This is your first day at extreme altitude," Roxana admonished coolly, her eyebrows up in a fine arch. "You shouldn't drink alcohol."

She really could be insufferable. Garrick opened his mouth to speak, forgot what he'd planned to say, and closed it again. When his rum and Coke arrived, he took a big gulp. It went down the wrong way and he wound up doubled over and coughing.

Slade threw

Chapter Thirteen
The Day at Munaypata

Towel over his shoulder, Garrick left the bathroom and walked up the hallway to the room he shared with Slade. It was just past 9:00 A.M. and the dormitory was quiet. Work shifts had changed over an hour ago. Most of the miners from the night shift had already eaten and gone to bed.

Slade stood at the window, but swung round when Garrick entered. Sunlight caught his face at an angle, moulding his features more sharply than usual.

"Are you sure you want to hang around here all day?" Garrick asked him. "Sounds pretty boring to me. Besides, Valdivia's a creep–did you see him last night at the dinner table trying to feel up Roxana?"

Slade issued one of his humorless grins. "I want to give you and your girlfriend some time alone together. I feel like I'm getting between you two."

"Go screw yourself!"

Slade studied him a moment before saying, "You're pretty touchy about certain things. You always been like that?"

Garrick put on his shirt, taking his time before replying. "No. It's a fairly recent development."

"The rear echelon pricks and the politicians," Slade pointed out. "We do the best job they let us do. I'm proud of my time in Iraq."

"Yeah, well, maybe. I still carry a lot around inside though."

"Yeah, I know," Slade sympathized. "Lots of my buddies went through the same thing." Then, he grinned again and said, "Let me tell you something else, pal. I was only half kidding a minute ago about you and Roxana. That broad's starting to get to you. Situation's getting a little serious perhaps."

"Nope. I prefer my women a trifle warmer around the edges. She comes on too strong for me. How 'bout you, anyhow? You got a girlfriend back home...or a wife, maybe?"

"No."

"Never felt like marrying?"

"No, I never felt like marrying. And I don't have a steady girlfriend either.... But if that worries you and if it'll make you feel better, I fucked four women in one day in a whorehouse once."

"Hey, man...look...I didn't mean to imply...." Garrick stammered in embarrassment.

Slade grinned. "Let's go get something to eat."

They met Roxana in the near-empty mess hall. As Garrick nibbled his fried eggs, he thought about what Slade had said.

Sitting opposite him in the bright, spacious mess, Roxana looked very appealing. She must have given her hair a stiff brushing for it shone glossily, cascading darkly onto her shoulders. Excited about the day's prospects, her eyes danced inside the curve of her face. While they dawdled over coffee, she chattered away with all the animation of a young girl planning her first party.

"Where's Domingo?" Slade asked her.

"In his office. He said to tell you he'll be busy this morning. The end of the week is payday–the payroll and the accounts have to be taken care of."

"They pay the men out here at the mine?"

She nodded. "The pilot and two guards flew the money in on the plane yesterday. That's the safest way to bring it here. Then, they lock it up in the strongroom."

"Oh...you mean that locked room across from Valdivia's office?"

"Yes, that's it." Her manner toward him was polite, but cool.

Slade leaned back casually in his chair. "Reckon I'll just wander 'bout this morning...amuse myself." He stretched luxuriously. "I don't want to be a bother to Señor Valdivia."

Later, as they jounced along the road to Coporaque, Roxana asked, "How much do you know about your friend?"

"Not much. I just met him. Why?"

"I don't like him."

"So I've noticed."

"I don't trust him. He gives me the creeps."

"Oh, for God's sake!"

"We don't even know his first name."

"So what? Look, Slade's all right. He's just a moody type. I admit he's a bit different–but he has a right to be. I can understand why that is...even if you can't."

"You mean the war? He uses that on you. He uses the war as leverage on you."

"Cut it out! What would he gain by doing that? And frankly, that's my business and not yours."

"Just trying to help."

The edges of Garrick's mind started to grind together.

When she spoke again, her voice was surprisingly gentle. "That war really affected you, didn't it?"

Stop! I don't want to talk about that.

She'd caught him in a state of *unpreparedness*. Also, he had heard her gentleness and didn't know how to deal with it. Lacking the necessary psychic armor, he withdrew, slipping into survivor mode.

Calmly, he said to the woman beside him. "The war doesn't bother me more than it does other men. Actually, I don't think about it too much anymore."

That didn't fool her, although they drove along silently for another mile or two before she ventured to speak again, saying, almost shyly, "I'm not always as bitchy as I may've appeared so far. Um...if you unbent a bit more, I probably would, too."

Then, astoundingly, her face colored a bright red.

A confused quiet descended between them. It was relieved only when she braked for a horse, ridden by a bare-footed, teen-aged boy using a folded blanket as a saddle. He kicked the beast smartly to one side.

Garrick managed a chuckle and the feeblest of jokes. "Ride 'em cowboy."

Blaring the horn, she accelerated past the startled boy, swaying down the road as if in flight from something that posed a danger to her.

~ * ~

"So, you want to know about Pachac Puquio," Mother Catarina said. "I've heard rumors about the place for years. Frankly, I'm not even sure it exists. If there is such a place, though, it's located somewhere downstream...somewhere extremely isolated."

They were seated on a bench near the church, in the shade cast by a wall. As on the previous day, there was little activity in the sleepy village. Swallows and wrens flitted busily about the kitchen garden nearby, despite the strips of shiny metal tied to the fruit trees to frighten them away. While speaking, the nun kept a cautious eye on the birds.

"The first I heard of Pachac Puquio was from the Alcalde of Chivay," Roxana reflected. "I wasn't quite sure at the time whether he was serious or joking."

"What's so unusual about this place?" Garrick asked them.

Catarina said, "The stories range from it being a village where renegade Spaniards settled, to a village so old and untouched that no Spaniard, in fact no non-Indian, has ever seen it." She smiled in her calm, deliberate way. "Take your pick. It could be another valley myth, and that's all."

"I wouldn't be so sure of that," Roxana demurred. "I have a gut feeling it does exist. I'd love to go there.... It'd certainly offer a more pristine view of pre-European Indian life than I could find anywhere else. It could even be a real archaeological find."

"If you intend to try and find Pachac Puquio, you'll have to prove another legend first." The nun's eyes twinkled. "That legend is Ampire, supposed to be the oldest man in the whole Colca basin. I haven't the faintest idea where he lives, other than it's high in the hills. His grandson lives not far off, though. In those old ruins at Munaypata, just east of here."

"Ampire knows Pachac Puquio?"

"I'm not sure what he knows. It's just that whenever I've heard the old people speak of the village, Ampire was usually mentioned as well."

Several blue and yellow tanagers joined the swallows and wrens in her garden. She regarded them disgustedly as they began to help themselves to her fruit.

"What's the grandson's name?"

"Cusi, I think." She rose to her feet, a signal she had things to do.

They bade her goodbye and left, leaving her to rush about her garden with a stick, chasing the birds from her almost-ripe fruits and vegetables.

They found Cusi at Munaypata, unloading a llama. The llama bolted as soon as the pack was lifted, cantering off with two children giving chase. They caught the animal and turned it into a stone corral.

Centuries earlier, a small town had existed here. The ancient homes, tombs, and storehouses were badly tumbled down, although some walls stood proudly as yet, monuments to the skill of their builders.

Cusi was forty-something, dirty, stoop-shouldered, with cheeks so shiny red they almost glowed. He fixed them with small, suspicious eyes.

Roxana's questions were answered in a slow, bitter-sounding monotone. He had a way of shaking his head stubbornly from time to time, as though what she asked amounted to a sheer impossibility.

Roxana became increasingly frustrated.

"It's no use," she concluded finally. "He doesn't want to be bothered. He doesn't know the way to Pachac Puquio himself, and he won't take us to his grandfather."

"Offer him some money."

The offer of money brought a crafty smile onto the Quechua's face. An interminable bargaining session began, at the conclusion of which he nodded his head in agreement.

"He's agreed to take us to speak to his grandfather," Roxana translated with a grin, pleased and relieved the marathon session had ended. "Then, on to Pachac Puquio."

"So, there is a Pachac Puquio."

"He says there is."

"I thought he didn't know how to get there?"

"He doesn't–not exactly that is. We'll have to get directions from his grandfather, Ampire. He lives in the mountains west of here. Cusi reckons Pachac Puquio is more or less a half-day's ride farther on."

"Ride?"

"Mules. He can bring them to the mine tomorrow, but he says they're very expensive. He's hiking the price up."

98

"How much?"

"It works out to about twenty dollars a mule. If your friend, Slade, insists on coming along, that'll mean four mules. Eighty bucks–too damn much."

"Tell him to bring four. I'll pay."

With arrangements completed, they started back to the Land Rover along a footpath between green bean fields. It was a perfect day, warm and sunny and you could see for miles.

"I wonder how Slade is making out with your honorary uncle?" Garrick mused aloud. "I think Valdivia sees himself as a sort of young Lochinvar. His Lochinvar to your fair Ellen perhaps." He chuckled. "This may sound nasty, but I fear he makes a more likely Iago."

"Who're they?"

"Iago was the villain in *Othello*, one of Shakespeare's tragedies. Lochinvar was the hero in Sir Walter Scott's ballad, *Marmion*.... He makes off with his lady love, Ellen, in dashing fashion."

"I can't quite picture you reading ballads and plays."

"I've read lots of ballads and plays. And literary fiction and poetry, too. I studied creative writing and journalism in college."

"Oh! You wanted to be a writer?"

"At one time I did.

"And?"

"I changed my mind. Nowadays, I write the occasional magazine article and that's all. I decided to become a soldier instead."

"You chose that over becoming a writer...a creative person?" She was incredulous.

"Yes, I did," Garrick replied shortly, wishing now he'd shut up.

"You were an officer, then?"

"No, I enlisted as a private."

She gave him one of those all-men-are-little-boys looks, and opened her mouth to start in again. He hustled to head her off. "What're your plans for the balance of the day?" he asked quickly. "We've the entire afternoon to kill."

"Poke around here. Spend some time at Yurac-Qaqa. That's the old Indian name for the long promontory you see just west of Coporaque. During

Inca times, it was an important ceremonial center."

They neared the Land Rover. A grey partridge exploded from a clump of head-high, plump chilca bushes with a whir of wings and a call: "Chirreep."

"Does Munaypata, the name of the ruins there, mean anything special in Quechua?"

"Munay in Quechua means love and will...or beautiful place...depending on how it's used. Pata means high, or above. By the way," she added dryly as they reached the vehicle, "*cusi* means happy."

"Happy!" Garrick hooted. "What a disappointment old misery guts must be to the people who named him. What's Coporaque mean?"

"I've heard various meanings. It probably comes from some Quechua words which mean place where the corn is dealt out."

"What are the other possibilities?"

She hesitated briefly, then looked him right in the eye and said, "Big cunt."

"What?"

"Some people I've met, the Alcalde of Chivay among them, swear that's what Coporaque means. The story is that one of the Incas found the women sent to him as concubines from Coporaque all had oversized sexual organs. So, he called the place 'Big Cunt.'" She dug out the car keys, got in the vehicle, and reached across to unlock Garrick's door. "Get in," she ordered.

But he was roaring with laughter and could not.

Chapter Fourteen
Night Moves

In the hours just prior to dawn, the part of Garrick's brain that acted as an alarm clock sent a message it was time to wake up. The same thing had happened last night–a reaction triggered by the lack of oxygen at high altitude.

Since Afghanistan, he had rarely slept a full night through in any case so, settling comfortably beneath the covers, he waited to fall asleep again. Few sounds intruded. Slade was a quiet sleeper, and the generator which provided the camp with electricity issued only a gentle hum in the distance.

His thoughts drifted to Roxana and how she had looked yesterday, clambering like an exuberant schoolgirl up the hill at Yurac-Qaqa. She could be a confusing person at times; abrasive one minute, kind and charming the next.

What was it she had said earlier? ..."*I'm not as bitchy as I've seemed. If you unbent more, I would, too.*" Or words to that effect. Words that could only be considered as an initiative of some kind.

As a rather shy man of only average physical attractiveness, he had never been terribly successful with women. He enjoyed women, though, the way they looked and moved, graceful with soft, rounded limbs. He liked the prettiness of women.

The sight of Roxana striding athletically along, raven's hair bouncing, remained with him like some optical echo.

A light rustle sounded on the far side of the room. A solid black shape floated across to the door.

It was Slade, feeling a need to visit the bathroom and doing his best not to disturb the other man.

The door opened, and light from the corridor filtered in as Slade slipped through. There was a barely audible click followed by silence once more.

A sliver of light remained behind at the base of the door.

Maybe it had been a mistake to bring Slade up here. The tension between him and Roxana made it awkward for all of them. And yet, the man was capable of considerable charm when he was in the mood.

At dinner, he had shown a ready wit not evident previously. Domingo Valdivia had seemed particularly impressed. Apparently, the two men had gotten along famously during the day. Still, the man's toughness, lying just beneath the surface yet clearly displayed, invariably kept people from approaching too close to him.

It struck Garrick suddenly that there had been a sergeant in Afghanistan who bore a certain resemblance to Slade. His name was Lionel Betts, referred to as "Betsy" whenever he was out of earshot. Betsy was an elemental man, and like others in the unit Garrick had stepped softly around him. His similarity to Slade was not a physical one; the sergeant had been red-faced and heavily-built. The likeness lay elsewhere.

They were on ambush patrol when they spotted the troop of Taliban crossing a stretch of broken, semi-open ground. Sergeant Betts called in the gunships with a happy grin on his face. It wasn't often the enemy were caught like this.

The crews on the helicopters didn't waste the opportunity. They brought a huge amount of firepower to bear, firing rockets and hundreds of rounds a minute from their chain guns. With devastating effect.

Garrick's unit filtered through the shallow defiles to commence the body count.

Bullet-stitched and smashed bodies sprawled everywhere. There had been no place to hide. The gunships' guns and rockets had chopped up the warm, dry soil, and sought out the baggy-clothed men wherever they had scattered to.

"I think I'll have some target practice," the sergeant had said, laughing at the sight.

He planted two shots neatly in the back of a man lying face down.

The man's body convulsed, rolling him onto his back. In his hand was a pistol he'd been hiding under his body.

He'd been playing possum, lying coy and astonishingly cool in a desperate ambush for the Americans. It enraged the sergeant so much he charged about firing into body after body, pulping the flesh of the already dead enemy soldiers with his M 4.

Christ!

Garrick's stomach muscles knotted. Shifting onto his side, he curled his knees up into his chest until, finally, the pictures faded and he was able to relax again.

Another half-hour passed before he noticed the sliver of light at the base of the door had disappeared. He listened, but could no longer hear the camp generator.

Slade was certainly taking a long time in the bathroom. Garrick sat up, uneasiness beginning to gnaw at him.

Feeling restless, he dressed in the dark and padded down the corridor to the bathroom. In the blackness he could see nothing, so he stood in the center of the big room with its shower stalls and toilet cubicles, and strained to pick out any noises.

Nothing.

Feeling his way to the door, he stepped outside. Pinprick stars and a pale moon painted surreal shadows across the landscape. A freshet of dark, cooling night air brushed his cheek. A door banged off to his left, and a flashlight's thin beam began an unsteady trip to the generator house.

Acting purely on impulse, he picked his way down the sloping walk to the administration building, crunching softly on the loose gravel.

With nothing but a few scrawny bushes near to it, the administration building stood stark and alone. To the rear lay a parking lot where both passenger and work vehicles spent the nights.

As he neared the building, he halted, undecided what to do next and feeling faintly ridiculous. Also, he recalled hearing that a night watchman stood guard over the place, and he was likely to be armed. There was no point in getting shot by a half asleep, jumpy guard. He was debating whether to return to the dormitory when a pencil beam of light flashed for an instant and then vanished.

It had been so fleeting, like a firefly, he wondered whether he'd imagined it. A depression in the ground sloped off to one side leading in the general direction of the building. He eased into it and slipped forward.

Ten yards on, he stumbled over a man's body.

He gasped, sucking on thin air, his whole body stiffening. Christ! It had to be the watchman. He slipped his hand underneath the man's shirt. Thank God! A heartbeat, shallow and irregular, but a heartbeat nonetheless, pulsed beneath his fingers. Further groping found a sticky substance on the head. Blood!

Something scraped the ground just ahead. Flick! The firefly light again. Someone was at Valdivia's office window.

Garrick strained forward to see, rolling loose a pebble. A shadow at the window crouched and froze. When he edged ahead, the shadow melted away toward the parking lot.

The faint sound of a door closing in the housing complex drifted down the slope. A slim beam of light approached.

Garrick slipped ahead to the building, worked his way along the rear wall, and stopped. For a full half minute, he concentrated on the vehicles parked fifteen paces away. No sound, no movement, nothing. He took a chance. "Slade," he hissed.

Sensing rather than seeing it, someone rose beside a small truck to ghost up the slope.

The flashlight beam bobbed and dipped along the walk. A voice called out. Valdivia.

Now what to do? It would be difficult to explain his presence here at this hour with blood on his hands. He paused a few seconds longer, listening and looking hard, then made a crouching run for the cover of the small truck.

The driver's door hung open. The truck's interior stood empty.

Valdivia called the watchman's name, cursing when he heard no response. His light sliced into the darkness along the side of the building nearest to Garrick. When he rounded the corner and started down the other side, Garrick made a break up the slope.

Distant, angry voices erupted by the generator house. Men arguing over something. A rending noise split the night just as Garrick slipped into the dormitory bathroom.

Hurriedly, he washed his hands clean of blood, and went down the corridor.

A door two rooms up from his opened, and a sleepy voice called out: "Que pasa?"

"No se," Garrick casually responded in his rudimentary Spanish. The door closed, and he went into his own room.

Slade stood by his bed, outlined faintly by the moonlight coming in the window.

"What's goin' on?" he asked, yawning cavernously. "What happened to the lights?" He moved to the window and peered out.

"Where were you?" Garrick demanded.

"How d'you mean?"

"I woke up and you weren't here. Where were you?"

"If it's any of your goddam business, which it ain't, I was using the bathroom."

"Yeah?"

"Yeah! Now it's your turn. Where have *you* been?"

Slade sounded genuinely outraged. Doubt began to seep into Garrick's mind. "Umm...I was poking around outside."

"Find anything? Taliban, mebbe?"

"No," Garrick replied, not knowing what else to say. "I thought something was going on. Figured I'd check it out."

"Good for you." More sarcasm. "I feel safer knowing you're on the lookout for things. Now we have that established, maybe we can get back to sleep."

His bed creaked as he climbed into it. Feeling a little foolish, Garrick did likewise.

A shout, muffled by distance, exploded from the direction of the administration building. But although Garrick listened intently, it was not repeated.

Quiet again enveloped the camp.

Presently, the sound of soft, regular breathing came from the other bed.

"Slade," Garrick whispered, then again, "Slade." The soft, regular breathing continued unbroken.

About twenty minutes later, the sliver of light reappeared at the base of the door accompanied by the gentle hum of the generator.

Suspicion would not let go of Garrick. All his senses told him Slade had been the figure by the truck. It must have been him! And yet he wished to believe otherwise.

Staring open-eyed and unseeing at the darkened ceiling above, Garrick Connolly wrestled with it. And he damned himself for a fool and a weakling.

~ * ~

"Hijos de putas!" Valdivia snarled, his tempered lips quivering with rage. Raising a skeletal arm, he pointed out again the bent and twisted wire mesh on the outside of his office window. "I arrived just in time," he stated dramatically to the crowd in his office. Switching to English, he told Garrick and Slade, "I scared them off."

"Lucky he didn't attack you...like he did the guard," Garrick said.

Valdivia sneered, just sneered. "Pah! They were cowards."

As the conversation shifted back temporarily into Spanish, Garrick studied Slade. His covert examination accomplished little, however. The man's facial expressions gave away nothing.

"What do you think they were after?" Slade asked in his flat way.

"The strong room across the hall has no windows. Thieves would have to enter through the door from inside the building. The payroll is locked up in there...and a number of silver bars also."

"Oh," said Slade.

Valdivia gripped a steel bar lying on his desk. "This bar was found in the parking lot. First, the pigs damaged the generator to make sure there would be no lights. Then, they came down here with the bar to break into my office."

Garrick was curious. "The door to that strong-room looks pretty damned solid to me. That outer security door I mean–it's steel. How d' you suppose he meant to get inside?"

"Possibly one of them hoped to pick the lock," Valdivia suggested. "As you say, that door is steel. Oh–and the ignition wires to one of the trucks

106

were found hanging loose."

"You think it was more than one man?" Roxana put in. She had one booted foot mounted on a rung of a chair while she leaned elbows on its top, sexy and tomboy-ish at the same time.

Steepling his fingers, reclining further into his own chair, Valdivia carried out a thorough examination of her while answering. "It would be next to impossible for one man to attempt so much," he insisted. "Shut down the generator, subdue the guard, break inside this office, pick the lock of the strong-room, steal a vehicle and load it up. And do all those things quickly and silently." He shook his head. "There had to be more than one man involved...working in different places simultaneously."

Garrick considered this. Valdivia made a good point. Maybe it hadn't been Slade, after all. And when you thought about it, his reasons for suspecting him weren't really all that solid. He pursued this line of reasoning a while longer, until he realized he was simply trying to talk himself into believing something he wanted to be true.

Slade said, "They were talented men, these thieves."

"You sound as though you admire them," Roxana shot at him.

Smiling in his icy, thin-lipped way, he gave a brief shake of his head.

"Putos!" Valdivia worked himself up into a rage again. "Cobardes– cowards!"

"No, Señor Valdivia," Slade admonished. "You're wrong there. Men with certain skills. Dishonest men, yes. But men with nerve–certainly not cowards."

Roxana threw him a funny look.

"Is there a suspect?" Garrick asked Valdivia.

"This is a mining camp," Valdivia snorted, "not a monastery. More than one man working here has spent time in jail. Which ones...?" He spread his hands in a gesture which said he had no idea.

Two security men came in for a discussion with Valdivia. The crowd in the office drifted back to their respective jobs, and Garrick, Roxana, and Slade wandered outside the building.

"Look at that," Slade said, waving a hand toward the gate.

Outside the gate were four mules. A thin, wizened Indian wearing a lugubrious expression sat near them on the ground.

"Isn't that the guy with the mules you were telling me about?"

Indeed, it was dour Cusi.

"Now what?" Slade went on. "There's the transportation. Is the archaeological expedition still on?" He glanced inquiringly at Roxana.

She returned the look reluctantly. "You're interested in coming along then?"

"Sure," he stated emphatically. "Sounds like it may be exciting. Wouldn't miss it."

Resignation settled over her. "Well, I haven't changed the plans I made yesterday. I'm leaving in a few minutes."

"Fine. I'll get my things." Slade strolled off toward the dormitory.

Garrick studied his back as he climbed up the gravel path.

"Tell me something," Roxana said. "Why did you keep insisting there was only one man acting alone last night?"

"Huh?"

"Everyone else referred to the *thieves*, speaking in the plural...using words like *them* and *they*. Not you, though. You kept talking as if there was only one man, speaking in the singular. What makes you think there was a lone thief?"

"I didn't even realize I was doing that," Garrick replied, honestly enough, while mentally kicking himself. "Stick to archaeology, Roxana. You make a lousy detective."

Something still struck her as being not right. She stared right at him. He kept his own gaze elsewhere until she finally cut short her scrutiny, saying, "Right. We should get moving. It's going to be a long day." Shouting a message to Cusi, she marched off to her quarters.

Uncertainty and indecision were written all over Garrick's face as he watched her walk away. For a long time after she had gone, he just stood there looking up the slope.

Chapter Fifteen
Cajamarca-Silent City

"Halt," a commanding voice boomed.

Yahuar Huaccac and his people neared a narrow pass in the sierra. An officer of the victorious Northern Army had planted himself in the road, blocking the way forward. His soldiers were stationed behind him, leaning carelessly on long lances.

The officer and his men had been busy. Beside the road, bodies hung head down from gibbets, houses smoldered not far off, roofs fallen in and walls blackened.

"State your business," the officer demanded, gazing bemusedly at the multitude of elongated Collagua heads.

He was a big man, Changa's size, and appeared even bigger because of a huge headdress he wore. When he ambled forward it was with a conqueror's swagger.

"Sodomites and adulterers," the officer snarled, flipping a casual hand at the evil fruit dangling from the gibbets. "We hung their families along with them. Afterwards, we burned their homes."

Huaccac's attention swung between hard bitten soldiers and hanging corpses. He appeared wan and haggard. He'd been through the most incredible and exhausting time of his life.

Upon arriving at Cuzco, the people of Coporaque had found the imperial city in chaos, with Atahualpa's armies still pillaging. Prudently, they didn't enter, remaining instead at one of the twelve satellite towns outside.

Prince Atahualpa was not present. They learned he had lingered behind, relaxing at the far northern city of Cajamarca, a place noted for its thermal hot baths. Some of the contingent urged a return home. Cuzco was unsafe, they argued, and Cajamarca too distant. Mayta Yupanqui would have none of this, however, peremptorily brushing such arguments aside. Brief consideration was given as to whether Huaccac should return home with a man or two to help get him there, but in the end, all had made the arduous trek north to the Inca's camp.

Along the way, they passed many burned and deserted villages. Troops of the Northern Army became a regular sight. Fighting persisted in some areas, forcing them into a number of detours. They were now travelling south on the Inca Road instead of north.

Mayta Yupanqui informed the officer, "We come from a province south of Cuzco. Our journey is to the court of the Supreme Inca, Prince Atahualpa, to demonstrate our loyalty."

Scowling fiercely, the officer strode along the column on a cursory inspection. Then, after a few more words with the governor, he waved them through.

Two more hours marching brought them to the edge of an escarpment overlooking a flat, lush valley. The thatched roofs of the town of Cajamarca peered up at them from below.

Vapors, mysterious appearing mists, caused by scalding overflow from hot sulphur springs, floated across the valley, filling it and lending to it a mystical, unreal effect.

The mists received little attention, however. Instead, they stared awestruck at the hills beyond the city. On the slopes, as thick as snowflakes in a mountain blizzard, were the white pavilions of Atrahualpa's army.

Mayta Yupanqui broke the silence. "Let us proceed," he said, in a voice lowered, but calm.

Descending the escarpment, they crossed the valley floor toward the city. From a distance, Cajamarca seemed strangely quiet, stripped of life.

Even at the Temple of the Sun and the *Aclla-huasi,* House of the Chosen Women, only a handful of people were briefly seen.

The curaca's heavy brow settled into a dark, brooding frown. This was a big city, of a size to support thousands. And many of the houses were fine and large, boasting of wealth and refinement. What had happened to its citizens?

Filing along empty streets, they entered the great plaza by one of its two gateways. It was almost triangular in shape and vast in size. The plaza of Coporaque would have nestled comfortably into it several times over.

They paused, gawking, as an empty silence greeted them.

Low buildings flanked three sides, a wall of sun-baked clay bricks with a tower in the middle the fourth. Commanding the town from the high side sat a stout fortress surrounded by a triple ring of walls. Both fortress and tower also appeared deserted.

A pair of ground doves landed with a flutter of black wings. They began to strut about.

Ollanta gave a sullen grunt. "This place has a foul feel to it...as though deserted by the gods."

"Be silent," growled Changa.

At a signal from Mayta Yupanqui, they continued on through the town.

A causeway led toward the imperial camp over a long stretch of green meadowland. They walked along the causeway for nearly an hour, coming to the first of the white tents and then to a stream with a wooden bridge across it. Here they halted, unsure how to proceed.

Hordes of people milled about: soldiers, vassals, nobles. Many different tribes were represented.

On the far bank of the stream, a band of six mahogany-skinned men, lithe and graceful in their movements, conversed in a strange tongue. They were armed with bows and arrows and their faces were covered with white clay masks–men from the lowland rain forests.

Mayta Yupanqui spoke briefly to two soldiers positioned by the bridge. One of them went off with a message while they waited, mingling with the crowd.

The crowd hummed with wild and excited talk of the bearded strangers, said to be within several days' march. The reason for the empty city was now made clear. Cajamarca had been evacuated to provide lodging for the white strangers.

The bearded men! Huaccac quivered with excitement. Soon, he would see the incredible beings!

Evening had fallen when permission finally arrived for them to make camp.

Squeezing into a tight circle by the stream, they lit cooking fires and commenced a meal–a soup of *charqui* and *chunu*, jerked meat and freeze-dried potatoes.

Everywhere, preparations for the night were underway. A soft vaporous glow hung over the vast encampment, the countless fires turning darkness into half-light.

Huaccac made secret plans to explore the surroundings. The huge mass of people, the mysterious mists, the pomp and circumstance, demanded a closer inspection. He attempted a sly withdrawal.

"Do not wander off, little brother." Ollanta seized a tiny arm and twisted, making the boy squirm in pain. "Return to the tents," he ordered roughly, a mocking grin showing mud-white in the firelight. He gave the arm a last excruciating wrench.

Rubbing the bruised member, Huaccac slouched back to the fire, fighting off tears.

"Fill my bowl. I find I am hungry," Ollanta rasped to a man hunched over the fire. Filled bowl in hand, he sat cross legged on the ground and began to eat.

The man at the fire offered another bowl to Huaccac. The boy refused with a shake of his head. "No, I'm not hungry right now."

From Ollanta's side of the fire came the sound of guttural laughter.

~ * ~

"The Supreme Inca is resting," a member of Atahualpa's entourage informed Mayta Yupanqui two days later. "However, he has expressed a wish to see some of you."

The official, a thin man of middle years and grim manner, frowned constantly as he spoke. The responsibility of serving the Prince weighed heavily on him.

"We'll prepare ourselves immediately," the governor told him, while signalling to the others to make ready.

Attire suitable for an audience with the Sapa Inca was brought forth.

Huaccac donned an ankle length tunic his mother had made for him, decorated with a large triangle in front. Underneath it, he wore short breeches of aloe fibres, while over all, he slung a fine cloak with the Collagua eight pointed star in red dye on front and back. His thick, black hair he left uncovered.

When all were properly garbed, they resembled a flock of gaudy forest birds.

The thin official with the frown led them through the camp to where a man of Inca rank, a plump fellow in gorgeous clothing, sat on a three legged stool. Although his fleshy limbs were festooned with weighty gold jewelry, his demeanor was so severe as to dull his flamboyant image.

The frowning official stepped close to the seated noble for a lowered discussion. After some minutes, the governor was beckoned forward to be put through a rigorous grilling. It ended with him indicating certain members of the band.

The official motioned to those Mayta Yupanqui had pointed out. Then, as if acting on afterthought, he went to where Yahuar Huaccac waited beside his father.

"Come," he said to the boy.

It had been expected that, on this occasion, Mayta Yupanqui alone would be granted an audience with the Lord of the World. Now, it was apparent that all of them who bore royal blood, even Huaccac with his small portion, were going before him.

Instantly, Changa became nervous. His hand dropped onto Huaccac's chest, restraining him. Ignoring the warning in the governor's eyes, he made bold to speak. "I am of the curaca class and the boy is my son. He carries but little of the blood of the Inca. In addition to which, he is very young. Let him remain here with me."

His temerity stunned the officials. The seated man appeared so enraged he seemed on the verge of apoplexy.

The hand on Huaccac's chest trembled slightly. With a shock, he realized his father was afraid. Changa was afraid! Never in his life had he considered such a thing even remotely possible. Until this moment, Yahuar Huaccac had been merely excited to see the Sapa Inca; now he felt the mortal chill of fear.

"The decision has been made," the seated noble bellowed. "The

Supreme Inca wishes to see people from the south. These will go before him now."

Then, the frowning man took them to the Inca.

Huaccac entered last, his heart thudding. All were barefoot and bore light burdens on their backs as gestures of submission. Softly lamenting, weeping at the enormity of being in the presence of the God King, the five men and the child crawled forward on all fours.

The Inca was seated on a low stool in a courtyard. A small, white-plastered building, or pleasure house, lay in the center with galleries running around it. In front of the house stood a bath, carved from stone and fed by both warm and cold water–the pool where the Emperor and his women bathed.

Many splendidly dressed, bejewelled nobles waited in attendance, although closest to the Inca were the ladies of the royal household. Dozens of wives and concubines hovered around and behind the royal stool. A dark-eyed beauty with responsibility for her master's drinking cup stood at his side, a goblet fashioned from the skull of one of Prince Huascar's generals in her slender hands–on top of the skull glittered a golden bowl, the teeth held the silver spout from which the God King drank.

Off to one side, blind musicians, drums and flutes in hand, quietly awaited their lord's pleasure.

An elderly noble near Atahualpa ordered the prostrating figures to proceed no further. They halted, heads down, buttocks up, not daring to gaze upon the Inca without permission. They also ceased wailing.

In the sudden quiet, birdsong trilled from a garden at the rear, joined by the murmur of water running in the aqueducts.

The Inca desired information from them. His spokesman carefully questioned Mayta Yupanqui regarding the current situation in the south. The question and answer session wore on.

His heart hammering a fierce tattoo, Huaccac thought, I must see the Inca. I must!

By all the gods, dare he? He knelt at the rear, largely ignored. Temptation eclipsed his fear. He risked a lightning glance over the raised buttocks in front of him, those of a thin, dark man called Sinchi.

A man of roughly thirty sat gazing off across the courtyard. He was dressed in sleeveless tunic and striped trousers of vicuna wool, with a brown cloak made from the fur of vampire bats over his shoulders. In contrast to his nobles, he wore few ornaments.

His grave, lordly bearing readily identified him as monarch, even if the *borla*, royal fringe, wound round his temple did not. A tuft above the red tasselled borla carried three small, black and white feathers of the sacred Curiquinque bird. He was a handsome man in the full flower of manhood, strongly-built, with a large, well-shaped head.

Enough, Huaccac warned himself. Down! Quick! Thrusting his face into the ground, he waited.... No one made any movement toward him. He'd not been noticed.

The governor explained the reason for their visit. "We have come to offer fealty to the most noble Inca. After hearing of his splendid victories, we could do no less."

In a quiet voice, the spokesman enquired, "You are all close kin to Prince Huascar. Are you not?"

Words softly spoken, yet fraught with danger.

"We are descended from the noble Huayna Capac," Mayta Yupanqui replied steadily. "We are blood kin to all members of his family." Without mentioning Atahualpa by name, the governor had reminded these people of his blood ties to the current Inca, as well. "And in the recent war, we took little part," he added shrewdly.

The noble fell quiet a moment, absorbing this, before intoning another question. The governor responded in measured fashion, and so the audience continued.

Unable to resist, Huaccac dared a second glance, and froze. Atahualpa gazed in his direction, the fierceness of his expression leaping across the intervening space. That hawk-like stare was made fiercer by round, black eyes, the outer parts of which were red-rimmed and bloodshot.

He looks like Ollanta, Huaccac thought, sagging in utter astonishment.

The Prince swung his head away, his cloak settled low on his neck, and an ear which had been torn in battle–a bad omen–was suddenly exposed. Swiftly, the Prince rearranged his cloak and the ear disappeared.

Huaccac's head had dipped into the dirt again, trying to take all this in, when someone nudged him. It was Sinchi, moving backwards on hands and knees.

The audience had ended.

At their camp, they were pounced on by an anxious group.

"Was the Prince receptive?"

"Describe the manner of the Sapa Inca."

"Will we be permitted to return home soon?"

Changa eyed his son with relief. "Did it go well?" he asked the governor.

Mayta Yupanqui shook his head wearily. The strain of the ordeal he'd just been through sat heavily on him.

"I attempted to convey to the Inca that we desire only to serve him in peace. His nobles made no reply to this, however. And as for the Sapa Inca...he spoke not at all."

Chapter Sixteen
The Bearded Men

In the week following the audience with the Inca, a great stirring swept the encampment.

Frenetic whispers flew about. "The bearded men are coming!"

The approach of the white men had been monitored for weeks, envoys even visiting their camp in an attempt to spy out their intentions. The envoys had returned with the reassuring news that the white strangers numbered less than two hundred.

In their turn, the strangers had sent one of their Indian allies as emissary to the Emperor. A poor choice of ambassador as it turned out. He had loudly demanded access to Atahualpa at a time when the Prince was fasting, and had been hustled unceremoniously out of camp for his insolence.

Now his masters had entered Cajamarca.

Some in Cuzco believed them gods sent by Viracocha, the Creator. After the creation, Viracocha had walked off across the ocean, but many of Huascar's followers believed he was now responding to their urgent need. Surely, the bearded men were sent by him to deliver them from Atahualpa.

The Sapa Inca cared nothing for these mutterings, having consulted the oracles and been assured of his invincibility. Besides, he was eager to see the white men. Here, within the security of his army, he would see the strangers and their amazing beasts for himself.

~ * ~

In the late afternoon, a low, menacing rumble like that of thunder swept along the causeway leading to the encampment. Atahualpa left his pleasure house with his nobles and women, and seated himself on a stool in front. Before him, tens of thousands of silent, brightly plumed and garbed soldiers lined the meadows.

A storm rode with the strangers. Earlier, the day had been fair, but now rain mixed with hail was falling.

The rumbling crested, then abruptly ceased on the far bank of the river. Sixteen hoofed monsters emerged from the mist to line the bank, tall men, armored and helmeted and bearded, bestriding them.

Shivering in the damp chill, Huaccac stared at them with fascination and dismay. How huge and fearsome they were! Were they really half-man, half-beast as so many insisted? In the mists and rain, they blurred together before his eyes, like figures from the nether world where sinners went upon death.

The monsters splashed across the stream and thundered closer. Trumpets blared brassily.

The man ahead of Huaccac flinched and fell sideways. It was thin, dark Sinchi, he who had been in front of Huaccac during the audience with the Inca. The governor fired a hard, fast glare at him and he stumbled back to his place in line.

The strangers halted some paces in front of the Emperor, hoofed beasts champing the bits. No one spoke. For a time it was as if the world had stopped. Both sides measured the other in silence.

One of the white men finally signalled forward a slim, young Indian in a bright headdress.

For one so young, he behaved haughtily, speaking directly to the Sapa Inca rather than to his spokesman, the *Inca Apu*, beside the royal stool. He spoke the language of the white men, he told them, and called himself Felipillo, a name given him by the strangers. He pointed out the leader of the troop, Hernando de Soto, an elegant looking man in his twenties with regular features and a neat, black beard.

As de Soto walked his horse up, a second troop of horsemen galloped in, led by a tall, heavyset man with thick lips and a red nose. This was Hernando Pizarro, brother of the Spanish general.

Reining in beside de Soto, he doffed his helmet and bowed

respectfully from the saddle. "I come as ambassador from my brother and captain to advise the noble Atahualpa of our arrival in his city," he said through Felipillo. "The fame of the Sapa Inca's military victories has brought us here...reaching even our country across the sea. It is our commander's wish to meet with him soon. Will the Lord Inca visit him in his quarters?"

Ataualpa sat unresponsive and still, his gaze lowered.

After a lengthy pause, the *Inca Apu* answered in his stead: "The Lord Inca cannot visit your general for he is fasting."

After a respectful pause of his own, Pizarro continued, undaunted: "We are subjects of a mighty prince and have come from him to offer our services and to explain our religion." He allowed Felipillo to translate this, then added in a softer tone: "Our general loves the Inca dearly. His enemies are ours. Only tell us and we will conquer those who displease him."

At this, Atahualpa glanced up, a faint smile on his lips.

Huaccac couldn't keep his eyes from the two young captains. They exhibited no slight signs of being cowed by the vast army encircling them. Rather, their confident bearings matched that of Atahualpa's.

"Our general would be greatly pleased if you would visit him in his quarters," Pizarro persisted, repeating his invitation.

On this occasion, the Inca Apu accepted for his master, saying simply, "It is well."

The two Spanish captains exchanged frustrated glances at Atahualpa's refusal to speak. Pizarro tried again, insistent yet gravely courteous. "Would the Lord Inca inform us in his own words, what is his pleasure?"

Condescending to reply, Aahualpa said, "Tell your captain I am keeping a fast which will end tomorrow. I will visit him then with my chieftains. In the meantime, let him occupy the buildings on the square, and no others. Tomorrow, when I come, I will order what is to be done."

He ended with a moment's curious examination of Hernando de Soto's restless warhorse.

Seeing this, de Soto suddenly wheeled his beast and spurred it furiously over the meadow. Wheeling, dashing here and there, he thundered past the ranks of startled onlookers, showering them with clods of earth.

Then, he turned and charged toward the Inca.

Stunned into immobility, Huaccac watched the beast streak closer. In front of him, Sinchi cried and dropped his lance.

Now de Soto was upon the Inca. Iron hooves clawed the air above the Prince's head. Foam from the beast's muzzle flew onto the royal garments.

Not one tiny movement betrayed the Inca. Atahualpa's gaze remained fixed stolidly ahead. Indeed, as de Soto backed his mount away, the Inca, with incredible aplomb, gravely directed his women to offer refreshments.

The Spaniards declined the foods, but accepted maize beer, served in cups of gold, drinking from horseback.

Handing his emptied cup to a lady of the harem, Hernando Pizarro bowed once again from the saddle. "We see you are a mighty prince and will inform our commander of this. He eagerly awaits your arrival."

Hernando de Soto also courteously saluted the Inca. Then, the bearded men rode back to Cajamarca.

Soon after, armed men came for Sinchi. For cowering before the strangers, he must pay the price. He and all those who showed craven were never seen again.

Chapter Seventeen
A Great Killing

Around noon of the next day, preparations for the visit to Cajamarca began.

Huaccac was aflutter with excitement. To the spectacular events of yesterday there was now added the splendor of a monarch on the move. Hopping around the fringes of the huge entourage, he tried to take it all in. Not until the procession was about to set out did he realize he'd become separated from his father and friends. They were swallowed up in the multitude.

He joined the mob preceding the Emperor. Around him were hundreds of menials sweeping away every particle of dirt and rubbish, chorusing songs of triumph. Men of higher station followed them, bearing maces of silver or copper and dressed in different liveries. A wave of nobles in azure liveries, ornaments flashing, marched around the Prince.

Atahualpa travelled above the host on a golden litter, lined with the plumes of tropical birds and carried by eighty great lords, headdresses and jewelry flashing in the sun.

The Son of the Sun glittered from head to foot. His robe was shot through with threads of pure gold, and his sandals were of gold. Golden ornaments adorned his hair, while a huge emerald collar of green fire encircled his neck.

Sitting in his litter in a manner lofty and dignified, the imperial *borla* about his head, a scepter of gold and silver in his sacred hand and a blazing golden shield on his arm, the Sapa Inca was about his royal business.

His entourage filled the plain. Praises, victory songs, the clamor of trumpets and drums and flutes and cymbals echoed off the surrounding hills. Proceeding at a sedate pace, the shifting, chanting, resplendent wave rippled toward the city on the meadow.

A thousand paces from town, Atahualpa gave orders to halt and pitch his tents. A messenger sent to the white men informed them he would enter the city in the morning.

Huaccac saw a Spaniard hurriedly arrive to speak with the Inca's attendants. When he departed shortly afterwards, the order went out to continue on to Cajamarca.

According to the European calendar, it was Saturday, November 16, 1532, and it was late in the afternoon. In a little more than an hour, darkness would fall.

The procession entered the plaza and halted. "Where are the strangers?" Atahualpa demanded, peering around.

A bearded man with dark, intense eyes, wearing a long, white robe and black hood, stepped from a doorway.

Huaccac hopped up and down to see. This man was the strangest person he'd ever seen. Yet he walked as all men should, on two feet, not mounted or part of one of the hoofed beasts. With him was the young Indian interpreter, Felipillo.

In the crush of humanity Huaccac suddenly spotted Ollanta, standing taller than the men around him. He carried out a brief search for his father and the others before giving it up as hopeless. They were probably outside with the greater mass of people and, in any case, he didn't want to miss anything. The man in the hood had reached the Inca's litter.

"This man is a priest," Felipillo explained in a loud voice, "sent by his governor, Francisco Pizarro, to explain the religion of the white men."

The Dominican Friar opened a book and, in a voice brimming with emotion, described the creation of the world and the crucifixion and resurrection of Christ.

Felipillo explained: "The white men believe in three gods–*The Holy Trinity*–although one is more powerful than the others, and is the One True God. The power of these gods lies in the hands of a man they call *Pope*. This Pope has commissioned the Spanish Emperor to conquer and convert all peoples in the world.... The Emperor's officer, Francisco Pizarro, has come here to carry out this important mission. When you have learned this new religion and have become a tributary of the white man's king, you will be entitled to his aid and protection."

To this incredible statement, the Dominican hurled the even more astounding warning: "If you refuse, we will make war upon you without mercy. All your idols will be cast down. Fire and sword and bloodshed will compel you to reject your false religion and to receive our Catholic faith. Pay tribute to our Emperor...surrender your kingdom to him."

Atahualpa was speechless. Then his eyes caught fire. His brow darkened ominously, enraged at the audacity of these men who dared to lecture him in the heart of his empire.

"I will be no man's tributary," he thundered, shaking with rage. "No greater prince than I exists upon the earth. When I see your emperor has sent his subjects so far across the waters, I do not doubt he is also a mighty prince, and I am willing to hold him as my brother. But as for this man, Pope, of whom you speak, he must be mad...my faith I will never change." He was quiet a moment, controlling his anger. Then he pointed to the sun sinking behind the mountains. "There is my God. From his home in the heavens, He looks down upon his children."

Aghast at such sacrilege, the friar held high his breviary. "Here is my authority," he insisted fiercely.

Atahualpa took it, turned the pages over briefly, and hurled it to the ground.

The Dominican sank backwards in shock and horror.

Gathering his imperial demeanor about him like a cloak, Atahualpa delivered a stern admonition. "Inform your people they must account for their doings in my country. I shall not go from here until they make full satisfaction for the wrongs they have committed."

Felipillo rushed forward and snatched up the breviary. The priest took it, automatically wiping it clean of dirt. Then, calling loudly on God, he ran inside a building flanking the plaza.

In full alarm, Atahualpa rose up on his litter, shouting to his men to make ready.

Not far from Huaccac, a tall, lean, hollow-cheeked Spaniard with a full, spade beard sprang onto the plaza waving a white cloth over his head.

Instantly, sounds like thunderclaps broke the air, coming from the fortress on the high side of town. Cannon balls whistled into the crowd. Scant seconds later, from the buildings around the plaza, the men in mail poured forth.

"Santiago! Santiago y a ellos! Saint James and at them!"

The guns belched fire again. Bugles added to the din.

Two Spaniards tore by Huaccac on foot, slipped in the blood already sliming the ground, caught themselves and hurtled forward, eyes riveted on the Inca.

Indian dead piled up in heaps, blocking escape routes and preventing the warriors outside from joining the fray. A cloud of artillery smoke rolled along the square.

Around the Inca, a convulsive battle raged. His unarmed nobles flung themselves upon the mailed horsemen, attendants threw themselves onto Spanish swords in a frenzied effort to protect the God King, and if a litter bearer's hands were severed by a Toledo blade, he still struggled to support the litter with his shoulders.

The golden vehicle heaved back and forth.

Tall, lean, bearded Francisco Pizarro, fighting on foot with dagger and sword, was one who clove a path close to the Prince. Desperate to capture the Inca alive, he stretched out his arm to take a cut aimed at Atahualpa, the while booming a warning to the man who had swung the weapon.

Moments earlier, Huaccac had been swept off his feet by a flood of terror-stricken men. Legs churning, he rode the human wave to the far side of the plaza.

They smashed against the adobe wall there. A man in a checkered white and red livery attacked it with his bare hands, splitting his fingers and dripping them crimson. All the while, he set up a keening wail heard distinctly above the uproar. A second later, he was gone from view, trampled by the horde into an untidy lump of pulped flesh and wet entrails.

The mob's frenzy finally burst the wall. A long, convulsive heave and the barrier collapsed. An escape route fifteen paces wide yawned, and thousands poured through the gap.

On their heels rode the devil horsemen, crying out in harsh Castilian.

"After those in the Inca's liveries!"

"Let none escape!"

"Spear them!"

"Ride them down!"

"Santiago! Saint James and at them!"

A tall Indian bounded forward, face wild, making for the gap in the wall. Huaccac recognized his condor's head and blood-streaked eyes with a leap of elation. Ollanta!

He sprang after him. "Ollanta! Ollanta! It is I, Huaccac. Help me. I cannot escape alone."

Ollanta got tangled in the entrails of a gutted man and went down. He rebounded quickly, but Huaccac had closed the distance to a few short strides.

"Help me!"

Ollanta heard, and looked. A grimace twisted his fleshy mouth, and that was all. Then he was gone, hurdling the fallen bodies, sprinting for the safety of the countryside.

The sound of more hooves rumbled just behind.

Huaccac squirmed under the nearest heap of bodies.

"Santiago! Santiago!"

In a thunder of blood and hooves, the Spaniards vaulted the gap.

Huaccac fell deaf to all except the thudding of his heart. For the space of a thousand heartbeats, in his horrid cocoon of dying men and twitching, still-warm corpses, he awaited the killing thrust. Indeed, he almost wished for it.

The battle had waned, however. When the realization came that he'd been passed over, he was still able to function again only gradually. More minutes had to go by before he could will himself to wiggle to a hole between the bodies and peer out.

Fighting yet raged around the Inca.

Seven or eight mounted Spaniards spurred up to the litter, grabbed the edge and heaved on it. Flung to the ground, the Inca was pounced on by Francisco Pizarro himself, bound and carried off.

With that last amazing act, all resistance ceased.

Mercifully, dusk fell soon after. The clear notes of a Spanish trumpet sounded recall from the plaza. Huaccac froze, hardly daring to breathe as he heard horses returning.

A horse blew his nostrils. Two riders approached. One of them laughed, leaned forward in the saddle and pointed with his lance.

A corpse had somehow become stuck upside down in a breech in the wall. Naked legs jutted stiffly upwards, spread wide like a giant prong.

The trumpet called again and the riders touched heels to mounts and left. Jubilant Spaniards continued to arrive, bursting loudly with self-congratulation.

The last of the white men came and went. Complete darkness descended, bringing with it a night chill to seep into Huaccac's hiding place and clam his skin. Another full hour passed before he plucked up the courage to leave his hideous refuge. Trembling with shock and cold, the child stumbled over the ramp of dead bodies and through the wall.

Not knowing where else to go, he headed back along the causeway.

As he went, wounded men occasionally called out to him. The boy trudged on, ignoring the pleas. A hand groped his leg once. Squealing horror, he squirmed loose and broke into an exhausted run.

He ran right into someone. A startled gasp, and a figure leaped off the road. Whether man or woman, Huaccac could not tell. He merely heard the pad of swiftly-moving feet on the grass of the meadow.

How he wished his father were here.

Yahuar Huaccac shambled onwards, leaving the last of the wounded behind him. The night became dead quiet. He snuffled a little; there was only that sound and no other.

With lunatic nerve, a mere handful of Spaniards had captured an Emperor in the midst of his huge army, slaughtering thousands of warriors in less than two hours. And not a single Spaniard had been seriously wounded!

The collapse of the empire had begun.

Chapter Eighteen
Flight to Coporaque

In the soft, gauzy light of the Andean dawn, the Inca's camp appeared little changed. The tents of the vast bivouac had not been struck. Warriors were yet present in their thousands. Human forms drifted in and out of the warm, sulphurous mists, ephemerally, like figures in a dream. But as the light hardened, a difference became apparent in the faces of the people, and in the way they moved. Men and women, they were a dazed and fearful lot.

On the damp ground by a huddle of royal ladies, Yahuar Huaccac lay crumpled, racked by a long, rasping cough.

A lovely, dark-eyed girl wept over the fate of the Inca. Her face was heavily rouged with vermilion and the tears ran streaks in it. Wrapped within themselves, the circle of long-haired ladies of the royal household paid her little heed.

The tall curaca with the oddly shaped head none of them noticed at all.

Changa had come. After prowling the edges of the camp for hours, watching and waiting, the sound of that racking cough had directed him in.

Bent double in a hacking fit, Huaccac didn't see his father arrive. The first inkling he had was when big, strong hands reached down to him.

He stiffened in disbelief. It just couldn't be! The nightmare had ended! His father had arrived, and now everything would be all right. He gave in to the terrors of the past day and allowed himself to cry.

"I thought you were dead," Huaccac sobbed, fat tears raining from his ridiculously long eyelashes. "So many were killed. I had to hide when...when...Ollanta...."

Changa searched him for injuries. "Are you hurt?"

A man ran by, shouting: "The bearded men are coming!"

Thirty of the dreaded horsemen approached in battle formation. Swinging Huaccac onto his shoulder, Changa marched swiftly off. Brawny arms clearing a path through the mob, he headed for the hillside to the rear of the camp.

The Spaniards splashed across the stream, the dashing, young cavalier Hernando de Soto in the lead. Not daunted in the least by the vast array of warriors present, he trotted his cavalry troop confidently forward.

Little resistance was offered. Obeying instructions sent them by Atahualpa, one after another of the Inca's captains made signs of the cross to signal surrender.

A number of warriors did show fight, although their lances and stone clubs proved ineffectual. Huaccac watched the white men easily drive them off. Then, they began gathering captives and livestock to drive back to Cajamarca.

The girl with the tear-stained face was thrown, squealing, across a saddle. Many of the Spaniards occupied themselves in a search for loot.

Changa reached the hill and started up. When he rounded a bulge, the picture disappeared.

"Hsst," he called as they neared a clump of squat, green chilca bushes.

A man crouching in the bushes waved them through. Farther up the grassy slope, more familiar faces appeared from around a huge boulder.

Sliding over the boulder, Changa dropped lightly into the hollow behind it. He was met by seven men. Of the fifty who had started out from the home valley, these were all who remained. Most had simply scattered, chaff before the Spanish wind. Some had slipped away to go it alone. Many were dead.

Changa had collected those he could, Mayta Yupanqui and Ollanta among them, and had hid them here last night.

He eased Huaccac from his shoulder onto the ground.

Ollanta offered no comment at sight of his half-brother. Instead, he moved moodily off to sit against a lichen-covered rock at the rear of the hideout.

Mayta Yupanqui lay on his back with a cloak over him. "What's happening?" he asked in a voice barely above a whisper. "We heard shouting." A partly crusted wound stood out lividly on his face, running up into his hair.

"The accursed white men are in the camp," Changa informed him, adding bitterly, "hardly a lance was raised against them."

"We must linger here no longer then," one of the others hastened to put in.

Changa glowered at the man who'd spoken those words unbidden, a bow-legged, sour-faced servant of the governor called Curipay. "Be quiet," he snapped. "For the moment there's no danger. The white men are busy plundering the camp."

Going to the boulder, he mounted it and cautiously raised himself to his full height to make out the camp. The white men were there still, although a cavalcade of captive men, women, and llamas appeared almost ready to set out. Extensive looting had gone on. Gold and silver plate, jewelry, and ornaments formed dazzling piles on the ground.

Spaniards clustered about the treasure, stroking and fingering the precious stuff.

Changa swore at the sight. "The bearded men are about to leave with their captives and plunder," he announced bitterly over his shoulder. Leaping from the boulder, he strode angrily up and down in front of Huaccac.

The boy was sitting up, feeling better by the minute now that he was with friends.

Ollanta stared poisonously in his direction. He would never forgive Yahuar Huaccac for witnessing his ignominious flight from the Spanish. Huaccac threw him a heated glance of his own. While recalling only too vividly his own unreasoning terror, he nonetheless found it difficult to forgive his brother for abandoning him.

"What will happen to the Prince, think you?" Mayta Yupanqui croaked.

"Any barbarity is possible," rumbled Changa. "These white strangers are killers. Cutters of throats."

"The flower of Atahualpa's army is intact at Cuzco. The Sapa Inca can be rescued."

Changa shook his head doubtfully. "The army won't move without instructions from Prince Atahualpa. The white men hold him hostage to prevent this. They are more cunning than other men."

Bow-legged Curipay boldly spoke up again, a rebellious expression on his ugly face: "We have tarried too long. We should leave immediately."

Changa swung on him, incensed, but Mayta Yupanqui said, "Yes, we must go. Organize the march home as soon as possible."

"Are you able to travel?"

In answer, the old noble struggled to his feet. He swayed there unsteadily, almost falling.

"You are our leader," Curipay said insolently. "Go in front, as always. We will follow."

Changa reached for his sling, meaning to whip the lout.

"Stay." Mayta Yupanqui raised a hand. "Let us proceed without further delay." He commenced a slow, laborious climb up the hill.

On the crest of the hill, Curipay, racing ahead, automatically headed for the main road.

"No, fool," Changa snarled. "Have you learned nothing these past days? On roads or level ground, the beasts of the white men run more swiftly than the fleetest deer. If you want to live, keep to the hills."

They headed south. Riding his father's shoulders and twisting his head constantly to look back, Huaccac kept the valley in sight the longest. Then, they dipped between two hills, and the lovely valley, with its warm, mysterious mists, its army of lost warriors, and its city of woe and infamy passed from his sight forever.

~ * ~

They camped that night not far from a burning village. The houses had been torched by Indians, not the Spaniards who remained in Cajamarca. With the iron discipline of the Inca in disarray, malcontents who had only recently been brought under the sway of the royal scepter gleefully carried out acts of vandalism.

Mayta Yupanqui had collapsed upon the ground, his brow fevered. Changa surveyed him glumly, wondering how his friend would ever manage the arduous journey ahead of them. Nearby, Yahuar Huaccac tossed in fitful sleep.

Aside from the curaca, the sickened noble, and the child having a nightmare, five more persons rounded out the company. Curipay had run off, and another man with him.

Ollanta sat a bit apart, gazing into the tiny campfire, his face flat and angular in the light of the flames. He'd not spoken a word since the flight began.

Lying down between his youngest son and the governor, Changa managed to doze off. Well into the night, he was startled into wakefulness. Mayta Yupanqui fought to sit up. The campfire was cold ashes. Everyone else slept.

A pale moon hung directly overhead. In its light, the governor's finger beckoned. Changa shifted closer to listen.

"Are we pursued?" came a barely intelligible whisper.

"No," Changa whispered back.

"Oh," the old man said, then launched into a rambling, incoherent account of a military campaign he'd fought in during the reign of Huayna Capac. He maundered on for a while, making little sense, until he suddenly leaned forward in a surprisingly swift movement, and said, "I would have liked to have seen the copper palace one last time."

Then he slumped back to the ground.

The curaca covered him with his own cloak. A wave of tiredness washed over him. Mayta Yupanqui was dying, and that loss was infinitely more meaningful to him than the loss of the Inca. The God King was impossibly remote to a man like Changa. The governor had been a close and respected friend. He sat brooding, too weary and dispirited to move, or even sleep.

When he next checked Mayta Yupanqui, the old man was gone, his body already growing cold.

Changa gently bent the corpse into a fetal position–his life cycle completed, he must end as he had begun inside the womb. Afterwards, the curaca settled down to a lone vigil. As a friend should, he would watch over the lifeless body during the first night of its departure from *Pacha Mama*, Earth Mother. In the morning they would build a burial mound. A simple pile of stones would have to suffice.

Intoning a song of mourning, he raised open hands in prayer to the Moon. It was fitting to pray to the Moon in this circumstance, he thought, comforted by the presence of the beautiful deity. The Moon was gentler, more approachable, more feminine than the Sun. Look, even now she was changing her appearance.

He watched, fascinated to see. Often, a message was given. What he saw abruptly ended his noiseless dirge. Above him, an orange-tinted halo slowly reached out to envelop the deity.

A certain sign of grave misfortune.

~ * ~

Mama Ocllo picked up the skirts of her tunic and ran downhill, quick and light on her feet, running like a young girl.

A chasqui had brought word of Changa's approach three days earlier. She had kept anxious watch from the hilltop overlooking the road ever since. At the foot of the hill, a small group of curious townsfolk also waited.

During the two days march through the home valley, Changa's tiny band had attracted something of a following. It now numbered two dozen or so. Ocllo made straight for the little figure slumped against his father's knee.

"Huaccac! Huaccac!" She swept him into a smothering embrace.

"Are our people well?" Changa asked her by way of greeting, his voice gruff, irritated by her public display of emotion. But she was off on her own, rocking back and forth, crooning to her son.

A burly chief of secondary rank answered his question: "All is as you left it. The plowing and the sowing went well. We expect an excellent harvest."

As if to underscore his assertion, the comfortable sound of a farmer at work drifted up from a field below them.

Unperturbed by the excitement above, a farmer was breaking clods of earth with a foot plow, raising it above his head by the handles and driving it into the ground with the aid of his foot.

Changa ran his farmer's eye over the freshly earthed-up field and the well-tended gardens on the slopes back from the river. A little sigh of satisfaction escaped him. The harvests, due in three to four months, did appear promising.

How good life was here, he said to himself, seeing again how beautiful it all was. How long would that life continue? Would the white men come? Just thinking about it caused the anger to boil up within him.

"A runner reported Mayta Yupanqui has died," put in the burly chief. "Is it so?"

Changa nodded curtly. "He's gone to Hanac Pacha, the upper world, to live with the Sun. Have any others returned?"

"Ten men all told, so far. Two with wounds." He ran off their names. "They said they became separated from the rest in the confusion after the fighting."

Changa asked specifically about one man. "Curipay, a servant of Mayta Yupanqui, accompanied us early on, but disappeared. Has he been seen?" The curaca's hands itched for the coward's throat.

"No."

The crowd swelled, people hurrying down the road in a steady stream. A barrage of questions poured out, which Changa waved off with his hand. A meeting of the senior officials from all the Collagua towns would have to be called. That would be time enough to answer questions.

He searched the crowd for Ollanta, thinking to use him as a messenger. His eldest son was nowhere to be seen, however, having wandered off without a word. The curaca wrinkled his brow, worried about Ollanta. The events at Cajamarca were acting like a poison inside his brain. Each day his behavior grew stranger.

"Come," he announced. "We are weary and would rest. We'll talk later."

Ocllo trailed behind with Huaccac, going slowly so as not to hurry him overmuch. One arm encircled his scrawny shoulders, while the other tried to control an overjoyed Piqui Chaqui from leaping up to caress his master.

Chapter Nineteen
Ollanta's Leaving

"It ill suits me to dally here when I could be fighting the bearded men." Fingering the hilt of a bronze battle axe, Ollanta stared hatred at the far off purple hills. In the bright, airy atmosphere of a peaceful day in the high pastures, his vitriolic mood seemed utterly out of place.

His companions, Yeure and Paonie, eyed him warily.

"To fight the bearded men," Yeure reminded him, "you must go all the way back to Cajamarca. The bearded men haven't left the city. Prince Atahualpa's ransom is not yet collected."

Those words set Ollanta's teeth on edge. The Inca had promised a vast amount of gold and silver in exchange for his freedom. A room, seven paces by six paces, would be filled with gold as high as the Inca could reach. Another room would be filled twice over with silver. Gold and silver plate, costly jars and pitchers and ornaments, were steadily making the journey to Atahualpa's prison. Holy places and palaces were being stripped to satisfy the Spaniards' lust for treasure.

While picking his teeth with a bronze dagger, Yeure twisted his swarthy face into a thoughtful examination of Ollanta. His lower jaw, broken in a fall as a child and not properly set by the bone-setter, protruded at an unusual angle so that his speech tended to be poorly enunciated.

"Where then," he asked sensibly, although in a barely understood mutter, "will you find white men to fight? As long as they hold the noble Atahualpa hostage, no army will move against them. Especially now that Prince Huascar is dead."

A somber silence fell over the trio of young men. Word had arrived recently that Huascar had been murdered while en-route to Cajamarca under an escort of Atahualpa's soldiers. Speculation immediately centered on Atahualpa himself secretly ordering his half-brother and main rival removed. This news, the latest in a series of calamities, had hit the valley like a lightning bolt.

"So," Yeure continued, "with the army sitting on its hands at Cuzco, and the bearded men in the far north, who do you propose to fight?" Delighted at being able to bait Ollanta, he barely managed to conceal a grin.

An empty laugh answered him, a harsh sound stripped of all honest merriment. "If the bearded men are too far off, then other opponents will do. Those who cower in hidden valleys like this one, for instance."

Yeure fiddled with his dagger again, trying to gauge the seriousness of those remarks. Turning outlaw, if that was the suggestion, would be contrary to everything they'd been raised to consider as proper. Yeure believed his boyhood friend capable of almost anything. But this? His thick chest rose and fell as he lay back to grapple with the problem. When he sat up again minutes later, his twisted jaw was bent into a grin. Changa's wild-eyed son was joking.

"You find a jest where none exists," Ollanta sneered. "I truly am leaving. Follow me," he challenged. "I'll take you to your fill of fighting...and also women and other delights. For men such as us there will be all manner of things to enjoy."

"We couldn't leave without permission," Yeure cautioned. "You know the law. I doubt permission would be granted."

"You talk as if your mouth was full of llama dung," Ollanta snarled, mocking his friend's speech. "Spit it out and maybe your brain will work properly. Permission! Permission! Things have changed. The old rules no longer apply." He swung abruptly on Paonie. "What's your opinion? Speak!"

Paonie was a trundling little fellow, much given to squinting against the sun, and right now he had his puffy, round face screwed up into a pensive knot. Like Yeure, he'd been bowled over by Ollanta's proposition, and seemed at a loss for comment.

"Give us your counsel," Ollanta insisted with a grin. "Although, maybe I shouldn't ask you. I can see you're frightened."

Paonie's coppery cheeks flushed an instant, dark red.

Ollanta barked laughter, and Yeure smiled broadly. Paonie's discomfiture in such situations was always predictable.

"Too much is happening to linger here," Ollanta went on. "Let us join the army near Cuzco. We would be made welcome." Hoisting his axe, he studied the half-moon blade as though seeing it for the first time. "Would I have had this that day at Cajamarca. We were tricked into leaving all but ceremonial weapons behind. We either ran like dogs or were cut down."

He began to rub his head up and down the axe handle in a curious manner, in much the way a condor cleans its head on grass after feeding. The fact he'd been forced to flee bothered him as much as the massacre itself.

Paonie stared at him, fascinated and unable to look away. Yeure, however, pointedly kept his attention on the thread of river far below, curling its way west to Cabanaconde and the great canyon.

"My father will grant us leave," Ollanta stated at length, seeming to assume the other two had already agreed to leave with him. "Changa has become the real governor of this province."

Yeure and Paonie traded quick looks. "T'is best not to be overhasty," Yeure put in hurriedly. "It will bear more thinking about." Paonie nodded swift agreement.

"If he refuses permission, we'll simply go," Ollanta persisted. He threw a stone at the llama nearest them. "These ugly beasts have eaten enough for one day. Besides, I'm hungry myself. It's time we went home."

They ran to round up the flock. Whirling slings about their heads, hissing, they moved their charges toward the path that twisted like a corkscrew off the near vertical mountainside to the valley below.

Ollanta charged them to say nothing until he'd spoken to his father. "Don't talk in your sleep," he ordered Paonie with a toothy grin.

Paonie assured him that he never talked in his sleep. Ollanta laughed. He enjoyed the power he exercised over his companions. If he wished them to accompany him when he left, he was confident they would do so. He pranced a little as he negotiated the steep path.

His mood had changed for the better. Lively prospects lay in store.

~ * ~

"No," Changa stated emphatically. "With the situation so unsettled, you must remain here."

The argument inside the family compound had been lengthy and heated. Mama Ocllo and two serving girls working on a loom glanced uneasily at one another.

"While we idle here, the white men swagger and plunder," Ollanta raged, his face suffused and contorted with passion. For an incredible moment he appeared on the verge of striking his father. "There's work for men to do. Important work!"

The curaca fought to control himself. "These are difficult times," he said sternly. "You are my son and will be curaca one day. You are needed here." To end the argument, he marched swiftly off into the street.

Piqui Chaqui raced around the corner of the house, chasing a ball of wool Huaccac had thrown for him.

The ball bounced past Ollanta with the dog in close pursuit. A vicious kick to the ribs sent the animal flying against a wall with a terrified yelp.

Huaccac ran to help him. The expression he levelled on his brother brimmed with hurt and accusation. "You fight Piqui Chaqui more eagerly than you fought the bearded ones at Cajamarca," he charged.

Ollanta leapt for him, but Ocllo was swifter. She sprang in front of Yahuar Huaccac, and rooted herself there. "Save your strength for the bearded ones," she screamed.

With a savage oath, Ollanta strode across the courtyard. A kick overturned the loom and a slow-moving serving girl was hurled aside. He stormed through the entrance and disappeared.

~ * ~

Cora, the prostitute, limped along the uphill path that led to the town center. At the main aqueduct, she halted to sit and rest.

In a field of *quinua* grain close by, a farmer labored over a break in an irrigation canal. He glanced up, noticed Cora, gave her a casual appraisal, then did a double take.

"What are you gawking at?" she shouted at him. "Your fields need tending–as does your wife." She glared at the farmer with her one undamaged eye.

This was one of the rare days when Cora wished she was simple mother and wife instead of the valley's most celebrated *pampairuna*. Attempting to concentrate on the more pleasurable hurt between her legs did no good either. She found herself stroking the gash on her cheek instead.

Last night had been a rough love-making, she reflected ruefully. Nothing she had done for Ollanta had satisfied him. Thanks to the gods he finally went in search of that friend of his, Yeure.

Angrily, she stamped her foot against the rock she was sitting on. It awakened the miseries in her back but she did it again, anyway.

A small boy dressed in good clothing walked up the road. "Piqui Chaqui," he called. "Where are you?"

Cora examined him with her one good eye, trying to place the child, then recognized him as Ollanta's brother. She was about to hurl an insult for him to take home to his family when he yelped in alarm and ran into the quinua field. A wail tore through the air. Cora heaved herself to her feet to investigate.

The child knelt over a small dog lying motionless in the half-grown grain. Shuffling closer, she saw the dog was dead, the back of its head crushed. Foul-looking matter slimed the mop of hair between its ears. The boy had fallen silent now, but she saw how his entire body shook. She watched a short while longer, then lifted her head to measure the sun. It was past mid-morning already, she noted, and she had things to do in town.

Groaning, she crossed the aqueduct by the steps and headed for the plaza.

Chapter Twenty
The Old Man of the Mountain

Roxana waited at the Land Rover, dressed for hiking in a pair of jeans and a heavy shirt. She eyed Slade narrowly as he arrived with Garrick.

"I'm looking forward to this," Slade offered pleasantly. "My first archaeological expedition." He tossed his things into the back of the Land Rover.

Garrick glanced around, looking for Cusi and his string of mules. "Where'd the happy boy go?"

"He headed off downstream toward the canyon with the mules to save time," Roxana explained. "We'll catch him up."

"What's this canyon like?"

"It could just be the deepest canyon in the world. Certainly it's one of the deepest."

His skepticism must have showed, because she immediately arched an eyebrow. "That just happens to be true. The Colca Canyon is almost twice as deep as your Grand Canyon."

"That's a fact," agreed Slade. "I've heard about it."

"Really! Should be worth seeing then!" Garrick attempted to sound enthusiastic, but preoccupied with the other concerns and more than a little distant, his enthusiasm came out appearing forced.

Roxana studied him, eyes slit slightly in speculation. Garrick found it easy to read her mind. *She's still wondering what really happened last night*, he mused, feeling distinctly uncomfortable under her gaze.

"The canyon most certainly is worth seeing," she said evenly. "As you put it in the States–it'll blow your mind."

~ * ~

A morose expression souring his face, Cusi slumped on a rock beside the broad trail, just past where the road ended. A tiny brook joined the river here. Roxana ground up to it in four-wheel-drive and stopped.

Lower down, where the brook splashed into a shallow pool, a woman was washing clothes. An olive-skinned child, the Quechua deep-scarlet blush aflame on his cheeks, played on the bank. After squinting briefly at them, the woman carried on with her washing.

Roxana parked the Land Rover at the base of a towering, flat-sided rock. The rock was moss-strewn in patches, and cactuses, wound all around with dainty, yellow flowers, seemed to grow right out of it. A mountain parakeet perched on top of the rock, standing on the needle point of a long cactus spine.

"Subimos," we climb, Cusi informed them, commencing the ascent to a break in the hills that offered sloping access to the high ground above.

A narrow footpath awaited them on top, worn into the timeless soil by centuries of human and animal traffic.

To save the mules a while longer, they set out along the path on foot, leading the mules and moving at a brisk pace. Understanding the benefits of a loose, regular stride on a long march, Garrick settled in quickly, as did Slade. Roxana, more comfortable than either of the two Americans at this elevation, also displayed little difficulty in maintaining pace.

As for Cusi, he slogged loose-kneed along as tirelessly as the mules.

They travelled up and down over rounded hills, over light, sifting soil. Except for an occasional, twisted quenua tree clinging to the more inaccessible hilltops, the terrain was treeless. The gentler slopes had been denuded of easy-to-reach trees centuries earlier.

Black-tailed, grey doves, always in pairs, exploded from patches of dwarf shrubs. A breeze chased itself, in spurts and circles, through the breaks and across the infrequent flats.

Sunlight pouring out of a nearly cloudless sky soon had perspiration running in rivulets down Garrick's face. He peeled off his jacket and tied it about his waist as they slowed to work along the base of a cliff. A cavity in the cliff had a huge rock overhanging it, and in that cold, never-changing shadow, years-old snow gleamed whitely.

At a rest stop, Garrick spotted a shadowy movement high up in a copse of quenua trees. A mere hint of something substantial and it was gone. But he had hunted deer in the woods of northern New York and identified something familiar about that movement.

"I just saw a deer," he declared.

Slade showed interest. "Yeah? Where?"

"See that patch of twisted trees between those two hills. In there."

"Can't see anything," Slade said after straining in that direction for a minute or two.

"It's gone now, but I saw it all right. You a hunter?"

"Back home in the States, I went hunting every year. Maybe you just thought you saw a deer."

"I only got a glimpse. I'm sure it was a deer, though."

"It could've been," Roxana said. "There were a lot of them once. They've been killed off over recent years. Used to be a fair number of pumas, too. Probably none at all left now. I haven't heard of any being sighted in ages."

Mumbling a few monosyllables, Cusi rose to his feet glowering at them, an announcement the rest was over.

Another hour's march brought them to a rocky outcrop strewn with cactuses, where a brook danced down a hillside.

A clutch of round, stone houses nestled on the level ground at the foot of the hillside. In a corral in front of the houses, a girl of eight or nine was trying to milk a small, brown cow. A calf stuck its muzzle over the child's shoulder and under the cow's belly, wanting the teat. The girl kept shoving it away.

Cusi mumbled and pointed, by which Garrick assumed they had arrived at his grandfather's, Ampire's home.

It looked a lonely spot, hugged in by purple ranges to form a small valley. Letting his eyes follow the brook upstream, Garrick saw, peeping over a ridge, the snowy spine of grand mountains.

Although the girl's hands worked busily, no milk came. Sitting back on her skinny haunches, she wiped her runny nose on a dirty sleeve while she considered the problem. The cow had chosen not to cooperate and would not relax the udder. Just then, a plump woman of early middle years emerged from a hut and saw the child's predicament. Going immediately to the calf, she pulled it forward to the teat. With the calf sucking, the cow let go of her milk bag. The woman twisted a rope around the calf's nose and pulled it away. Then, she motioned for the girl to begin once more.

The cow lowed. A rich, yellow-white stream splashed into a pail wedged between the child's feet.

Cusi called out. The woman straightened and spun around, shielding the sun from her eyes with a work-roughened hand. She seemed startled–visitors were extremely rare in this remote place–but visibly relaxed when she recognized Cusi.

Her name was Warmi, married to a nephew of Cusi's called Osco. They lived here together with their children and old Ampire. Osco was absent, high in the mountains with their young son and their flock of llamas and alpacas.

All information had to be gleaned from her by way of the reluctant Cusi; Warmi spoke no Spanish and Roxana's Quechua was spotty at best. The woman seemed friendly, however, bunching up cheeks like frost-ripened apples in a wide-gummed smile of welcome.

"Ampire's up in the mountains with some other men," Roxana reported. "They're after a condor. Warmi isn't sure when he's coming back."

"What do they want the condor for?"

"The skins fetch good prices, and body parts are used for medicine. They're after a live one this time, though. A town near the coast is having its one hundredth anniversary, and they need a live condor for the ceremonies. It's fairly common. The old culture isn't completely dead–the condor represents the triumph of the Indian spirit."

"So," Slade put in. "What's next...scour the Andes Mountains of South America in hopes of stumbling across them, or sit here and vegetate?"

Roxana gave him an irritated glance. "How were we supposed to know this would happen? We'll just have to wait."

~ * ~

It was late morning when muffled sounds accompanied by a splash of color directed their attention to a cleft in the nearby rocky hillside. A strange cavalcade dropped down toward them.

A slender, young man about Garrick's age, apparently of mixed blood, dressed in worn trousers and a checkered shirt, led a burro by a rope. He was trailed by two men, both lean, short, mountain Indians wrapped up in ponchos.

A huge bird of piercing gaze and evil-looking beak rode the burro, tied in position.

The bird struggled against its bindings, managed to partially free itself, and commenced to flap its wings. The little grey burro brayed a desperate call of alarm. The two mountain Indians rushed forward to re-fix the straps, and the great bird settled down once more. The young mestizo spent a moment calming the burro, stroking it, before resuming the descent.

Garrick stared at the winged predator. If ever a creature could appear totally evil and yet noble at the same time, it was this one.

Pebbles bounced down from above, and a wrinkled creature materialized. For one crazy instant, Garrick thought, *it's a monkey*. It moved as such, stooped and bent, scrabbling on all fours. A thatch of dirty white hair stuck out from beneath a crumpled, black Stetson. Ampire.

Observing him crabwalk lower, it occurred to Garrick that this was the first Indian he'd ever seen with white hair.

Ampire's small black eyes gleamed intelligently as he took in the three visitors. Sliding the last few feet to the bottom, he sat there quietly, looking as dry and brittle as parchment. He glanced up at last to mouth a few words in Quechua. His face, collapsed by time into a soft spider's web of wrinkles, worked gently as he spoke.

Garrick threw up his hands in amazement. "I can't believe a man as old as this climbed those hills."

Roxana repeated this in Spanish to the young Mestizo. Grinning widely, he translated it to Ampire. The ancient fellow's face moved gently once more, his narrow, fleshless mouth opened, and low, rasping noises emerged.

"Ampire," the Mestizo explained, "says he began climbing mountains a very long time ago, even before the strangers came. Each day since then he has climbed mountains. He believes when he stops doing this he will die."

Roxana was full of curiosity. "What strangers?"

Garrick fancied he detected a twinkle in the old man's eyes when he spoke again. The Mestizo bent over him to listen.

"Mistis—strangers with beards," he translated, straightening up with a laugh. The two Indians also sported broad smiles.

"What's so funny?" Garrick wanted to know.

Slade explained: "Misti is a slang term for white man. The bearded strangers...that's how the Incas initially described the Spaniards, four and a half centuries ago." He chuckled. "The old boy's pulling our legs."

Garrick joined in the laughter. He was curious to know how they'd captured the condor, and got Roxana to ask the Mestizo.

He came from the village where the condor was headed, and his excitement over its capture was still evident. His voice rose as he described what had happened.

A dead llama had been deposited in a small valley surrounded by high hills. The condor visited the stinking carcass and gorged itself to the extent that it was unable to fly over the encircling hills. The two Indians and the Mestizo had chased it, wings flapping helplessly, up and down the valley, until it was exhausted and finally caught.

The young man examined his prize proudly. "I've been four days here and will probably spend two more on the return journey to my village, but it's been worth it. The whole village will be pleased. Our festival is next week."

Ampire climbed to his feet, and the procession continued on to the huts. Roxana questioned him as they walked, employing the affable young man as interpreter.

At the mention of Pachac Puquio, Ampire mumbled, "Ah, the place of the *Mistis*. Close to where the young *villca*, priest, and the things from the temple lay."

Roxana started. "Mistis! Is he saying that white people live at Pachac Puquio?"

Ampire replied that the inhabitants of the village were not of the *people*–by that seeming to mean his own pure Quechua stock.

"Sounds like a fairy tale to me," Slade scoffed. "They're common in the Andes. Someone tells a story, it gets repeated over and over until eventually it's accepted as fact. All along, though, it's nothing but bullshit."

"Ask him about the priest," Garrick urged.

The old man's face clouded. He spoke grudgingly. "A young villca of Coporaque, a man of royal blood, sleeps with the things from the temple not far from Pachac Puquio."

When pressed to give the location, however, he insisted he didn't know. When Slade guffawed loudly at this, Ampire clammed up.

Roxana was furious, but Slade's cynicism continued unabated. "At least we're having a pleasant hike in the mountains," he gibed. "The entire day won't be wasted."

The two Indians knew little of the priest. But of Pachac Puquio, they said, "Oh yes. We've heard of it often. Strangers are not welcome, so we've never gone there, but it lies somewhere in the great canyon."

"There. You see," Roxana stated triumphantly to Slade. She marched off, her back stiff and straight.

"Y'know," Garrick offered to his compatriot, "when a legend persists over a great number of years, such as this one seems to have, there's usually a grain of truth to it. Don't be surprised if we find something pretty damn interesting."

Chapter Twenty-one
Pachac Puquio–Place of One Hundred Springs

"The old boy's quite a character." Garrick chuckled as he watched Cusi wring directions to Pachac Puquio, a painful sliver at a time, from his reluctant grandfather.

"He's more than an interesting character," Roxana corrected. "He's a repository of knowledge. Important knowledge. And that creep friend of yours, Slade, upset him sneering that way. That's why he doesn't want to talk."

"Oh, I dunno. Whenever it suits him, Cusi's as stubborn as that mule over there. Maybe mulishness runs in the family. But you speak Quechua well enough to make yourself understood. Use that feminine, terribly sweet charm of yours on him before we go. Leave him in a friendly mood."

That made her laugh. She did as he suggested, though. Just prior to their departure, Garrick also walked over and shook hands with the old gentleman.

They worked through a jumble of rounded hills to the south-west, emerging onto a small plain. The only sign of life, a *rhea*, an ostrich-like bird, regarded them briefly in astonishment before sprinting off on long legs. Dark-green swells of land hemmed the plain in, running eventually into grey-blue mountains.

Outcrops of brownish granite soon appeared, along with the first glimpses of the canyon. Cusi took them in what seemed to be circles, hunting for the path that led onto the rim. After an hour of searching, he located it. A small heap of pebbles and coca pellets marked the spot.

A slender trail, easily missed by anyone not on the lookout for it, led onto the wall. And there, hugging the cliff face, two short strides in width, lay the sloping path to Pachac Puquio! The river leapt into view almost two miles below, spectacular and dizzying, surging through the narrow, twisting canyon in a torrent of mud and stones.

One quick look, and Garrick drew back. He had not expected anything as hair-raising as this. "Jesus!"

Slade was visibly shaken. A single timid peek over set him trembling. His expression loosened, became elastic. You got the distinct impression his brain was spinning.

The man's terror of heights was laid bare for all to see.

Once he got over his amazement, Garrick found it a bit amusing. Weakness of any kind seemed so foreign to this strong, cold man. He couldn't resist grinning at him. "Ain't gravity a bitch, buddy. How far down did you say it is?" he asked Roxana loudly.

She wasn't amused, sharing at least some of Slade's fear of heights. She squared her shoulders, however, and declared firmly: "We've come all this way. I'm going ahead."

"Whadd'ya say, buddy?" Garrick grinned at Slade.

With a terse nod, Slade agreed. He could hardly do otherwise when a woman was willing to make the attempt.

Garrick just let the mule do it, going behind Cusi and Roxana and ahead of Slade. He fought the urge to close his eyes and discovered to his surprise that, after ten minutes or so, he was able to relax. A further ten minutes and he was casting about with interest.

The old, familiar world of puna and craggy mountains had vanished. In its place were encompassing cliffs shaped and curved by nature over millions of years. A clean breeze blew, wafting aside his last concerns. Over the past days he had felt the pull of this strange land. Now, he surrendered to it, letting the *feel* of the country settle about him.

Exhilarated, he swung in the saddle to look behind. "Hey, Slade," he called. "Isn't this something?"

Slade's face shone wax-like with fear. Both hands were around the pommel of his saddle in a death's grip. Garrick hadn't realized the man's phobia was quite as bad as this, and experienced a twinge of guilt. Rocking along in the saddle, he was trying to think of what to say to him when they came unexpectedly upon a broad, flat-bottomed ravine carved by nature out of the canyon wall.

The basin had two occupants. A man conversed with himself in front of a crude hut. A pink and black piebald pig lay close to him dozing in the sun.

Utterly incredulous at the arrival of visitors, the fellow's pointed, rat-like features screwed up into an expression of comical astonishment.

"Huh-huh-huh," he babbled moistly.

After speaking briefly with him, Cusi announced his name as Titu.

Titu shuffled closer, bringing with him a body odor so rank even the leathery Cusi pulled away. Tall for a mountain Indian, he was sparely built and somewhat stooped. He could have been any age between thirty and fifty.

"Look at his eyes," Garrick said. "They don't focus properly."

"Light-colored eyes, too, for a Quechua," Roxana added.

"Huh-huh-huh," Titu gibbered with his wet, mobile mouth.

"A babbling idiot," snorted Slade. He'd undergone a dramatic transformation in the few minutes since exiting the narrow trail. Relief flooded his face, his body relaxed in the saddle.

A quick scrutiny of the roomy ravine provided Garrick with a surprise. The cliff top loomed much closer than he ever would have expected. "We've been dropping down steadily. I thought we'd be lower by now. The rim must dip down at this point."

"Filthy sonuvabitch! Get outta here!"

Garrick spun round to see Titu scrambling backward from a kick, his hand on his ribs. He mewled in pain.

"Easy buddy," Garrick said quickly. "He's harmless–like you said, an idiot."

Slade's expression had gone ugly. A sullen, eager-to-hurt look had settled across his face. Circumstances had provided him with a focus for certain frustrations. The wretched Titu must accept the blame for Slade's recent failures, and for the terror filled trip along the canyon wall.

Keeping a wary eye on Slade, Garrick asked Roxana to find out whether the fellow lived here alone. "Jesus–there must be someone else around!"

Poor Titu! Rolling his eyes fearfully at Slade, he seemed hardly able to comprehend he was being spoken to. It took repeated attempts for Cusi and Roxana to get any information from him.

"No, he lives all by himself...except for the pig," Roxana announced at last. "He even grows his own food here, apparently."

Titu transferred his attention from Slade to Roxana, watching her intently as she spoke, an untidy gleam in his unstable eyes.

Awakened by the unaccustomed noises, the pig finally got to its feet and wandered about the immediate area. It was a bony, runty thing with ludicrously short legs. It didn't walk or run, it skittered.

Titu's scrutiny of Roxana didn't waver. Uncomfortable before it, she made the obvious comparison: "It's hard to tell which one is the pig. Isn't it?"

"Let's take a look around," Garrick suggested.

There was not much to see: the miserable hovel, a pathetic garden of potatoes and a little maize. At the tip of the ravine was a heap of refuse where, presumably, the pig was obliged to scratch a living. The cliff face, against which the hut leaned, had been heavily striated by water and wind erosion. Fanciful statues and castles had been sculpted out of the rock.

A general outward curve threw the whole area into shadow. With a breeze fluting among the rock columns, it was a brooding, darkling place.

"Unusual looking rock formations," commented Garrick in lowered tones. "Eerie, in a way."

"Quite beautiful, actually."

For several minutes they were quiet, subdued by the frowning cliffs.

Then, Roxana said, "I still don't like your friend. You saw what he just did."

"Aw, he's all right," Garrick mumbled, hoping she wasn't getting started on Slade again. "Don't worry about him. He'll be okay." He gave a last glance at the cliffs. "Not much of archaeological value here, is there. Let's go back...see if we can find out anything else from our weird, new friend."

Slade met them with an announcement. "Laughing boy here says he won't go any farther. Him and the idiot had a long talk. I couldn't figure it out."

Cusi gazed stubbornly off across the canyon. Other than muttering something about, "Mistis," he refused to even discuss the matter.

"There's that word 'Misti' again," said Garrick. "Titu has sort of a fairish skin and light-colored eyes. You wouldn't call him white, though. Wonder why he lives here by himself, anyhow? Why doesn't he live in Pachac Puquio with the others?"

"That's not hard to figure," Slade snorted. "Look at 'im, smell the bastard. His own people couldn't stand him. They threw his smelly ass out."

Titu's slavering gaze was fixed on Roxana once more.

She didn't like it in the slightest. "Let's go," she demanded. "I can't stand this place. The village can't be far. We don't need Cusi."

They both looked at Slade.

You could tell he hated the thought of going deeper into the canyon, but he gave in nevertheless, snarling: "All right. All right. Let's get this goddamn operation over with."

To everyone's huge relief, the track soon broadened out. Also, it was warmer than Garrick would've thought possible at this altitude. The canyon flowed almost directly east to west, accepting the full brunt of the sun's rays throughout the day. Having soaked up the sun's heat for hours, the rock walls in their turn radiated warmth. Jackets and heavy shirts not already removed now came off.

A few miles onward, they were brought to an abrupt halt.

A brook cascaded beneath a natural stone bridge. The sound and sight of water foaming under the slender arch of stone provided disconcerting reminders of the awful drop below.

"Easy, Roxie." Garrick reached over to pat her shoulder. "Wait here. I'll go first."

Shaking her head stubbornly, she kicked her mule the twenty yards to the far side and dismounted, trembling.

"Nice going, Roxie," Garrick sang out, fighting down the urge to call her *honey*. He followed with his mule, crossing easily.

For Slade, it was terrible.

"C'mon, buddy," Garrick encouraged. He got off his mule to watch. "Just keep your eyes straight ahead."

"Shut the fuck up!" Slade screamed. His lungs taking in air like a bellows, he ventured onto the bridge.

The mule clopped unconcernedly to the far side.

Safe across, Slade fumbled his hat from his head with a shaking hand.

Sweat lathered his head and face, standing his short hair up in peaks, giving him a look of such desperation and bewilderment, Garrick couldn't help laughing.

Slade snapped bolt upright.

He was a proud man, prizing his strength and coolness above all other things. These attributes had been under serious assault during the ordeal on the mule path. A certain erosion of will had occurred. This was difficult enough in itself to accept, but to be laughed at by a man who shared many of his own values simply could not be tolerated.

He tumbled from the saddle, his face stiff with rage.

Garrick said the wrong thing. "See," he soothed. "It wasn't so bad after all."

For once, Slade's expression told it all. His mouth tightened into a grim, bloodless slash, and his eyes, suddenly gone dark, glittered with such intensity that it amounted to a promise of violence.

A dog barked at that moment, from up the trail.

"Listen to that. Listen," Roxana said in a rush, throwing words between the two men. "We must be at the village." She looked nervously from one man to the other.

"Yes. I guess we must," mouthed Garrick levelly, not dropping his gaze from the other man's. "What d'you say? Should we go and take a look?"

Slade was half-crouched. A long, silent minute passed before he slowly uncurled, but when Garrick gathered up his mule's reins to go, he told him softly: "You don't know how lucky you were just now."

"Yeah? How's that?"

"Don't ever push it again."

Roxana tugged at Garrick's arm. "Come on."

They walked to the next bend in the trail and arrived at Pachac Puquio.

The village lay in an oval valley, perhaps thirty or forty acres in size, sloping gently from the base of the cliff down to a small pond. A collection of stone and adobe houses sat on the high ground farthest from the road.

Bridal veils of spring water slid down red-brown cliffs wherever one looked, appearing golden in the sunlight

"Roxie, do you know what Pachac Puquio means?"

"Puquio is the word for a spring of water. Pachac means one hundred."

"That's it," concluded Garrick in a soft voice. "Place of one hundred springs. It's well named."

A short-legged dog, almost hairless except for a mop of hair between its ears, bounced around the pond barking furiously. It kept glancing over its shoulder, apparently hoping for support from the village. At a flicker of movement from the terraced gardens near the cliff face, the dog gave a little wiggle of triumph. People were coming.

"The one in the lead's carryin' a gun," Slade said when they came into full view.

A group of approximately thirty men, women, and children approached warily. One little girl about six, unable to contain her curiosity, raced ahead of the rest. A tall woman, presumably the mother, hurried after her, but stopped suddenly, uttered a loud cry and bent down to pick up a stone. Her throw was awkward; the stone flew past yards distant from Garrick and his companions.

"Better get back," Roxana cautioned.

With a harsh laugh, Slade jerked a thumb back the way they had come. "Look at who she threw the stone at."

Poor, unwashed Titu had secretly followed them. He surveyed the crowd with an idiot's slack-jawed grin.

A second stone bounced at his feet, which he ignored. He had seen the little girl and edged toward her. Shrieking, the mother rushed forward, seized the child by one arm, and dragged her to the rear. Shouted threats from the villagers coupled with a heavy shower of missiles eventually forced him to retreat back up the road and out of sight.

The dog added to the uproar, bouncing up and down and barking frenziedly in obvious enjoyment of the situation. One of the men growled an order, and gave it a swat on the rump. Thereafter, the dog contented itself with silent wriggles.

Quiet ensued, both villagers and visitors attempting to measure each other.

Slade appeared to have regained control of himself. At least some of his humiliation from the stone bridge remained, however, for he gave the impression of a man in search of an opponent. A means by which he could reassert himself. Rocking gently back and forth on his heels, he examined the crowd facing them. His examination ended at the tallish, sinewy man holding the gun.

A confident grin in place, he strode forward. The sinewy man's weathered features twisted in annoyance. Up snapped his old rifle in clear warning. Unconcerned, Slade carried on, breaking stride only at the last moment.

"Buenos dias," he said in greeting, sticking out his hand.

The man's face darkened. He mouthed a couple of low, angry words, but seemed unsure what to do next.

"Come ahead," Slade called casually over his shoulder. "Just act like we're in charge. Nuthin's gonna happen."

Then, he leaned over and pinched the little girl on an ivory cheek. She escaped behind her mother to peep back, wide-eyed, at the strange white man. The mother giggled uncertainly.

Slade laughed, enjoying their confusion.

An ancient, stooped woman shuffled closer, rheumy eyes alight with curiosity. She found Roxana of particular interest and questioned her at length in Quechua. This was beyond Roxana's ability in the language, obliging her to merely smile and shake her head at the old lady. The woman smiled in return, patted her on the arm, and offered all manner of encouragement for her to speak. She couldn't seem to grasp the fact that someone was unable to speak the language of her people.

The little girl shouted something then, which brought a titter of laughter. A couple of the bolder children pushed forward.

"These people aren't dangerous in the slightest," Roxana exclaimed, fairly bubbling over with excitement.

"It seems not," agreed Garrick. "Except for maybe Pancho Villa there." He nodded towards the man brandishing the gun.

"Don't worry 'bout him," assured Slade in his old, flat manner. "If he was goin' to do something, he'd have done it by now. Let's take a closer look at the village."

Clearly pleased with his minor triumph, he ambled off up the path between the fields.

Ignoring a baleful glare from the man with the gun, Garrick and Roxana followed. In ones and twos, the villagers trailed after them.

Gardens and fields were in full bloom, divided by irrigation ditches into neat rectangles about thirty feet square.

"Ingenious method of farming," Roxana commented. "We've seen how hot the sun is here–the water in the ditches heats up during the day and then provides warmth for the crops at night. Damned smart!"

Garrick agreed. "Better looking crops than in Coporaque wouldn't you say?"

Under the blazing sun, the well-tended fields of beans, corn, and potatoes appeared lush and fat.

"Take a look up there and tell me what you see," Slade broke in. "I've seen enough mango trees to recognize them when I see 'em. I still can't believe it, though!"

A dozen trees with spreading branches of dark-green foliage formed a small grove between the fields and the houses. The branches hung heavy with half-ripened fruit.

"Well, I'll be damned!" breathed Garrick. "Whoever would've thought it was possible at this altitude!"

A big red and white and black duck left the grove and headed for the nearest ditch, ducklings strung out behind her. They slid into the water and paddled leisurely in the direction of the pond.

The village itself, with all its inhabitants trooping along silently to the rear, had a curiously empty feel to it. Only animals occupied the place. An adorable months-old burro crowded next to its mother, fluttering long eyelashes at the approaching mob. Domesticated guinea pigs were in evidence everywhere, and a dog, grey in the muzzle but otherwise resembling the short-legged dog, slept against a stone wall. Atop the thatched roofs of the houses fat, white pigeons strutted.

There were no streets as such; homes were situated any which way. Head-high walls, with tiny cactuses lining the tops, surrounded each establishment. Garrick creaked open the wooden door to one of them. Inside was a neatly-swept courtyard with an oval, stone-encrusted garden in the center, growing both flowers and shrubs. One whole corner of the yard was devoted to the cactus-like "tuna" plants, spotted with prickly, green fruit. A house occupied each end of the courtyard, and on their grass roofs–sprouting green in spots–chili peppers were spread to dry in the sun.

"I can't get over this place," Garrick exclaimed. "I feel like an explorer. A lost village in a hidden valley in an unexplored canyon. See whether anyone speaks Spanish."

One of them did. Somewhat reluctantly, a weedy, pale-skinned youth of roughly eighteen slouched forward to speak in halting Spanish to Roxana. Averting his eyes from the man with the gun, he introduced himself as Paullu. The man with the gun was Peque, the village leader and his father. Although his people rarely left this place, he, himself, occasionally worked in the big valley outside.

"How long have people been living here?"

Shrugging, he said, "This village is very old–no one knows how old." Then, he asked her: "We are wondering why you have come here. It's very strange to see visitors."

"We're interested in archaeology...umm...the history of the Colca Valley and the Canyon at the time of the Incas."

As Paullu conversed with Roxana, translating her comments to his own people, the old lady disappeared through a doorway, reappearing moments later sporting what could only be described as a clever smile.

Garrick grinned back at her. "I think the old girl wants to tell us something. Get the kid to speak to her."

A row broke out between Paullu and Peque. It continued briskly for a minute or two, after which the young man refused to talk any further. He retreated a few steps to stand beside a young woman bearing a strong resemblance to him.

Most of the villagers were of a size, tallish and regular-featured.

"They all look alike," Garrick said.

"Pretty goddam hard to avoid in-breeding in a place like this," grunted Slade.

"Notice they have the same light-colored eyes and skin as Titu," Roxana added. "Rather European type facial features, too. Hmm...most interesting...in northern Peru, on the eastern slope of the Andes, there's a light-skinned people, some of them even with blonde or red hair, that have always been a puzzle."

"This bunch isn't exactly what I'd call white," snorted Slade.

"Roxana's got a point, though," argued Garrick. "Okay, they're not real 'Mistis,' whites, but we're not looking at one hundred percent Peruvian Indian either. There's more than a germ of truth to those old legends. What d'you...." His voice trailed off. The old woman, her foxy smile intact, went up to Roxana with her hand held out. "Roxie, you've made a big hit with the old girl. See, she's brought you something."

It was a small object, wrought of metal. Roxana held it up to the sunlight. "It's made of silver," she stated, nose bunched up in concentration, "and seems to be the hind leg and part of the back of a small figurine...of a llama or some other animal."

Garrick took it, and turned it over in his hands. "Well-l-l, you could be right," he said in a voice lacking conviction. "Here. Take a look." He tossed it to Slade.

Slade glanced at it and, possibly as a joke, put it in his pocket.

The villagers didn't like it. Up jumped Peque's battered rifle. He barked something and, instantly, threatening rumbles sounded from all sides.

"Time to go, Roxie," Garrick ordered, stepping between the villagers and a combative-appearing Slade. "Make some soothing noises to our hosts. If we leave before things get real nasty, we can come back another day." He jammed his hand into Slade's pocket, feeling muscles knot in protest. "Easy. Easy, goddammit!" Garrick handed the silver trinket back to the old woman. "Gracias, Mama," he said in his basic Spanish, smiling apologetically at her. "Adios."

Roxana added a few words of Quechua and, escorted by the entire village, they marched back through the mango grove to the mules. The short-legged dog joined the group, stirred into action once more and barking furiously.

Roxana led in front, her body rigid with anger. At the stone bridge, with the village out of sight, she rounded on Slade so rattled she could hardly form words. "Just what did you think you were doing?" she spluttered. "Those people aren't used to strangers. After that stunt of yours, we won't be able to go back."

"Big fuckin' deal," he sneered in a voice low and mean.

She turned and left. Her straight, slender form stayed well ahead of the two men, vanishing then reappearing around the bends of the trail, bobbing up and down in the saddle.

Ahead of her slunk Titu, a slouched, furtive figure barely made out in the distance.

They paused at his hovel. Wordlessly, Cusi began unsaddling the animals. A rest was required for them before the return journey.

They had been there about fifteen minutes, with Roxana sulking by herself, when Titu emerged from his hut and headed in her direction.

"Watch out for the creep, Roxie."

Titu fell to his knees gabbling unintelligibly, a dirty hand thrust under her nose. In his open palm was an offering for her, a metal object in the shape of a llama's head, neck, and front legs.

Garrick walked over for a look. "It's beautifully made," he said admiringly. "How old do you think it is?" Then, he stopped, slapping his thigh in wonder. "Jesus H. Christ!"

"Exactly," Roxana crowed. "The piece of carved silver we saw at Pachac Puquio would fit onto this one to form a complete llama."

"Lemme see it," demanded Slade.

"No, you don't," she said swiftly, closing her hand around it. She called Cusi over to interrogate Titu.

It took a painful, slow half-hour before they persuaded him to divulge his secret. Taking them to a spot by his hovel, he jabbed a finger upward.

After studying the cliff face long and hard, Garrick gave a rueful shake of his head. "Can't see a thing. He could be lying, or–"

Slade suddenly shot an arm up, finger aimed. "There," he shouted. "Fifty feet below the top, directly underneath that weathered rock that looks like a castle."

The area lay in shadow, bare rock covered by a fuzz of vegetation. Standing behind Slade, Garrick sighted along his arm.

In the rock face was a perfect, black circle.

"That's no geological fault," Slade stated. "Geological faults don't come in perfect circles."

"It's a black stone sealing up the entrance to a cave," Roxana declared, her voice rising. "It can't be anything else."

Garrick pictured workmen dangling precariously from the cliff top

157

and threw his hands up in astonishment. "You're right. I can't imagine what else it would be. Whatever they were sealing up...it must've been damned important."

"What was it the old man, Ampire, said?" Slade cut in. "Near Pachac Puquio is where the *villca* lies...."

"Yes, yes. That's it," broke in Roxana. "The young man of royal blood, the villca, priest, of Coporaque, and the *things from the temple*!" She waved the broken silver llama under Titu's nose. "Inside. Are there more of these inside?"

Cusi translated, but an expression of actual cunning came over Titu's face, and he refused to acknowledge the question.

"Genuine Inca artifacts are worth a lot of money," Slade mused aloud. "Especially gold and silver artifacts. Wealthy collectors will pay damn near anything."

"Genuine artifacts go to the museums in Peru," Roxana corrected him. "Where they belong."

Garrick smiled wryly. "Before we can sell or donate anything, we'd have to open up the cave and see what's inside. Could be nothing. Or, maybe there was something of value in there years ago and it's gone now. Anyhow, it'd be a helluva operation even reaching the cave mouth...let alone breaking open that seal."

Roxana's expression was rapt. When she spoke, her voice quavered slightly. "I'm getting inside. Somehow or other. With or without you."

The lure of buried treasure was irresistible. Neither of the two men argued with her.

"We should be able to get the ropes and tools we need at the mine," Garrick said slowly. He took a deep breath. "Let's do it, then."

Chapter Twenty-two
Ambush

A wolfish, leering grin enlivened Ollanta's face as he surveyed the mass of warriors on either side of him. Thousands of men lay in ambush along the crest of the Sierra of Vilcaconga, a march of a day or two from Cuzco.

Almost to a man, they were warriors of the Northern Army from Quito. Aside from Ollanta and his two companions, Yeure and Paonie, few southern men had joined the Quitans. The still festering hostility between north and south prevented any hope of a united front against the bearded men, and for those like Ollanta who despised the Spaniards, the sheer stupidity of it all was enraging.

He directed his attention below and soon grunted softly in pleasure. Tiny figures had entered the pass, men on foot leading horses.

Crouched by Ollanta's feet, Yeure heard the grunt. "How many?" came his whisper.

"What difference how many?" Ollanta taunted him in lowered tones.

Yeure's Adam's apple bobbed up and down. "It is good to know," he mumbled in his imprecise way, wiping his streaming whopper-jawed face with a grubby forefinger. The afternoon sun had turned the pass into an oven.

"It appears to be an advance patrol," Ollanta told him. "Forty white dogs, more or less...with some of their accursed Indian allies. They proceed as though they suspect nothing." He showed open palms in gratitude to the Sun. *Inti*, the Sun, giver of all good things, had delivered the devil horsemen into the trap. "Inti looks down upon his children," he murmured. "This is a good day...a good day for the white dogs to die."

A year had passed since the slaughter at Cajamarca. Those twelve months had added layers of muscle to Ollanta's frame. Well-sinewed before, his broad form now rippled. And his loathing of the white men had grown commensurate with his strength. He seethed with rage whenever the bearded invaders were mentioned.

When he stalked the camp, men turned aside from him.

Now the white men were on their way to Cuzco. The Inca Atahualpa was dead, garrotted like a common criminal once his captors had extracted an immense ransom from him. For that, and for all other crimes they had committed, they must pay. With each day that passed, Ollanta swore this oath.

He squinted cautiously over the lip of the hill again.

The Spanish patrol had neared, the men trudging and the horses plodding wearily in the heat. One man, a bow shot ahead of the others, passed just underneath, heading for a level place with a tiny brook running through it.

Something about him seemed familiar. Under his helmet was a young, handsome face with a neatly-trimmed, black beard. His movements were athletic and graceful.

Where had he seen this man? Then it came to him. Hernando de Soto! The very same cavalier who had raced his horse before Atahualpa's pleasure house in the valley of Cajamarca.

Ollanta's heart leaped. What a prize! He marked him down with the deliberation of a hunter carnivore targeting a specific animal out of a herd.

"Hssst." Yeure's hand plucked at his tunic. "What's happening?"

Ollanta squatted to face him. "They are well into the pass," he whispered hoarsely. "The arrogant one who reared his horse before the Sapa Inca has just passed below. Ready yourself."

Gripping his battle axe, he ran his eyes once more along the lines of tense warriors. Then, he stiffened.

Offspring of a diseased bitch!

A few paces off, Paonie, rigid with fear, stared blankly at the dirt in front of him.

Quivering with silent fury, Ollanta leapt the distance separating them, and seized Paonie's throat in a steel grip.

"Ready yourself," he commanded in a terse whisper.

Paonie tore at the iron fingers, but to no avail. His windpipe was being slowly, agonizingly crushed. By the time the grip relented, pinpoints of light danced crazily before his eyes.

"The bearded men are here. Do exactly as I instructed you."

Paonie gasped for air.

With a final, warning snarl, Ollanta lifted his battle axe high. "Make one mistake and...." The axe dipped to gently kiss the smaller man's cheek. A thin, red line appeared as if by magic. Blood painted his chin.

"Yes! Yes!" Paonie managed to gurgle. "Yes, of course." He readied his sling and fumbled his shield onto his arm in a show of determination.

Satisfied, Ollanta glided back to his position.

He was dressed in the knee-length, quilted cotton tunic common to an Incan warrior. A round protective plate of hard wood slats hung on his back, a helmet of wood protected his head. A crest of parrot feathers on the helmet and bright woolen fringes decorating his legs from knees to ankles added color and flair.

To the Spaniards, he might have resembled an ancient Roman or Greek soldier. The small, decorated shield he carried on one arm added to the picture.

The ring of iron-shod hooves on rock drifted up. An oath sounded as a horse slipped on a loose stone, pulling the reins free from the man leading it. The main body had arrived. Ollanta tensed, his body bowstring taut.

A harsh cry in Castilian split the air!

Hernando de Soto had spotted them. He vaulted into his saddle, shouting to his men to form battle lines.

With a wild cry, Ollanta plunged over the edge. Thousands charged with him, thundering down the slope. Javelins filled the air, scattering the Spaniards like flung pebbles.

An exultant roar went up as horses fell kicking and screaming. The dreaded riding beasts were vulnerable after all!

The Spaniards who managed to mount their horses spurred up the hill toward level ground, through flying stones and darts and javelins. One stocky Indian warrior bounced along behind a horse like a child's toy, hanging on to the horse's tail and letting go with a banshee howl at each jump.

Five Spaniards were trapped in the crush. One mounted man, although savagely pressed by a dozen attackers, appeared about to break through. Ollanta made for him.

The horseman lunged at a shrieking, plumed warrior to his right, exposing his sword arm for brief seconds. Axe whirling, Ollanta darted in. The Spaniard's sword, with his hand and forearm still gripping it, clattered to the ground. In disbelief and horror at his spouting member, a scream bubbling from pale lips, he was dragged from the saddle. In an instant his helmet was torn loose, and the dripping axe rose again. With the full weight of Ollanta's arm behind it, the man's head was cloven to his chin.

In a frenzy, Ollanta swung again. Now the horse screamed as blood gushed from its rump. Another blow and the animal dropped kicking and thrashing. Again and again the axe swung. He continued hacking the animal, long after it was dead and the heaviest fighting had moved elsewhere.

"Santiago! Santiago!"

Ollanta lowered his axe and peered up the hill. Hernando de Soto, recognizable even in the midst of the storm, rallied his men for a charge.

With a wild yell, the Spaniards charged the tightening noose, trying for the level ground by the brook. The clash of arms, the screams, the din of battle rolling down the pass had an almost physical feel to it. High above the swarm of warriors, the bearded men slashed downwards, cutting Indian flesh with their steel weapons.

"Saint James and at them!"

Throwing warriors to the right and left, they broke through.

Howling his own war cry, Ollanta fought upwards through the melee and came, suddenly, upon a group of men cowering behind a boulder. Paonie crouched among them.

Paonie's eyes flew wide when he noticed the brawny figure looming over him.

"I warned you what would happen," Ollanta grated. The axe rose.

"No! No!" Paonie's sling slipped from nerveless fingers.

"I warned you!"

Standing with shoulders sloped forward, arms hanging loosely, and his face ashen, Paonie looked like a miniature caveman with terror-filled eyes. He puffed out his lips a little, but could manage only a bleat.

"Please!"

A quick movement of the axe, almost a flick, and a crimson fountain jetted from his severed neck.

Ollanta turned his back on the twitching body, and forced his way upwards once more. As he did so, a relative quiet fell. As if by mutual consent, both sides had drawn back. At the tiny brook, the white men rested their heaving horses. The Inca's army waited, also resting.

This sudden calm in the midst of battle was as if a great, hammering earthquake had crashed abruptly into stillness. In the unexpected quiet, even the cries of the wounded sounded distant and not quite human. Everyone ignored them.

In a fever at the halt, fearful it would allow the Spaniards to recover, Ollanta's gaze never departed de Soto. A predatory stare accompanied the Spanish captain as he moved among his troops, exhorting them to one last effort.

So, when the horsemen mounted up, formed a line of battle, and unleashed a charge, Ollanta crouched in the front ranks of the waiting army. An almost irresistible wave swept forward, big men mounted on big horses. The Inca's army took the shock and held.

The Spaniards fell back, stunned. A grim retreat commenced, a descent of the hillside to more open ground below.

Three times, Ollanta carved a path toward de Soto. But the cavalier had the devil's own luck. Or a devil's skill and courage. He remained unscathed, always just out of reach of spear or club, struggling down the rocky gorge with his men. Miraculously, they made it out of the pass.

There, the Spanish captain lured a part of the army onto level ground and killed over twenty of them.

Darkness fell soon after. Few of the Spaniards, or their horses, had escaped unhurt. When they took up a station on a hillock two bow shots off, a torrent of jeers pursued them. Exultant, the thrill of battle yet raging within, the people of the Inca waved severed heads of Spaniards and horses high in the air on spear tips.

Yeure sought out Ollanta. "On the morrow," he vowed, "I will have a Spanish skull for my drinking cup." He was agog with excitement. "What a victory! The bearded ones are defeated. I, myself, struck down one of the foreign Indians accompanying them." Then, stopping to catch his breath, he thought to ask: "What happened to Paonie? Have you seen him?"

"Bah!" erupted Ollanta, frustrated by the inconclusive end to the day's fighting and furious at the escape of the Spanish leader.

De Soto...the white men's gods must have rode with him today. How else could he have escaped? The man was as dangerous and as elusive as a snake.

Near them, a dead horse filled with gas made funny hissing noises. Ollanta attacked the animal with a knife. With its body opened up, the horse finally stopped hissing.

But Ollanta's assault on the dead horse continued. And when he saw Yeure staring open-mouthed at him, he lunged half forward, snarling: "You babble like a loose-headed woman. Bother me no more with such prattle."

Yeure left him, brooding by the mangled horse, alone in the midst of thousands of jubilant warriors.

The wait for dawn was well-advanced when a strange music rang through the mountains. Soon, a similar sound from the Spanish camp disturbed the night.

The noises were repeated at regular intervals. A distant, clear note would ring out, quickly answered by the nearby Spaniards.

The Indian camp became nervous.

"A message to us from the gods," one young man ventured hopefully, gripping his mace and peering, unseeing, into the darkness. "They watch over us and lend support against the bearded ones."

"Maybe the bearded men pray in this manner to their own gods," offered another. "They know well they will die tomorrow."

"It's the music of men, not gods," growled a grizzled veteran. "Although I admit I've never heard such a sound before. A trick of the white men's possibly...."

Yeure sought out Ollanta once more. "That's a strange noise...clear yet cold." Squirming deeper inside his cloak, he asked nervously, "What do you think it is?"

"I heard this sound at Cajamarca," Ollanta spat. "It's the music of the white men's trumpets."

"But it comes from two places, and the white men are all on that hill over there."

Ollanta hissed in bitterness: "It means the cunning and luck of the white men are unmatched."

~ * ~

Throwing back his condor's head, Ollanta laughed long and loud.

"It cannot be," cried Yeure, gasping in amazement. "Overnight they have doubled in number. Who can hope to defeat such an enemy?"

All around them warriors gaped, thunderstruck. Already, many were drifting away.

Cheering erupted from the Spanish lines. The reinforcements which had arrived during the night–guided in by the blowing of trumpets–were lined up stirrup to stirrup with the battered troop of yesterday.

The arrival, at that moment, of a thousand additional warriors from Cuzco did nothing to save the situation. In formation, the Spaniards advanced up the hillside.

Only a heavy ground mist prevented an outright slaughter. As the mist reached the lower slopes, thousands faded into it.

Yeure went with the others, after urging Ollanta to come with him and receiving no reply. He scrambled up the hill to the relative safety of a cleft in the rocks. From there, he observed the Spaniards rout the last of the Inca's army. Ollanta's tall, broad form was nowhere to be seen.

~ * ~

The Spaniards walked their horses along the empty trail, bantering back and forth, hugely pleased with the morning's events.

"Quiet there, and keep your wits about you," growled a diminutive, one-eyed man. "Do you want to blunder into another trap?" He was the leader of the reinforcements, a scarred veteran of New World campaigns and not one to let his guard down.

Some members of the troop threw sly glances at Hernando de Soto, riding his horse more quietly than usual. The one-eyed man's implication was clear–the dashing, young captain had blundered the previous day. A chastened de Soto accepted the rebuke without comment.

A half-league onward, as if to underscore the leader's warning, a hurled lance missed by inches the head of a huge, red-bearded man mounted on a deep-chested sorrel stallion.

"See, there," the rider cried, whipping his sword out and levelling it toward a tall, powerfully-built Indian bounding up a narrow ravine.

"Get him," barked the one-eyed man.

Horsemen pounded up the ravine. The red-bearded man and three others found a narrow path farther down the road, and spurred up it to higher ground.

They reached the top just as Ollanta leaped out of the ravine. With a cry they were after him. A pack of wolves after a swift-moving stag in full flight.

The wolf pack brought the stag to bay at the base of a steep hill. For a second or two nothing happened as the Spaniards took in this unusual looking specimen–far larger than most Indians they had seen, blood-shot eyes burning out of a misshapen skull.

"Cut him down," the red beard shouted, driving his sorrel stallion forward.

A battle axe struck the sword from the bearded man's hand, then cut through harness and leather into the horse's side. The sheer force of the blow shocked him. Numbed hand dangling, he wheeled his horse and dug spurs in deep to avoid another stroke. The horse galloped painfully off a short distance.

Staring wildly about him, Ollanta roared in triumph.

The three remaining Spaniards closed in swiftly from different sides, wolves on a stag.

A sword cut started blood flowing under Ollanta's chin. Then, a rider charged his horse in, knocking him down and sending the axe spinning. Ollanta bounded to his feet immediately, reaching desperately for the lost axe while fending off a sword cut with a bare arm.

The bearded riders crowded in, slashing down into his face and upper body. Weaponless and outnumbered, Ollanta lashed out blindly with clenched fists.

The fight became simple butchery.

Ollanta's great strength kept him on his feet long after other men would have gone down. He fell at last, blood streaming from countless cuts, his eyes sunken and glazed as life drained out of them. He jerked spasmodically once or twice, and was still.

The Spaniards rode back to the troop.

The little captain questioned them with a glare from his single eye.

"Dead," they reported. "We left him like a piece of butchered beef."

"Un diablo," growled the red-bearded man. He couldn't stop thinking of the wild figure who, twice, had nearly killed him. "Un loco!" He began a thorough examination of his horse, cursing when he saw how deep the axe wound was. Now he would have to walk until the animal healed.

De Soto gave the order to march on. The big man with the red beard allowed the others to pass and, bridle in hand, trudged along in the rear.

Chapter Twenty-three
Ollanta's Return–1547

His priest's robes flapping about his legs, Yahuar Huaccac left the temple and descended the seven carved-stone steps to the square. The square was small, a dozen long paces both in width and length, and yet it fully occupied the topmost terrace on the sacred hill of Yurac-Qaqa. A chest-high stone wall surrounded it.

He paused at the wall to spend an indolent moment or two. Every day he attended the temple he did this. The view was stunning from here.

Coporaque filled the close horizon a short walk away, yet he could also make out individual houses in Ullo-Ullo, the big town on the far bank. From the base of the wall, the hill fell away sharply, tier by tier, to the Inca Road, before sloping down gradually to the high bluff above the brawling river.

How very peaceful it all was, he thought. His attention ventured to the copper palace, then beyond and to the left, to where *Umachiri,* sacred mountain, protector and special deity of Coporaque, gazed down upon the town.

His long, fine eyelashes did a slow close and open. His expression became almost dreamy. Umachiri's reassuring bulk had that effect on him. The sacred mount's very presence provided a huge comfort.

When he looked back at the temple, however, a frown tugged at the corners of his mouth. The ceremonial and religious center of Yurac-Qaqa had been of great importance once. Now, Huaccac counted only a handful of visitors, few of them young. The white priests sternly forbade the worship of the old gods. Indeed, it was only because no Spaniards were currently present

Gregory Gourlay

in Coporaque that even this meager number of worshippers dared to attend the small, pyramid-shaped temple on the promontory.

Under the Incas, sixteen priests had provided for the spiritual needs of the people. Nowadays, only Huaccac and a few older, more senior priests persisted in that duty. And always when the white men were absent.

All the people gathered on the square were Collaguas. Square-headed Cabanas were not often seen these days. The Cabana country was now the *encomienda*, the fiefdom, of two Spaniards, and they had proved harsh rulers. Families had been forced from their isolated farms and villages into towns laid out in the Spanish manner. Travel was restricted.

Although the Collaguas had also been subjugated, divided and granted to different Spanish overlords seven years earlier, change had come more slowly to this upper part of the province.

Gonzalo Pizarro, current master of all Peru and brother to the conqueror, Francisco Pizarro, presently counted Yahuar Huaccac's people among his innumerable vassals. Mighty Gonzalo had been too active elsewhere, however, to fully secure his yoke upon them.

Times were turbulent for conquered and conquerors alike. Francisco Pizarro himself was dead, assassinated by fellow Spaniards. His brother, Hernando, rotted in prison in Spain, another brother had been killed in fighting near Cuzco. And now, Gonzalo, last of the brothers of doom, led Spanish settlers in a rebellion against the Crown of Spain. The rebellion had raged across the Andes for the last three years.

Deep in thought, Huaccac started across the square, sandals slapping the stone pavement. People nodded deferentially to him as he passed; the gentle, little priest in the headdress of bright feathers was extremely popular. Although he was yet very young, they found his calm manner reassuring. A priest's chaste life, coupled with an ascetic diet of roots and herbs and water, fasting often, suited Yahuar Huaccac perfectly. It also provided him with a considerable measure of dignity for a man of his few years.

A rain squall had just ended, hissing its way down valley and shielding the sun, peek-a-boo, in a gauzy veil of mist. It was early in the season for rain. On either side of the big river, the newly-sown fields and gardens glistened under the rich sheen of moisture.

Huaccac pursed thin, finely-curved lips in pleasure at the sight.

A bent old man stood facing the temple, a boy of five or six at his side. The child concentrated upstream. At a point where the river rounded a bend and dropped from view, a rainbow had appeared. The little boy let out a happy cry.

Huaccac immediately stretched forth his arms toward the flaming arch, hands open. He kissed the air and then the tips of his fingers in reverence. The Rainbow, Cuichu, with all its surpassing loveliness, was a deity he had adopted for his own long ago. In gratitude for its appearance, he plucked hairs from his eyebrows and blew them in the direction of the iridescent god.

Seeing the tiny *villca*, priest, pray thus, the old man followed suit, as well as others who were present. All offered their thanks to the beautiful deity.

Yahuar Huaccac, priest of the Sun, clung tenaciously to the old ways. This firm resolve, as much as his gentle nature, formed the wellspring of the affection and respect granted him by his people.

When the flaming arch faded from the sky, he made his way, from terrace to terrace, down the twisting path to the road. The appearance of the Rainbow had left him feeling buoyant, but then, like a cloud passing before the sun, his thoughts turned to Changa and, instantly, his mood darkened. The frown came back, tugging at the corners of his mouth once more.

The Spaniards had founded a city they called Villa Hermosa de Arequipa on the far side of the mountains. Two years ago, the principal curacas were summoned to a meeting there. Changa attended, and contracted a disease of the white men. He had barely managed the journey home. For days, he had burned with fever, his skin covered with red blotches. When he recovered, it was with much of his strength and vitality gone. Still, he was luckier than many others. Death by foreign disease was common all over the country.

Changa's declining health made Mama Ocllo very quiet these days. Although, so was just about everyone else. The coming of the white men had cast a shadow over the verdant valley.

His frown more pronounced than ever, he reached the bottom of the hill and stepped onto the road. He was about to head to town when he noticed a man a little ways off.

The fellow started toward him, a tall, strongly-built Indian dressed in plain tunic and sandals. A Spanish sword bounced on one hip, a bronze battle axe on the other. Over his left shoulder hung a small, round shield.

An Indian so heavily armed was a rare sight. Also, the carrying of Spanish steel swords by Indians was strictly prohibited.

His head was tapered in the Collagua manner. Wondering if he knew him, Huaccac examined the man's face. Immediately, he wished he hadn't.

The approaching face was a ruin. A huge, hooked nose jutted from a visage so seamed and scarred his own mother would probably not have recognized him. Wattles of scar tissue covered his throat and chin like the scales on a fish. At first glance, his chin seemed fused to his chest. Perhaps he'd been burned in a fire? But no, as he neared Huaccac could see that a sharp edged weapon had done the damage.

Poor creature, Huaccac murmured silently, his heart going out to the man. He nodded pleasantly to him. "Welcome," he said. "We don't have many travellers on the roads these days."

A hoarse sound spewed from the man's wattled throat. "By tomorrow, this road will be filled to overflowing with travellers."

Huaccac started nervously. The fellow's harsh speech was no surprise; not coming from that throat and mouth. It was the delivery he found more unsettling–the stranger had thrown the words at him, using speech like missiles. Also, his whole body seemed as tight as a drum head. The overall impression was of a man on the very edge of violence.

"What travellers are coming tomorrow?"

Blood-shot eyes surveyed Huaccac, taking in his ankle-length, woolen cassock and wide, grey-brown cloak.

"So, what I heard is true," he croaked. "You became a priest. To what end, villca, were your prayers directed this day?"

"Yes, I am a priest," Huaccac said slowly. "And I directed my prayers to the Sun and the Rainbow this day...that this valley will be left to its rightful owners...the children of the Sun, and those of the sacred volcano, Collaguata."

The man's big head tilted back, the mouth opened, and a rasping sound issued forth that Huaccac took as laughter.

"I would have been disappointed if you said otherwise. Bah!" He spat on the ground between Huaccac's feet. "A stunted, puling priest beseeching help from gods who deserted us years ago. A man I passed on the road knew your name and said you were at the temple, so I waited until you came down the hill. It has been many years little brother, but your mincing form I found easy to recognize. You were runtish as a boy...as a man you remain the same."

Stunned by the import of these words, unable to speak, Huaccac stared and stared at this man.

"Ollanta," he breathed at last. "It is you. We...we thought you dead these many years. There was no news."

"No, little brother. As you can see, I am very much alive. Even though the bearded dogs tried to kill me–and nearly succeeded."

Huaccac's mind wouldn't stop spinning. Questions he wanted to ask, needed to ask, tumbled about his head. In the end, however, gazing anew at the terrible damage his brother had suffered, all he could think of to ask was: "Where did that happen?"

"Where did what happen?"

"The wounds on your throat and face. Cuts from a weapon they look like. Are they from the bearded men you say tried to kill you?"

"Bearded dogs," Ollanta corrected him. "They left me for dead at Vilcaconga. You see, though, little brother, that I do not die easily. We killed many of *them* at Vilcaconga...and in other places." His eyes flashed fire as he spoke.

"The Battle of Vilcaconga! That was fourteen years ago! A long time to remain absent from your home."

"This valley is a small place. I always found it so. I preferred living elsewhere."

"Where?"

"Many places. Hidden places. Places the white men have never been to. Some of these secret places even have large cities, with many people. There, the old ways are still practiced."

Huaccac made a quick guess. "Vilcabamba?"

Ollanta delivered one of the hard stares Huaccac remembered so well, followed by a humorless flash of teeth.

So, that's where he's been, thought Huaccac. Stories of Vilcabamba, a

172

neo-Inca state built by Manco Inca, had floated persistently around the Andes for years.

Prince Manco, half-brother to the unfortunate Prince Huascar, had been anointed by the Spaniards to succeed Atahualpa. They proved abusive, however. The humiliations he suffered at their hands were frequent, finally proving intolerable. He led a formidable rebellion against his former masters, but it eventually collapsed, forcing him to flee to the mountain fastnesses in the east. There, he created his rump empire, Vilcabamba. From this redoubt, his warriors waged a guerrilla war against the white men. However, Manco Inca was now dead, assassinated by renegade Spaniards living with him.

"What's happening at Vilcabamba now that Manco Inca is dead?" Huaccac asked curiously. "His son, the new Inca, is very young and inexperienced." When there was no reply other than another hard stare, he gave up and gestured toward the Spanish sword instead. "It's against the law for us to own or carry such weapons."

"A law of the white dogs. I don't acknowledge it."

"There are severe penalties—"

"Think you, little brother, that I lay awake overnight worrying about foreign laws, and the penalties for disobeying them? This sword is better than the weapons we make. That's why I killed a Spaniard for it."

A question that had to be asked popped into Huaccac's mind. "Often, we have wondered about you, and about Yeure and Paonie, also. Since they left with you we have heard nothing of them either."

"Both dead. Paonie at Vilcaconga, and Yeure, of a white man's disease, a year later."

He had spoken while gazing off at Coporaque, but now he quickly turned and leaned forward, sticking his hooked nose to within inches of Huaccac's face. "Does Changa still live?"

"Yes, although he has been sick."

"Is he yet the principal curaca?"

Huaccac nodded.

"Are there dogs of white men presently in Coporaque?"

"No. In Cabanaconde there are. Here no. Sometimes white men visit, but they never stay long. One of their priests came about three months ago with two Indians who understand the religion of the white men. They stayed for almost a month...explaining every day that their god is superior to ours. Then they departed...to return to their town called Arequipa."

At the mention of the Spanish priest, Ollanta stiffened. "The white dogs with their accursed priests. Always it is the same: their religion, their cross, and their lust for gold." He leaned forward into Huaccac's face again. "What happened to the gold and silver from the temple and the copper palace?"

"Some of it was seized by the white men. Most of it, though, is hidden in a secret place in the rocks up there." He gestured upward at Yurac-Qaqa.

This pleased Ollanta, for he made another rasping attempt at laughter. Huaccac listened to the sound with relief. Now that the initial shock of finding his brother alive and in Coporaque was wearing off, he found his company exhausting.

"Come," barked Ollanta. "There is much to do." He started toward town in a swift, powerful stride that forced Huaccac into a half run to keep up.

~ * ~

To Changa and Mama Ocllo, the sudden appearance of Ollanta was as astounding as if they had awakened one morning to find that *Umachiri* had moved to the far side of the river.

And while Changa attempted to grapple with the fact that this scarred creature was indeed his eldest son, Mama Ocllo saw beneath the ravaged exterior to the more profound transformation underneath. She wore a troubled frown when Ollanta and Changa, with Huaccac hurrying along behind, marched off to a hastily called meeting of the curacas.

An emergency was upon them. Gonzalo Pizarro approached with his army.

~ * ~

Striding powerfully up and down the courtyard of the copper palace, his battered head jerking impatiently from side to side, Ollanta made a dominant, commanding figure, paid close attention to by the officials seated

174

cross-legged before him. When they heard his message, however, and what he wished of them, they could hardly believe their ears.

"Gonzalo travels with a huge army," sputtered one chief, a little monkey of a man with a scar running white along his jawline. "Hundreds of white men on horses and thousands of Indian allies. We would all be killed."

Ollanta abruptly ceased his pacing, and squinted at the speaker. "I remember you. Your name is Ayabir."

"Yes, Ayabir, the father of Paonie. Paonie went away with you many years ago, and still his mother talks of him. She wishes to hear of her son. Does he live?"

"He died in the fighting at Vilcaconga," Ollanta said shortly, wanting none of this. "Yeure also died...later, of sickness."

Ayabir's intelligent face hardened, the only overt sign of his distress. A wheedling man of slight physique, he used cunning and political skills to maintain his authority. That shrewdness told him this man was not speaking the full truth.

"And you expect us to follow you, to wage war against this great army?" he said, laughing, trying to use ridicule as a weapon.

"Explain again what it is you wish," Changa put in.

"The white dogs will journey up the road tomorrow on the way to Cuzco. We must select a suitable position for an ambush, gather boulders into piles, and await the bearded ones with slings and lances. A fine killing is ours to be had. Only the young men need come with me. Afterwards, it will be easy to escape into the mountains where their horses cannot follow."

"Madness," protested Ayabir. "Our young men are not fools. Ask them and see. They won't follow you."

The semi-circle of seated curacas murmured in agreement.

Ollanta stiffened, a certain look appeared.

"Easy, brother," cautioned Huaccac.

Ayabir shifted uncomfortably under Ollanta's savage glare and glanced around him, hoping someone else would speak up. One chief quickly did, followed by the others. They were in full assent. The plan was suicidal. One by one, they rose to their feet and departed, filing through the trapezoidal entranceway.

Soon only Huaccac, his father, and the incensed Ollanta remained.

"Look you," Ollanta spat at the retreating men. "Watch Ayabir tremble as he goes. The father is as brave as the son. Paonie was a coward."

"Ayabir spoke the truth, nonetheless," Changa stated bluntly. "Retribution by the white men would be terrible. Every town in this part of the valley would cease to exist."

"Stage the ambush elsewhere along the road then," Ollanta flung back at him. "In the Cabana country. Let the Spanish hack off square Cabana heads in reprisal."

"Impossible! We could never do such a thing. Nor would that fool the white men for long. Eventually, they would find out it was us who attacked them."

Huaccac was equally appalled. "In all these years, we hear nothing from you. How can you come home now and ask these things?" He wondered if the man was not unhinged.

"This is man's talk, priest. Do not interfere."

"You don't care what happens to the people here. You're obsessed with your hatred of white men, brother. You ask too high a price...a price for others to pay. Ayabir is right. No one will support you."

The glare Ollanta directed at him oozed venom.

Huaccac maintained an unwavering gaze, even though his stomach jumped in secret nervousness. To his huge surprise, Ollanta suddenly dropped his head in thought, then said simply, "Let us remove the gold and silver then. Deprive the white dogs of that which they covet most."

"No need," Huaccac exclaimed in swift relief. "Everything of value has already been hidden where no one can find it."

"Until now, you have dealt with white men of limited authority. They did not press the matter. Tomorrow, Gonzalo Pizarro arrives with his soldiers. Move the treasure deeper into the mountains or lose it!"

"There's really no need–"

"It is an affront not to be borne, that the thrice accursed white men be allowed to defile the sacred objects from the temple."

~ * ~

Changa visited the curacas, going from house to house, to argue for

176

the removal of the gold and silver. Ollanta accompanied him and, with his intimidating presence as added weight, the necessity of a more secure hiding place was agreed upon.

A troop of young men was conscripted to assist in this. Further, following Ollanta's suggestion, it was decided that Huaccac would accompany them, to ensure proper handling of the religious articles from the temple.

Chapter Twenty-four
Gonzalo's Army

Fourteen strong, young men struggled down Yurac-Qaqa with the last of the treasure, and pushed through the crowd of onlookers to the waiting llamas. Ollanta roared at them to hurry.

He'd climbed the hill along with them, to examine the slopes while they worked; his quick, searching eyes missing nothing. When he had climbed back down the hill, a satisfied expression creased his savaged features.

Huaccac walked up with Changa and three other men, Ayabir among them. "All is ready," he announced.

Ollanta flashed his teeth at Ayabir. The little curaca gazed sourly back at him, his resentment openly displayed.

"The sun has entered the western sky," Changa reminded him. "You must move swiftly."

Ollanta addressed the men supervising the llamas. "Let us be off," he rapped. "Quickly now. We must be off the road and well into the hills before the bearded dogs arrive."

They swung west on the road, pushing the llamas forward at a swift pace. After a short march, they turned into a defile that led off the road up to higher ground. On top, Ollanta motioned to the man who served as guide, a fox-faced fellow of thirty with the thick chest and sinewy legs of those who are born and raised at great altitude. They struck off in the direction of the canyon.

Periodically, their winding path took them within view of the Inca Road. Toward dusk, from high up on a mountainside, they looked down and saw Gonzalo's army.

From around the shoulder of a mountain it poured, twinkling and bobbing in the slanting rays of the sun, thousands of men; mounted Spaniards accompanied by Indians on foot. High up the mountain and with a wind blowing away from them, not a sound reached the small band from Coporaque. Armor gleamed and pennants snapped in the breeze, yet the grim, deadly column snaked on in perfect silence.

They watched, transfixed.

One of the horsemen in the van stood out, even from this distance. Bestriding a tall, richly-caparisoned bay horse, plumed and jewelled and wearing a cloak of slashed red velvet over shining mail, he shone in the late afternoon sun.

Gonzalo, last of the Pizarros, was a figure of legendary panache. Reckless, handsome, in his mid-thirties, he was the hero of countless native wars. An extremely vain man, rumors persisted that, not content with being the most powerful man in Peru, Gonzalo desired to crown himself king.

"The one near the front on the big horse," Huaccac asked his brother. "Is that Gonzalo?"

But Ollanta was held fast and made no answer. Hunched over with his whitened underlip quivering with tension, he appeared, for all the world, like a baby set to cry.

The fox-faced guide said, "See there...in the middle, surrounded by soldiers...those women and children and the men who walk with them. The men are not armed."

"Gonzalo gathers workers–no, slaves, as he travels," Ollanta ground out in a hate-filled rasp. "His holdings near Cuzco require labor." He flung an arm at the pitiable collection of non-combatants. "Behold the slaves who will till the fields and labor in the mines of the mighty Gonzalo Pizarro."

The armed multitude finally passed from sight, trailing a huge dust cloud in its wake.

Ollanta shook himself. "It's nearly dark," he grated. "A meadow lies a short distance up the road. They'll camp there tonight and reach Coporaque early tomorrow morning."

"We're well away then," blurted Huaccac, shaken by the sight of the army on the march. It was the very face of war.

"Yes, little brother who trembles like a leaf. We're well away." To the guide, he snapped: "Take us to a camping place for the night. There is important work to be done...work for tomorrow. Tomorrow, the bearded dogs...."

~ * ~

Huaccac shook in a nightmare. His father and mother were trapped on the puna during a storm. Lightning bolts struck all around them, smashing the ground and splitting huge boulders. They ran back and forth in frightened confusion, until at last Changa turned his face skyward. "Great *Illapa*, God of Lightning," he pleaded, "why do you threaten us so?"

Laughter like thunder answered him. A figure materialized out of a dark cloud. The visage of a bearded white man, evil and heartless, smirked at them. Raising his fist, he hurled a last bolt that ripped the sky.

An instant before it struck them, Mama Ocllo cried out in anguish: "Huaccac! Huaccac! I will not see thee again!"

Huaccac awoke quaking like a man with the ague. He sat up, bathed in sweat. Around him, men whistled softly in sleep. A mist had settled in, adding a damp bite to the chill and deadening the occasional night noises.

Dreams had meanings! And clearly, this one warned of terrible danger! The reason for it must be connected to the white men's army. Trembling, he lay back down to try to think.

The image of the silent army on the march was burned into his brain. A cold, clinging apprehension laid hold of him. What was about to happen to his family? The cruelty of the white men was unimaginable.

Perhaps he should awaken Ollanta to tell him of the dream? He directed a worried glance at his brother's sleeping spot, and found it empty. That was odd, although he could be taking a look around.

Time passed and Ollanta did not return. It was then that something he had said surfaced in Huaccac's mind with a sudden burning clarity.

There is important work to be done...tomorrow...tomorrow the bearded dogs...!

The meaning of his dream was now clear.

No, brother! By all the gods, no!

180

~ * ~

Yurac-Qaqa was deserted. With the white men so near, the citizens of Coporaque kept within the confines of town.

A yellow finch flew to the temple square to search for morsels of food left behind by visitors. As it probed the stone flagging, a man executed a careful descent from the above plateau, easing down the last thirty feet of near vertical cleft with the help of a knotted rope. At the bottom, he moved swiftly to the square.

The bird flew off, its plump, yellow body flicking displeasure at having been cheated out of a meal.

Ollanta bounded across the square, dropped down to the next terrace and commenced piling boulders from the stone walls into a mound near the pathway. When he finished, he carried on to the next level to begin another mound.

A mist hovered above the river, hiding the water and reaching up to the very foot of Coporaque. The copper palace appeared to be floating on wispy, grey waters, even as the early morning sun burned brightly on Yurac-Qaqa and the amphitheater opposite.

It was surpassing lovely, although Ollanta saw none of it. Nor would he have in less harried circumstances. He had never, by choice, sat on a rock to admire a splendid view, or cocked his ear for the call of a songbird. Having lived and fought in all manner of country, he was always unaffected by it. The freezing snows of the high sierras, the moist heat of the eastern jungles, this misty alpine morning–they were all one to him. Nature was benign or it was not. A thing either to be ignored, or battled against as an implacable foe.

In the place of these simple pleasures, he hated well. He loathed all white men, although some more than others. Hernando de Soto, stalwart of Vilcaconga, had been one which he'd valued above all others. When de Soto departed Peru, however, rich and admired, Ollanta readily transferred the malice once reserved for him to other, more available targets. Often he had done this, developing an easy facility for it.

And so, Ollanta labored on the terraces of the sacred hill, a short walk from the town of his birth, to prepare a welcome for Gonzalo Pizarro, because of all men in the world, he hated him most.

He'd just straightened his back from the pile of boulders on the lowest level when he heard the trample of a horse's hooves on the road. Noiselessly, he dropped behind the boulders.

Armor clad figures appeared, swaying on horseback, men's feet and horses' legs hidden in the mist.

Two riders passed. If the army was proceeding in the same formation as yesterday, the target he most longed for rode among the trim troop of cavalry just back from the head of the column. Another horse went by, dancing in the morning freshness, followed by a larger body of cavalry.

Ollanta's chest thumped raggedly. Now! Now!

Putting his shoulder to the mound, he heaved. A miniature avalanche cascaded onto the road, tearing a hole in the army's order of march and filling it in behind with dust and debris.

His heart soaring with the screams of the horses, Ollanta leaped up to the next level, going straight through a thick clump of cactus and never feeling the thorns.

Crested helmets edged into view beneath him. He showed himself deliberately, waving his Spanish sword as an added challenge.

A line of white men and Indians started up the hill. A crossbow bolt whooshed past Ollanta's head. The bowman bent to reload his piece, exposing himself as he did so.

Whirling his sling, Ollanta caught him just under the chin. He fell like a collapsing house. An angry shout sounded, and the line of skirmishers plunged ahead. Ollanta tumbled a second cascade to meet them, then dropped a squat, heavily-bearded man with another well-aimed rock from his sling.

The Spaniards covered the breadth of the slope by this time, advancing in a disciplined manner. He had to make his leap to the next level under a barrage of crossbow bolts and lances. Crouched behind the last mound of boulders, gulping air into his lungs, he readied himself for the final test.

A yell rent the air. An arquebus spat fire, and the Spanish charged. The third and last avalanche bought a few precious seconds. He made the most of them, sprinting for the top, his big body weaving and dodging.

Racing past the temple, he bellowed a challenge in the language of his people. The cleft to the upper plateau loomed straight ahead and he sprinted for it.

Inside the cleft, he was safe. Bolts and darts and lances rebounded harmlessly off the sheltering rock. He scampered up the knotted rope like a monkey.

On top, he screamed down insults, laughing uproariously. He played with his male parts in long, obscene strokes, and pretended to defecate onto the faces of the enemy.

The Spaniards and their Indian allies could only watch and fume. Their last sight of him was of a powerful figure bounding along the rim top.

~ * ~

Changa awoke to a world of pain. Rough hands shook him out of warm unconsciousness. They continued to bully him until he became dimly aware of sounds and movement. He experimented a little, struggling to move his arms and finding he could not. Upon forcing his eyelids open, a pain almost of fire threatened to split his skull.

Recoiling from it all, he attempted to retreat into the warm, comfortable darkness he'd just left.

"Throw that water on him," ordered a distant-sounding voice in heavily-accented Quechua.

A pot of water dashed onto the curaca's face.

His eyes stayed open on this occasion, seeing a sky tilted at a crazy angle. Fuzzy objects swam about. He concentrated on the sky and after a while the fuzzy objects faded away. Then his head cleared and he saw the copper palace. Swiftly, he searched behind it, and relief flooded in. Great and good Umachiri gazed down upon him.

Changa breathed a word of thanks to the sacred mountain, his silent companion since infancy, comforted to be within that watchful presence.

"He's conscious now." There was that voice again. "Douse him once more to make sure."

Water splashed onto his head, ran down his face and chest. He was bound and spread-eagled on the ground in front of the copper palace. Under his back, elevating his head and shoulders, was what felt like a pile of wood.

It was coming back now.

When the army poured into town and he proceeded to meet the commanders, he'd been seized and bound. It did no good to protest. A blow from the hilt of a sword struck him unconscious.

As he struggled to arrange these events in his mind, the voice spoke once more, coming from a handsome, young officer dressed in red velvet. His manner bespoke an ease with authority.

"Proceed," he said in his accented Quechua.

A woman's familiar voice called out then, reaching Changa above the background noise. Twisting his head a little, he saw Mama Ocllo, squeezed between two foreign Indians, waving her arms, making herself seen to him.

The plaza overflowed. Even during the most important festivals, the square had never held such a multitude. And certainly, Changa had never seen such a massing of white men.

The officer said something in the incomprehensible babble of the white men and a pale, thin priest, dressed in a long, white robe, advanced to stand over the curaca. With the hood of his robe thrown back, hair the color and texture of corn silk fell to his shoulders.

"There is certain information we require from you," he stated softly in Quechua far more fluent than the officer's.

"Why am I bound like this?"

The priest smiled faintly, shaking his head in mild disapproval. "Two things we must know. First—who was the warrior who hurled boulders upon us from the mountain? Some of our men were hurt. One of our crossbowmen may die. You must tell us where to find this man so we can punish him. Second—we want all objects of value. All gold and silver and the location of the copper mines." His speech slowed, became stern. "Give us this information and you may live. If not, you die...a number of your friends with you."

To make his point absolutely clear, he snapped his fingers at an Indian holding a smoking brand of wood.

The Indian leaned forward and, in a deft, practiced motion, thrust the burning brand between Changa's spread legs, under his tunic. The fellow knew his work; he entered the anus before the curaca realized what was happening.

184

Changa's shrieks filled the square. Hot, blinding colors swam before his eyes. Then, he passed out. Water was again dashed on him. When he came to, he once more desperately sought out Umachiri.

Mama Ocllo screamed and screamed. One of the Indians holding her rapped her on the head with the butt of his lance. She dropped to the ground, blood oozing from her temple.

"This pain you endure is completely needless," crooned the priest to Changa, bending over solicitously to speak. "First, who was the warrior and where can we find him? Second, tell us where the gold is hidden. When we know these things the pain will stop."

"Do not ask these things of me," Changa gasped. "I cannot tell you."

"You must!"

"I cannot!"

"You have this information. You're the principal curaca of this town. That man over there identified you as such."

He pointed out little Ayabir standing with a group of tall Spaniards. Ayabir nimbly directed his eyes elsewhere when Changa levelled a pain-filled gaze on him.

"It's true I am a senior chief," Changa stated with great dignity. "My answer must remain the same, however. I cannot tell you what you wish to know." Then, fixing his attention on Umachiri, he refused further speech.

The priest hurried over to the officer. A discussion ensued, with Ayabir being ordered forward to divulge whatever additional information he possessed.

The meeting was brief. No more time would be wasted. The officer issued commands with an air of finality.

A troop of cavalry, with Indians running alongside, clattered from the square with two directives: capture the temple treasure, and capture or kill the warrior who had caused so much mayhem.

Indian smiths were put to work stripping copper from the palace–the cavalry required horseshoes and harness parts.

As vassals to work Gonzalo's estates near Cuzco, two score healthy, young families were singled out. Several of the more beautiful women were chosen also, for the officers.

With these matters in hand, the handsome officer strolled to the nearest aqueduct. The sun's glare had become harsh and the aqueduct promised shade and cool water to drink.

Before he went, he issued a curt order to the priest.

The priest walked over to Changa. "This makes me very sad," he told him in his soft voice. "I don't wish to see you die. It's unnecessary and foolish. You see, my captain is not a patient man, and his authority is important to him. You were wrong to defy him as you did.... Only tell us what we wish to hear, and I will speak to him on your behalf."

Changa gave a terse shake of his head.

With an angry gesture, the priest directed additional wood to be heaped about him. "I offer you the opportunity to accept the One True God before you die," he said, his voice turning flint hard. "If you do so, you will receive salvation."

Complete calm settled over Changa. He replied courteously. "Thank you, priest, but I wish to live with the Sun, in *Hanac-Pacha.*"

Squaring his shoulders in annoyance, the priest flicked a wrist at a man holding a flaming torch.

With the flames mounting, Changa called out.

The priest moved closer in anticipation. Perhaps the curaca had changed his mind, after all. In this last moment, the heathen's redemption was yet possible. But when he understood what the curaca was saying, he leaped back in disgust, his cassock swirling about his legs in a petulant fan.

Changa joyously invoked the name of Viracocha, the creator of the universe.

Chapter Twenty-five
Roxana

"I'm tired. This has been an absolutely exhausting day. I think I'll turn in," Roxana announced, scraping her chair back in the mess hall. She looked weary, but excited. It would be a real coup for her, a mere student, if the cave contained an important archaeological find.

Garrick yawned. "I'll go along with you. I'm completely beat." Nodding to Domingo Valdivia and Slade, he rose from the table.

"Good night," Valdivia said, his eyes lingering on Roxana.

"See you both tomorrow morning," Slade called pleasantly after them. "We'll get an early start–lots to do."

At the door, Roxana glanced back. Valdivia had plunged deep into conversation with Slade, the American smiling amiably at him.

"I don't like him," Roxana stated flatly.

"Your admirer, Domingo? Can't say I blame you."

"Your friend, Slade."

"You're repeating yourself, Roxana. And he's not really a friend. You know that."

"He uses people. Like Domingo, for instance. See."

Valdivia was recounting a story he obviously considered amusing. Slade laughed heartily, slapping the table as if it was the most delightful thing he'd ever heard.

"Your friend's a cold fish, except when it suits him not to be. Then he's pleasant all of a sudden. I don't trust him.... And you know what else?"

"What's that? I'm dying to hear."

"He doesn't like women."

The exasperation in her tones—as though no man could possibly understand the horrors of misogyny—was so totally female he burst out laughing. "You can sense that, can you?"

"Damn right, I can. He has some hang-up concerning women." She considered it briefly. "He doesn't like women because women don't like him." When another burst of laughter greeted her, she lashed out. "And you, stupid! That man uses you all the time. He knows exactly which levers to pull to influence you."

Now Garrick flared up. "That so? Your woman's intuition at work? It's amazing what women can sense that men can't."

"It's true," she snapped, hitting full stride. "The war is your vulnerable point. You couldn't handle the pressures during the war—or after. Could you? Eh? Or, maybe you just like running away. Well, he knows that and uses it."

His face blanched. Not trusting himself to speak, he pushed by her through the door.

Seeing his hurt, she ran after him grabbing at his arm. "I'm sorry I said that, Garry. That was mean and bitchy."

He strode on.

"Garry. Garry. Forgive me. I don't know what got into me. Go ahead. Smack me one across the face. I deserve it."

He jerked to a stop. "Roxana, the war *is* my problem...always has been. I've been trying to work my way through it. Everything's still all crammed up inside, though." A weak smile crinkled his eyes. "It's going to take some time yet. You're gonna have to cut me a little slack. Okay?"

It struck him, landing as a thundering shock, that he was acknowledging his problem aloud for really the first time. Aside from a few tentative phrases to Harry Alexander and Slade, he'd not done so previously. His eyes did a slow blink to try to cover his confusion.

Standing very close to him, Roxana had concern stamped all over her. He blinked again, and shame flooded her face. "I *am* sorry! Really, I am!" She stroked his arm in a tender, soothing way.

Her extreme nearness only increased his confusion. "Forget it," he said quickly. "We'll pretend it never happened."

"But...uh...."

"Just forget it."

"Sure." They walked along quietly for a minute or two before she spoke again. "Can I speak now? I'd like to know what we're going to do about Slade."

"What do you expect us to do? The man said he wants to help open the cave. We can hardly order him not to come. He'll be okay."

She gave a loud sniff.

"He had some good ideas tonight on how to do things. And don't forget he was the one that got all that stuff we need from Valdivia."

Outside her dormitory, she wanted to stop and talk awhile, but he said good night and carried on to his own building. He walked slowly, his brain tired and overly full of thoughts. Sucking softly on his lower lip, he tried to think.

A struggle tumbled about inside. A rationalization was forming, had been forming over the past number of days, that he had a need. A deep, cutting need he must acknowledge and deal with.

It meant trusting another person, however, and that was the difficulty. The danger in reaching out could not be underestimated. He would be vulnerable, soul-laid-bare vulnerable.

Garrick studied the stars in the cold, clear sky, and waited. Eventually, a picture of Roxana emerged: how minutes ago she had demonstrated amazing hurtfulness, followed immediately by gentleness.

Women most love to help men when they've been hurt. And particularly when she was the one who inflicted the damage.

He wondered if he was falling in love with her.

In a moment of decision, hardly believing he possessed the courage to do this, he retraced his steps to her dormitory, strode down the hallway to her room, and knocked boldly on the door.

"Oh, Garry. What?"

Her hand covered her mouth in surprise. Then she saw the expression on his face, and said, "Oh," again. "Wait."

She shut the door. When it reopened, the nurse she shared the room with, a wide-hipped, middle-aged woman wearing a knowing smile on her face, exited the room and walked off, carrying a few articles of clothing.

"Is she coming back?" His voice was little boy nervous.

"No," Roxana smiled. "Not tonight. She has a friend she can stay with."

He stepped inside and closed the door. "Roxie...Roxie. I guess I need some help!"

"I know that. I've been waiting for you to ask me. Maybe we can help each other."

"Oh...umm...."

"Let me," she said suddenly, and slipped inside his arms. They stayed that way, not moving, each getting the special feel of the other. Then: "Come, Garry. I want this, too." She led him to the bed.

She began to undress, but he stopped her to bury his face in the soft flesh separating neck and shoulder. "Let me do that for you," he whispered hoarsely.

"Quickly then, Garry. Quickly."

~ * ~

Later, lying coupled together like spoons, her back to his front, and with Garrick's hand babyishly grasping one of her breasts, she thought of a day in the United States, years ago.

For Roxana Carpio, the single most important day of her life, the day which taught her everything she was ever to call pain, was that sunny day in Santa Cruz, California when she entered her father's bedroom and found him lying quiet and still on the bed.

"Papa," she called softly.

He didn't answer.

One day, her father was a robust man with a ticklish mustache who filled the house with his keen intellect and sensitive ways. Now, his stiff body lay before her on the bed. Ignacio Carpio, dead of a massive coronary at the youthful age of forty-four.

She had only to reach out and touch cold flesh to realize her world had ended.

In the presence of death, the very young react with a sense of disbelief. In Roxana's case, she experienced more than the usual numbness. Papa had been very nearly her whole life.

The months leading up to his death had been exciting ones for her.

She had at last begun tentative steps into womanhood. Her menses had flowed regularly for a full half year, and with its arrival, her body began to change. Small, hard breasts appeared–which she examined before the mirror in her room each day–and her angular lines took on a more rounded shape.

The woman changes delighted her. She found it astonishing now that she'd ever wanted to be anything other than a girl.

Boys suddenly had a definite appeal. Not clever at small talk and not witty, though, she lacked an easy facility with the other gender. That stiffness with males had persisted into womanhood.

Ironically, that very awkwardness was what had initially attracted her to Garrick. His own difficulties made him ill at ease in certain situations, and she could identify with that. There existed an odd oneness between them.

Her father had died at the start of summer, with school just ended for the year. Showing her father's academic bent, she had done well. Her English was nearly perfect by now, and she loved California. Her summer vacation stretched ahead perfectly.

Then it was all ended, and she could never be happy again.

Back in Peru fourteen months later, her still-grieving mother, Isobel, subsequently died also, of a variety of ills.

Her brother, Donaldo, three years old, went to live with one set of relatives, while she went to live in Arequipa.

One day before they'd gone to California, she and her father had been out in Lima when a crowd of shoeless beggar children surrounded them. Papa gave them coins. They pressed forward, jostling her and knocking her down. For a terrifying minute or two she was trapped under their bare feet, actually being trampled. Papa picked her up and swung her onto his shoulder before she could be seriously hurt, but it was the first occasion in her life she could recall being really scared.

"Garrick," she whispered, looking over her shoulder at him.

"Ummm." He stroked her flank.

"On the day of the tour in Arequipa, you kept giving coins to the beggar children...even when they were bothering everybody so much your friend Harry told you to stop. Remember?"

"Yes."

"Well, why did you keep on?"

"They had no shoes."

"What did you say?"

"They were shoeless. I felt sorry for them."

"Oh, Garry. My father used to talk that way." She turned around and laid her head on his chest. "I can hear your heart."

Chapter Twenty-six
The Stone Seal

Slade's face darkened in anger. "The sonuvabitch insists on going to the old man's place first," he rasped.

"Why?" Garrick asked with a questioning glance toward Cusi. "That'll take too long. It'd be faster to go directly to the canyon."

"By Christ, what an incisive mind you have," Slade snapped. "Of course, it'll take too long."

He had assumed command over the expedition, apparently regarding it as his rightful position.

The tall American's newly-acquired authority had little impact on Cusi, however; he wore that hell-won't-budge-me expression on his face. Garrick chuckled to himself. Good! Slade's cavalier assumption of command rankled a bit, even though he didn't particularly want to take charge himself.

"We may just have to do what he wants. You know how stubborn he is," Roxana said, cool amusement in her tones.

Slade caught it and directed a glare at her. But after darkly eyeing the Quechua for a moment longer, he decided he had to do as she suggested. "Bien. Vamonos entonces," he informed Cusi, bellowing at him even though the man was only a few feet away.

Garrick chuckled again, and gave Roxana a huge, lascivious wink. He felt good today. Damn good! Residue from last night bubbled happily within.

It kept him on a high during the hike to Ampire's valley.

Ampire was outside his hut braiding a leather rope when they arrived. Cusi instantly whisked him off for a private conversation.

"What in hell's he up to?" growled Slade.

"It's pretty obvious, wouldn't you say," offered Garrick. "He's telling the old man what we came up with yesterday."

"That's exactly what he's doing," agreed Roxana nervously. "Ampire mightn't want the cave opened–especially by non-Indians. My guess is Cusi figures the same. He's checking with his grandfather before he goes any farther."

The discussion with his grandfather ended, Cusi slouched over to them, a sphinx-like expression on his face which let them guess what he was about to say even before he opened his mouth.

"What!" Slade exploded upon hearing him.

"We go back," the Quechua reiterated, shaking his head in that stubborn way he had.

"If the canyon trail wasn't so hard to find, we wouldn't need him," Garrick complained.

"I can find the entrance to the trail," Slade announced.

"You sure about that?"

"I just said so, didn't I?"

"There's not much else we can do," Roxana said quickly, supporting Slade for a change. She was visibly upset at the very suggestion they give up the expedition.

"All right, then," Garrick agreed. "Let's go ahead on our own. We need the mules, though. Tell 'im to wait here for us."

Predictably, Cusi objected. "No!"

"Shit!" Slade growled. "You're wasting time." Gathering up the reins of two mules, he strode away.

"Here," Garrick said, stuffing some banknotes into Cusi's shirt pocket. "Let's go," he told Roxana, and they walked off before he could argue further.

True to his assertion, Slade had the gift of finding his way in strange country. With a skill Garrick was forced to admire, he guided them, with minor detours, to where the canyon path met the plateau. They arrived at mid-morning.

"Okay, then," Slade announced, planting a commanding foot on a prayer heap of coca pellets and pebbles by the trail. "One of us'll have to go along the path to the creep's hut while the others stay up on the rim. The one below can direct where to throw the ropes over." He looked pointedly at

Garrick.

Garrick would have to go. He understood that, but hesitated to leave Roxana alone with Slade. "I'll go if you like," he offered, "but Roxie should come, too. Just in case we need Titu's help for something. He's more likely to oblige her than me. We'll leave the mules here and go on foot."

"Sure," grunted Slade, willing to agree to anything that allowed him to stay on top. "Guess I can handle the mules alone."

Roxana shook her head in a firm no. "There's no need for two on the bottom and there may be up here. The mules for one thing. And connecting with you will be a lot easier if there's two of us looking." She ended with a quick, little smile that told him not to worry.

With further argument rendered pointless, Garrick began his cautious descent onto the path, sliding his feet rather than walking down the initial, steep slope.

"Be careful."

Five minutes brought him to a bend. He rounded it and, instantly, as though a light switch had been thrown, he was alone and plunged into the wild world of the canyon: towering rock walls, pale dust puffing up at each step, and a sheltering silence penetrated only occasionally by the soughing of the wind.

A rock the size of a small burro crashed down, bouncing off the path like a huge rubber ball. The noise it made became swollen by its own echoes into a series of ear numbing cracks and roars.

The reverberations fell with the big boulder. Pristine quiet returned. After that, the hike was uneventful. On this trip, knowing what to expect, he rather enjoyed his solitary journey. When he arrived at Titu's hovel, he was almost sorry it had ended.

As before, the stunted pig dozed in the sun-warmed dust, Titu sat contemplating nothing. He snapped out of his reverie when he noticed Garrick, and ran, wet-lipped and gibbering, up to him.

"Huh-huh-huh."

Dodging his outstretched claw with something like a shudder, Garrick marched past him to the weather-seamed cliff. Positioning himself directly beneath the mysterious black circle, hands cupped around his mouth, he shouted upwards. A bird nesting in the cliff flew off with a scream, but there was no answering reply from the top. And so it continued.

Finally, his voice hardly more than a croak, he went back out to a sunlit spot on the trail, stripped off his shirt, and remained there waving it for nearly an hour. He was on the verge of giving up when he spotted a flutter on top, some hundreds of yards to his left. Roxana's slender figure was signalling a reply. He returned to the base of the cliff, and waited for her to pick her way to a spot above him.

"Everything okay?" he shouted up.

"Fine." Her answer floated down, faint echoes distorting it.

"Where's Slade?"

"We spread out. He's 'bout a half mile down that way. Hang on while I get him."

Her head soon reappeared, cautiously peeping over the edge. Slade was just made out to the rear. "Throw the rope over," Garrick bellowed.

A rope curled in the air to slap against the side of the cliff. The rock curved outward here, the rope lay over a bulge. Swinging it from side to side, Roxana worked it lower.

Garrick directed her with waves of his shirt, at last hollering: "There, that's it!" He whirled his shirt in a victory circle about his head.

Eighty feet over his head, the rope split the round, black stone. "I'm coming up now." Donning his shirt, he commenced the long trek to join them.

He arrived in late afternoon, tired and breathing hard. Roxana and Slade sat a little apart. One mule was at hand, tethered to a stake driven into the ground.

"Everything okay?" he enquired of Roxana. She nodded. "Where's the other mules and equipment?"

"Over there a ways. While we were waiting for you we made camp."

"Good." He turned to Slade. "Any ideas what to do next?"

"Might as well go down and take a look. After that, we'll know more. The mule can walk you down."

"Come again?"

"We can snub the rope onto the mule's pack saddle, walk her toward the face to lower you, and walk her away to haul you up. You'll just have to steady yourself as you go."

"If it's so goddam easy why don't you go?" Garrick snapped at him. "Tell me something. How'd you ever manage to fly an airplane miles up in the sky?"

"That's different. You're inside something you control. It's not the same as this."

"It seemed so easy when we discussed this yesterday," Roxana put in worriedly. "Garry, it's not worth getting you hurt. I would never forgive myself if anything happened to you." She gave him a tender look.

Slade broke into a wide grin. "Oh, I see," he said. He puckered his lips and blew. "Kissy, kissy, kissy."

"Let's get going," Garrick growled.

It turned out to be relatively easy. *Sitting* in a loop of rope, he *walked* down the face with the mule's help.

The face was not quite naked rock. Lichens of various colors grew on it and, amazingly, cactuses had secured tenuous holds here and there. Swallows, nesting in the numerous cracks and fissures, swooped about the weathered columns, flashing blue and white in the sunlight.

The black stone inched into view over the bulge. It was not quite a perfect circle, he saw now, and it was chipped and scarred by metal tools. A hole in the cliff face approximately four feet in diameter had been shaped first and then fitted with the seal. At some period in the past, masons had plied their trade here.

"Okay," he shouted, excitement knocking in his body. "Hold it right there."

With his nose almost brushing the surface, he examined the seal. Up close, the cracks between the fitted stones were clearly visible.

Jesus! Jesus!

Bouncing up and down, he brought his booted heels down hard onto the surface. No sign of weakness. The ancient masons had done their work well. It would take a deal of labor to break through. He jarred his heels down again.

A wind sprang up. It plucked at his body, curling inside his jacket with chill fingers and sending shivers throughout. When it passed on, whistling across the face, a soft wail trailed in its wake.

In an instant, that sound, like the cry of a child, robbed him of movement. An insane notion seized hold, that the mournful cry emanated from the other side of the stone seal. Cold and enfeebled, he clung to the rope with stiffened fingers. A buzzing started behind his ears.

"Hey," Slade called irritably. "What's going on?"

"Pull me up," Garrick croaked, and then louder and more shrilly: "Pull me up! Now! Quick!"

He was hauled over the edge, limp, his belly scraping dirt.

Roxana stooped over him. "Garry, you're as white as a sheet. And you're trembling. Is everything all right?"

"Everything's fine," he mumbled, gulping air and feeling ridiculous. He'd panicked unnecessarily and he knew it.

"How'd it go?" Slade wanted to know.

Garrick strove to gather himself together. "Well...it's um, what we thought."

"What?"

"Dressed, black stones fitted together to make a strong seal. It's going to take a lot of work to open it up."

"Hmmm," Slade thought aloud. "We brought those planks, and we have a lot of rope. It won't be too difficult to make a scaffold to work from. May as well get started. We'll need some things from the camp." He headed for the mule.

The mule was grazing on a patch of grass and, true to its breed, refused to move. Slade commenced a tug of war with the animal. They churned up the soil, sending things flying.

Something landed near Roxana. She picked it up. "Look at this," she said slowly, turning it over in her hand. "It's a piece of rusted metal." She walked over and kicked at the ground, then used her fingers. "There's something else here. Something big."

Scraping busily with a sharp-edged rock, she soon bared a piece of curved metal. It proved to be a few feet long by almost as much wide, and so badly corroded the edges crumbled in Roxana's hand.

"Some kind of cooking vessel?"

"No. It's the wrong shape for that, and it's too big."

Slade came up with the answer. "Looks like one of those breastplates the Spanish conquistadors wore."

"Yes," Roxana breathed. "A cuirass. That's exactly what it is."

"Y'know," Slade said slowly, squatting to run his eye along the ground, "this patch here is slightly higher than the surrounding area. A bit greener, too." He stood up. "I'll get some tools from camp." He strode off swiftly.

Seizing the sharp rock, Garrick attacked the earth.

"Easy, Garry. *Easy*. You might damage something."

"Yeah. Yeah." Slowing his efforts, he peeled away the soil in thin layers. A foot down, he scraped on a hard object.

They cleaned around it with the Land Rover keys, then sat back, astonished.

Sticking up were two bony fingers in a V for victory sign.

~ * ~

"That's it, I guess," Slade said. Leaning on his shovel, he studied the curiosity at his feet. "Jesus Christ Almighty! Five skeletons, Spaniards from the looks of 'em, laid out head to foot in the shape of a cross."

"With the longest arm of the cross pointing toward the cliff, at a spot directly above the cave," added Garrick. "Someone sure had a macabre sense of humor."

"This was no joke," Roxana argued. "It was a statement of some kind."

"Damned definitive statement," commented Slade flatly. "These guys didn't die of old age. Look at the cleft in that skull there. A weapon did that...with a strong arm behind it."

"All of it directed at the cave," repeated Garrick.

Slade nodded. "Too late to find out what's inside that cave today." He began collecting the tools. "It'll be dark soon."

"I hate just leaving them like this," Roxana said.

Slade smiled thinly. "They've been lying here for centuries. They won't mind spending another night alone."

"You know what I mean. It's...it's just that it seems...well, not right, somehow, to expose the graves then leave them unattended."

"You keep vigil overnight, then. I'm going to camp."

Garrick put his arm around her. "C'mon, Roxie," he coaxed, "we have a big day tomorrow."

~ * ~

Setting aside his emptied tin of frijoles, Garrick drank from a bottle of water and eased back, sucking on a scraped knuckle. The light was fading, the snow on a mountain top to the west glowed salmon pink.

The camp–a single tent–was pitched in a sheltered valley a half mile long by half that in width. High, rugged ridges boxed it in on all sides but one, where a broad opening faced the canyon. An evening breeze blew.

No one spoke. Having finished eating, each of them digested the curious events of the day along with their simple meal of tinned rations. Slade puffed on a cigarette.

Seen through the tent flaps, dainty-footed creatures glided along a ridge.

"We have some visitors," remarked Roxana. "On that ridge. The troop of vicuna."

"Yes, I see them. Pretty things."

"I suppose they were down at the far end foraging. They'll spend the night in the high country."

Long-necked and graceful, the troop ghosted higher up the ridge to the mouth of a narrow ravine. Into it, six lovely ladies of the puna vanished. The last animal, the troop male, looked back briefly, his white bib showing grey in the failing light. Then he too disappeared, trailing after his harem.

Slade finished his cigarette and left the tent. There was the sound of him urinating outside, then he returned and crawled into his blankets without a word.

Garrick sat with Roxana, hugging his knees against the chill, thinking about the cave and his experience there this afternoon. He'd panicked. No doubt about it. Well, he'd have to keep his head tomorrow. They must uncover the long-held secret.

The breeze picked up, bringing colder air with it and chasing them to their blankets. Garrick positioned himself between the other two, resting his head alongside Roxana's on the bundle of clothing they used as a pillow.

Although tired from the long day, wondering about the cave and its contents kept him from sleep. And when he finally did fall off, it was into a sleep made restless by dreams of ghostly creatures that flew at will through living rock.

Chapter Twenty-seven
Cross of Cavaliers

Yahuar Huaccac's legs wobbled and gave out. He sagged wearily to the ground.

"Get up, little brother," Ollanta sneered, kicking him contemptuously in the buttocks. "Keep up, or be left behind." He marched off, rasping commands to the men ahead.

The sun angled in from the west. Cotton wool clouds scudded across the sky before a light breeze.

Huaccac drove himself to his feet, his face screwed up in pain. That kick had hurt! Massaging his rump, he fixed an angry look at his brother's back. Ollanta had pushed the band mercilessly, ever since catching up with them in late morning, trotting across the plain with a look of savage elation on his face.

He had refused to explain his absence, despite his brother's earnest entreaties to do so. And when Huaccac recounted to him his dream, of Changa and Mama Ocllo caught in a violent storm, and the concern he harbored for them, only coarse laughter answered him.

Ollanta oozed satisfaction, and it filled Huaccac with dread.

They came upon a small bog with bright green, bubble-like *yareta* growing around the edges. An Andean flicker, a woodpecker, hammered away at the brain coral-like vegetation, gathering nesting material for its burrow.

"Do you wish to camp here?" the fox-faced guide enquired. "Water is available–both men and animals are weary."

"How much farther to this place you're taking us?"

They were on the canyon rim now, the river a brown, slim cataract a heart-stopping drop below.

The guide cast knowledgeably around him. "We could reach there soon after dark...perhaps before the moon rises."

"Continue. We'll camp there."

Ollanta was pleased with the guide. He'd kept them on hard-to-follow, rocky terrain whenever possible, and had set a cracking pace. If the white men were on their trail, they would be a good distance to the rear. At the least, that would give them tomorrow morning to dispose of the treasure.

He laughed aloud, causing the guide to blink curiously at him, wondering at the cause for merriment.

~ * ~

In the uncompromising light of early morning, the prospect became particularly unnerving. Huaccac shivered on the edge of the cliff, afraid even to look down.

"Come, little brother," Ollanta jeered from below. "You are the custodian of the things from the temple. You must oversee their disposal."

The responsibility could not be denied. Fitting the improvised sling about him with nervous fingers, Huaccac eased over the side. He squeezed his eyes shut all the way to the cave entrance, where he was hauled in roughly by Ollanta. Slumped on the floor, breathing in the fine, silty dust, it took a minute or two before he was able to sit up.

The guide and a wiry, sure-footed man called Papo, had gone ahead to help receive the treasure as it was lowered. Courteously, Papo assisted Huaccac to his feet. Like most people who knew the tiny villca, he had a deal of affection for him.

Brushing dust from his garments, Huaccac peered about, approving of what he saw. The cave appeared ideal for their purposes. Unless its location was divulged by an informer, the temple treasure would remain safe here. Bidding wiry Papo assist him, he commenced, lovingly and respectfully, to position the religious objects in a large basket on the floor.

Finished, he extended his arms in prayer at the impromptu shrine, plucked eyelashes to blow at it, and kissed the air. He also made an offering of coca and maize. Later, when there was time to conduct ceremonies properly, he would sacrifice a pure black llama here.

Before leaving, he made a quick trip to the rear of the cave, unable to resist probing the blackness. He'd a horror of dark, confined places, however, and that soon sent him hurrying out to the entrance. His brother waited there alone.

"Where're the other two?"

"Up top. Their work is completed here."

"Let us go also, then," Huaccac urged, eager to be in sunshine once more. "At any moment, the bearded ones–"

"Little brother–nay, prince of royal blood, I said *their* work is completed here. Not yours." He smiled in his strange manner, playing with his axe.

If a condor could smile, thought Huaccac, that's how it would look. "I don't understand. The religious articles are deposited safely. I've prayed over them. There's nothing more for me to do here."

"You are of royal blood, are you not?"

Huaccac nodded warily. "You know I am. A small part."

"In that case, can you do less than your illustrious ancestor?"

"Which ancestor?"

"Ayar Cachi."

Ayar Cachi was one of the legendary brothers of Manco Capac and his sister-wife Mama Ocllo, founders of the Inca dynasty.

On their journey from Lake Titicaca to Cuzco, Ayar Cachi proved the most troublesome of the four celestial brothers, creating danger for them and their divine sister-wives. He carried a golden sling with which he flung great rocks about, smashing mountain peaks, gouging out mighty ravines at will.

His brothers tricked him into entering a cave to retrieve some golden vessels. They then sealed it up, ending his earthly existence. He reappeared again, miraculously, but never in earthly form.

The implication Ollanta made was too appalling to be taken seriously. Huaccac looked blankly at him, for a second or two almost laughing. But the uncompromising, glassy-eyed stare of the unfathomable man opposite was so suddenly and violently intense, it utterly shocked him. It was the rudest, most brutal expression he'd ever seen. Totally hate-inspired.

"What do you mean?" he asked, his mind whirling.

In answer, the condor's smile flashed again.

The realization of what was about to happen struck like a blow. He stared and stared at his brother, this sudden stranger. "Why do you hate me so?" he implored. "You're my brother. Why–?"

With a soft *thunk*, Ollanta's axe leapt forward and met Huaccac's head, the flat side striking just above his left ear.

Darkness rushed in.

~ * ~

On the cliff top, Ollanta met chaos. The man he'd posted as lookout had just sped into camp, gesticulating wildly.

At sight of him, the lookout ran up. "The bearded men are almost upon us!" he shouted.

Ollanta, a part of him not fully departed the cave, asked hollowly, "How many?"

The lookout wiggled the fingers of one hand. "Pichqa, five."

"No more than that?"

"And one Indian. He runs in front with his nose to the ground like a dog, smelling out our trail."

With an effort, Ollanta wrenched himself free from the cave and struggled to think.

The immediate area was relatively open, good for horses. Not too far back along their trail, however, the country was more broken. He'd marked it down last evening with exactly this contingency in mind.

"Follow me with your weapons," he ordered sharply.

Papo, the wiry man, spoke up. "But the villca. Your brother is yet below."

Ollanta knocked him flat with a blow of his fist. The *"wheep"* of steel being drawn from scabbard sounded, and the Spanish sword appeared in Ollanta's hand, brandished in meaningful manner.

From the ground, Papo blinked in hurt and amazement.

"I said to follow me. Now!"

They set out at a rapid trot, Ollanta in the lead, Papo at his heels.

~ * ~

The man nosing out the trail was tall for a mountain Indian, and he moved tirelessly among the rocks and cactus as only a man born to the high country can. Close behind him were five horsemen.

They proceeded in the supremely confident manner of conquerors, displaying scant caution. Men and llamas had passed this way, that much was clear. Maybe it was the bunch they were after, maybe not. They had split off from the main troop to investigate.

So, when floundering across a sandy ravine, they didn't react swiftly enough to the tracker's whistle of alarm.

Well-thrown lances, boulders, and a hailstorm of slung stones rained down on them. A hideously scarred warrior charged through the dust swinging a sword. Hard behind him, spurred on by their leader's example, hurtled a pack of men howling like wolves.

Two of the Spaniards were slain outright. The remaining three were quickly overwhelmed and bound. The lone Indian paid the price for his allegiance to the white men. Kicked, bludgeoned with maces, one ear torn off, stoned, he was reduced to a quivering lump of lacerated flesh.

~ * ~

Ollanta laughed hugely. "That's enough," he told his men, smiling fondly at them as they dug in the soil above the cave. "Now that the plowing is completed, we will begin the sowing." He roared with laughter at his own joke.

The two dead Spaniards were dragged to the hole and flung in. The other three were then forced, struggling fiercely, to the side of the mass grave and dispatched with Ollanta's sword.

Whump! went the sword. Blood pumped, and a Spaniard rolled lifeless into the pit. Twice more this was repeated, an ululation going up from the onlookers on each occasion. Waving captured swords and halberds and helmets, they cheered each chopping blow of the executioner.

With grisly humor, Ollanta arranged the bodies in the shape of the

Christian cross. Then the grave was filled in. Afterwards, horses and llamas were walked back and forth over it until the soil was as packed and hard as the untouched ground surrounding it.

The horses, plunging at the smell of blood and the strange hands on their bridles, were then forced to the canyon rim and driven over with blows from the bloodied sword.

Ollanta vastly enjoyed it all. What a fine joke, he congratulated himself as the horses caromed off the face of the cliff.

After the last horse had gone screaming to its death, he reluctantly turned his attention to other matters. He could savor this triumph later; right now there was a need to get clear of the area. Gathering the llamas and ordering his men to follow him, he set out on a brisk march.

Cowed by their leader and in deep admiration of his prowess, the men obeyed without question. None even made mention of the prince-priest in the lonely cave.

In early afternoon, the main body of Spaniards spotted them. They were traversing flat, open country perfect for horsemen.

A score of mailed riders trotting in formation toward them proved too much for the band. They broke and ran, giving themselves away immediately as the party the Spaniards hunted. Made certain of his quarry, the Spanish captain ordered a charge.

Whooping, they galloped the fleeing men down, intending to take them prisoner. But when they saw the bloodied Spanish weapons among them, their own swords bit furiously into Indian flesh. The grim reaping continued, in spite of a shouted command by the captain to keep some alive.

One man refused to run. Legs firmly astride, sword in hand, Ollanta screamed his disbelief that this could happen. He had been clear! Clear!

A tall rider confidently bore down on him. Right up to the last moment, he expected the warrior to run from the horse. They always did. Instead, Ollanta sidestepped neatly and swung his blade into the horse's neck with such fury he nearly decapitated the animal.

It collapsed thirty paces off, one of the rider's long legs pinned underneath.

Ollanta sprinted after him.

The pinned rider was young, a mere twenty, and arrived from Spain only six months earlier. Terrified, he observed the wild-eyed horror heave closer.

A crossbow bolt saved his life. Ollanta was no more than a leap or two off when the bolt entered his eye. It thudded in up to the fletches, the steel tip coming out under his ear.

It spun him in a circle. The tip of his sword drooped, digging into the soil. For a few seconds he hung there, not quite dead, weaving slightly.

The captain was closest. Setting the point of his lance onto the center of Ollanta's chest, he clapped spurs to mount. The horse lunged forward and the point exited between the shoulder blades.

The cavalry troop trotted back over the trail, coming at last to a place at the canyon top where a camp had been. All the signs were present: llama droppings, trampled earth, a dead fire. The Spaniards had been overzealous; only one Indian had survived, a fox-faced man. He was dragged forward and brutally interrogated.

Although wounded and terrified, he still resisted talking, so a fire was lit to put him to the torture.

The young rider, still badly shaken by his bare escape and more squeamish than his older, harder comrades, strolled to the canyon rim to avoid witnessing the Indian's agony.

It was now late afternoon. The setting sun cast huge shadows in the canyon and on the mountains above. Through the canyon, a pair of condors planed. He tugged at his beard, impressed as always by the majesty of the huge, winged predators.

Wind twisted among the cliff columns. It gusted, and a soft wail drifted up, sounding oddly akin to a child weeping.

At the fire, a short, sharp yelp of pain sounded. The rider turned in time to see the fox-faced Indian slump into a lifeless heap against his bindings. The man who'd been interrogating him bent over suspiciously, peeled back an eyelid and poked at the eye. No reaction. Cursing, he directed an angry kick at the offending corpse.

The procedure had barely begun. To have died so quickly, he must have been more grievously wounded than thought.

In the canyon, the wind wailed louder, tearing at the young rider's clothing and whistling mournfully about his head. It finally proved too much for his frazzled nerves. He left the rim and walked over to rejoin the troop.

~ * ~

Huaccac awoke to find the day dying. Instantly, all that had occurred flooded back.

"Ollanta, my brother. Why? Why?"

Then he was still, listening to the wind outside, his mind refusing to think further.

After a time he did begin to think again, and it came to him fully the very awfulness of the place he was in. Always, he had hated the dark. And in all his life, he'd never been away from friends and family.

He offered a prayer to the Sun. But as he did so, the blazing light winked out, dipping below a mountain peak and plunging him into darkness.

A wail escaped him, ending in a racking cough. He'd not coughed since childhood; his mother would be worried.

"Collaguata! Mighty Viracocha! Why have your children been treated thus?"

Chapter Twenty-eight
The Prince

Busy sounds invaded the tent. Morning light streamed in. Garrick stretched under his blankets, cramped from a night on the hard ground.

Beside him, Roxana stirred and abruptly sat up. "The cave," she announced, as if presenting a revelation. "Today we find out." She reached for her boots with eager hands.

Garrick trailed her outside. "Mind givin' me a hand," Slade called out, sarcasm dripping from his lips. "I'd do everything myself except I hate showing off."

He was trying to strap a wooden platform onto a mule's back and the animal wasn't cooperating. Garrick held the mule's head while the contrivance was lashed into position. Slade seemed pleased with himself.

"This morning, while you sleeping beauties were snoring away, I rigged this up. It'll provide somethin' steady to work from." He indulged himself in a superior look.

"For *me* to work from you mean," Garrick reminded him.

"Let's go."

At the cliff, Slade bustled about with great authority. He'd brought a number of steel drill bits and pieces of scrap metal from the mine, which he had Garrick drive into the ground with a heavy hammer. They secured the platform to them with ropes and slid it over.

He'd fashioned a rope ladder as well, and throwing an end over, he turned to Garrick. "All ready."

"I'm gonna get a bite to eat first," Garrick declared stubbornly, experiencing certain misgivings now that the moment was here. "Besides, it's too cold to go over that cliff right now. Give the sun another half hour or so."

Slade shrugged and offered no comment. Garrick opened a tin of food and seated himself to eat. Roxana poked around the mass grave.

"Okay. Let's do it," Garrick said when his thirty minutes were up. He strode past a worried Roxana to the rope ladder, and started down.

"For heaven's sake, please be careful, Garry!"

The scaffold hung too high and at an angle. He shouted up instructions to correct the problem.

"Okay, that's good there. Lemme know when you have it tied off."

"All tied off," came the signal a few minutes later.

With one steadying hand on the ladder, he stepped to the platform and jammed a heel down hard on the seal to see what would follow. Two or three minutes passed. His boot thudded onto the black stone once more. Nothing! The air remained still. The sun shone as always. A black billed shrike-tyrant flew unconcernedly by.

"You fallen asleep down there, or what?" Slade roared.

"Okay. Send that stuff down."

A hammer and a pair of sharp-pointed steel bits slithered downwards on a rope.

Below, Titu conversed with the piebald pig. Aside from a single glance at Garrick, the unusual sight on the rock over his home appeared to interest him not at all.

Under Garrick's touch, the stone felt smooth and beginning to warm from the sun. Four stones of different sizes formed the seal, fitted together with delicate precision. Running his hand one final time over the polished surface, he commenced work.

It took an hour of patient chipping, with increasingly exasperated demands shrieked at him from above–"How's it coming along?"...."How's it look?".... "Goddammit, man, why don't you answer?"–before the first slight quiver occurred.

He swung mightily with the hammer. One stone buckled. Another blow and it fell inside. Heart pounding, he pressed his face to the opening. Stale, sour air greeted him. Within, the cave appeared roomy, although he could make out scant details.

The screeching from the top reached a crescendo.

"I've broken part of the seal," he shouted. "I can't make out anything inside as yet, though. I'm going to do the rest now."

With one stone gone, the others succumbed readily. Within minutes, the opened entrance beckoned. Garrick stared at the hole, feeling a curious reluctance to enter.

The rope ladder began to slap and writhe. A pair of rounded buttocks headed toward him. "I couldn't wait any longer," Roxana burst out, breathless and flushed from the fearsome descent.

Her eyes wandered down to Titu's ravine, and to the awesome depths beyond. Her grip tightened on the ladder.

"Don't look down," Garrick warned sharply.

"I know. I know. You don't have to remind me," she snapped, angry with herself. Brushing hair from her face with a nervous hand, she held up a flash light. "You forgot this."

He took the light. "Slade comin'?"

"Don't know. I didn't bother asking." Her eyes were glued to the cave. In a swift movement, she ducked and entered. He went after her.

Once beyond the mouth, the cave widened out, becoming four to five paces in width. The floor was smooth and sloped gently toward the entrance. To the rear lay a black void.

They inched ahead, kicking up fine dust. It set them both coughing. Also, the air was bad–their chests were soon heaving.

Slade stumbled in. He'd attempted the rope ladder after all, and the terror of that brief journey showed clearly on his face. But he recovered fast; it was his quick eye that spotted the heap on the floor, thirty yards in.

"Bring the light," he ordered.

The remains of what appeared to have been a basket lay by a wall, filled with articles of differing sizes and shapes. Some had spilled onto the floor. Slade picked one up to examine under the light. Dust undulated upwards, and through it the thing in his hand gleamed dully.

"Gold!" he sang out.

"Gold and silver," Roxana corrected, her voice quick and low. She ran a shaking hand over the foot long artifact, wiping it clean of dirt. The workmanship was exquisite, tassels and leaves of silver combined with kernels of gold to create an ear of Indian corn perfect in every detail.

"Beautiful," she breathed, unable to take her eyes from it. "Beautiful! We've made a real find, Garry. Imagine that! Oh, just imagine!"

Slade sorted through the heap. Most of it was gold and silver plate, but there were beautifully-crafted figures, also, in the shapes of humans and animals. With an exclamation of, "Christ Almighty!" his hand darted to an object larger and heavier than the rest.

A statuette eighteen to twenty inches high, shaped like a man with his hands folded on his chest, shone butter yellow under the flashlight's beam. A huge, straight nose jutted from a head fully one-third of the statuette's bulk. From the eyes, large emeralds spewed forth a cold, green fire.

The figure was compelling, beautiful, savage, the unmistakable image of a heathen god.

"This alone is worth a pretty penny," Slade said slowly. He hefted it in his hands, trying to gauge its weight. "There's collectors in the States and here in South America who'd buy this and the other stuff in a minute. Museums, too...they turn a convenient blind eye to legality when it comes to this kinda stuff. You'd be amazed at the amount of artifacts sold on the black market each year. The gold and silver on its own is worth a lot–then multiply that by the archaeological appeal and...." Leaving the sentence dangling, he thoughtfully eyed the pile at his feet. "Not exactly a king's ransom, I suppose. Enough, though, for a man of modest needs to live on for a good many years."

"That's impossible," Roxana cut in. "You'd never get these things out of the country. There's laws against removing valuable artifacts from Peru."

Slade smiled pityingly at her. "Tons of artifacts are shipped out of South American countries regularly, laws or not."

Roxana grabbed for the statuette. Slade let it go, his superior smile intact.

Wrestling with its weight, she held it up for closer inspection. "This was an offering to one of the ancient gods. Maybe *Apu*, the origin of water and fertility of the earth...or, well, never mind. The point is, its value is far greater than mere money." She glared at Slade. "You wouldn't agree, though, would you? Someone like you wouldn't appreciate that."

"Let's check out the rest of the cave," he suggested mildly.

"Yes," agreed Garrick. "The arguments can wait." He led the way

213

with the light, Roxana, cradling the golden man, and Slade, a few steps to his rear.

Sixty yards in, the cave pinched out.

"That's it," said Garrick, stabbing the light into the blackness. Feeling distinctly uneasy for some reason, he was about to suggest they retrace their steps when the beam caught and held the outline of an object he'd assumed to be a rock.

On a ledge, a contoured shape waited.

He leaned closer to bring the light fully into play. It found the face of a child.

"Jesus! Oh, sweet Jesus!" He snapped upright in shock.

"What is it?"

"It's a child! Not a statue...a real child!"

The other two bumped up beside him.

On the rock shelf, the lonely figure–seated leaning forward, one leg crossing the other–stared sightlessly ahead. Tiny hands adorned with gold bracelets stretched across the knee in a supplicating manner. The small, round head lay uncovered and completely hairless. The lips, drawn back in death, seemed to direct a tremulous smile at the strangers who had invaded its solitude.

"Another offering to the gods?" Garrick whispered.

Roxana shook her head helplessly. "I don't know...possibly...that happened sometimes. And both Collaguas and Cabanas understood the science of mummification."

"His head is round," Garrick pointed out. "You said both Collaguas and Cabanas, in ancient times, were head-binders. Maybe he was placed here more recently? He *was* dead when he was brought here, wasn't he?"

"Sometimes offerings of live humans were made to the gods. He could've been brought here alive, and then mummified later." She pressed closer to Garrick, trembling.

"Only a monster would abandon a child to die alone in a place like this," he murmured. "Can you imagine the horror of dying here *alone*!"

They all fell silent. In the perfect quiet, he clearly heard the beating of his own heart. His chest heaved noticeably, also; this far in the air was very foul.

"I must see," determined Roxana. Placing the golden god on the floor, she took the flashlight and commenced a thorough examination of the figure.

"It's a male...and not a child," were her first conclusions. "See, he's wearing gold pendants in his ears. Adult male members of the upper classes wore those. No one else was permitted to."

"He's so tiny," objected Garrick.

"Many of the Quechuas were. And still are. You've seen that yourself. He was even smaller than average, though. Prob'ly a good bit under five feet tall if he was laid out straight." She shifted the light lower. "There, where his torso is exposed–you can see how the body cavity had the organs removed and then stuffed with grass and strips of dry cloth."

Bits of fabric peeked out coyly from the chest cavity.

"What's that stuff at his feet?" Slade asked.

The man's eye didn't miss much. Neither Garrick nor Roxana, absorbed in the drama before them, had noticed the things strewn at the foot of the ledge.

Speaking in reverent tones, Roxana went over them one by one. "This feathered pouch probably contained coca leaves," she said of a dirty, white pouch adorned with red feathers. "Oh, look at this, isn't it beautiful–an image of a goddess, made out of silver and dressed in a doll's costume." Her light swept over the remaining items. A red ceramic bowl with the Collagua eight pointed star in white colors on its sides lay upside down, its contents spilled out long ago. By it were two tiny llama figurines, one of gold the other of silver. The silver llama was identical to the one shown them by Titu. A handful of sea shells formed a small pile beneath the lonely man's feet.

"Not much to accompany him to the afterlife," commented Garrick, his voice gruff.

"It's a lot more than most were provided. Also, he's richly dressed. And see those golden bracelets–commoners didn't wear those."

"He was of high rank then?"

"Almost certainly."

"That long robe he's wearing looks similar to the robes Catholic priests wear."

"The robes worn by Inca priests and Catholic friars were something the same, at least in Cuzco. Don't forget though that the Collaguas and

215

Cabanas had their own cultures. It's never been clear how much Inca Cuzcueno culture was imposed on the Colca Valley."

"We're looking at a holy man," Garrick stated with conviction. "I get the damnedest impression he's praying.... And don't forget that Ampire did say 'the little villca' was with the things from the temple."

"He also said the 'man of royal blood,'" Slade reminded them.

Garrick was suddenly and ineffably sad. "Poor little princeling. Whatever happened? Who did this to you?"

Chapter Twenty-nine
Trapped

"There," said Slade. "That's the last of it."

Piled at the cave entrance and gleaming in the sunlight, the once secret horde of the ancients made an impressive sight.

Slade's eyes took on a dreamy expression. "Damn pretty to look at," he murmured, speaking as much to himself as to the others. "I couldn't even venture a guess as to the overall value. It'd be a helluva lot of money, though, however you cut it.... I'll rig up a basket of some kind to haul the stuff up."

"We're not disturbing the little man," Garrick stated flatly. "This is his burial place, his tomb. He deserves to be left alone. And that includes his burial things, gold bracelets and all the rest of it."

"It would outrage your notion of right and wrong, you mean?"

Garrick ignored the clumsy attempt at humor. "You got that right," he said.

Slade guffawed. "We're in agreement then. He stays. And he can keep his trinkets. I was talking about this stuff here." He prodded the lustrous heap with his foot.

With a last, fond look at the treasure, he grabbed the rope ladder to ascend to the rim and begin preparations. Along his jawline the muscles bulged nervously. His handsome face whitened and became ugly. Venturing up or down the cliff was as terrifying as ever for him.

~ * ~

Garrick helped Slade pack the artifacts into the bag fashioned from

217

tent material. With the load ready, he straightened up to find the other man staring at him.

"You or me?" Slade asked.

"You or me what?"

"Up top. One stays here to load, and one hauls the load up from the rim."

"Me up top, you down here," Garrick stated unequivocally. "And Roxie, you come with me."

With an exaggerated bow, Slade conceded. His laughter chased them up the ladder, a raucous sound they'd not heard him use before.

"We have to do something about him," Roxana demanded, sticking her head into Garrick's face as soon as they'd reached the top.

"Yeah. Why's that?" Garrick drawled. "Because he just laughed funny?"

"You know what I mean. I can't stand him. He's *your* friend. What're you going to do about him?"

"What in hell's name do you want me to do? Throw him over the cliff? He hasn't done anything yet. And for the last time, stop calling him *my friend.*"

"He gives me the creeps."

"Help me with the mule."

Soon, the first bulging sack eased over the side. The treasure of Coporaque had left its centuries-old home at last.

"Good," declared Garrick, a bit later, when the last of the sacks safely joined the first. "That's accomplished. Now then...." He stopped. Roxana eyed him strangely.

Appearing somewhat embarrassed, she said, "Before we go, let's say good-bye to the Prince."

"Prince, eh! You want to go back down there? I can't believe it."

"Prince, priest, or hapless sacrifice to the gods, I want to see him one last time before we go."

"Uh, uh. It'd be better to come back on our own later. We can bring more equipment and supplies...really investigate the cave. The whole works. The little man, and these, too." He pointed to the cross of skeletons. "Today, though, let's just get the hell outta here."

"Just five minutes."

"You were positively ranting and raving about Slade a few minutes ago. And now you want to go back down there with him! I thought you were scared of him?"

"I didn't say that exactly. I said he gives me the creeps. Look, we won't even talk to him. With the both of us there for the couple of minutes it'll take, what can happen?"

"Jeez...I dunno."

"Why don't you know?" she snapped.

"Okay then," he said levelly, "if that's what you want. I'll keep an eye on Slade while you say your good-byes. We'll have to go right now, while he's still down there. Just in case he does have some strange ideas, I don't want him up here all by himself. And listen, buster, don't start an argument with him. Just go see the Prince and that's all. Understand?"

Slade didn't seem surprised to see them arrive. He offered no comment.

"Roxie wanted to say farewell to our friend. Go ahead," he told her. She vanished into the darkness.

For a while after she had gone both men simply stood quietly, awkward in each other's presence. Finally, Slade said softly, "It's really too bad."

"What is?"

"I like you as well as I've ever liked anyone. If the situation was different we could've been friends. Guys like you, though...you're too easy. You almost invite people to take advantage of you."

His voice droned in a curious monotone, reminding Garrick of a psychologist he'd gone to for counselling once, after Afghanistan. It was difficult to know what to make of his remarks, so he decided to ignore them.

An uncomfortable minute passed with Slade, quiet now, staring across the cave at him, his eyes penetrating and as colorless as rain. "I don't really need friends," he said finally. "I suppose you realize that." He sounded apologetic, as if he felt obliged to explain things.

The stabbing gaze, the unusual statements; these signs and more told Garrick what was coming. Afterwards, when he'd had time to reflect, he was amazed the man handled him so effortlessly when ample warning had been given beforehand.

Another moment passed, with Slade apparently waiting for something. His head was lowered slightly and the fingertips of one hand were over a wrist. His lips moved as if counting.

"Tick-tick-tick," he said softly, looking up and smiling a lover's smile.

With that, he reached around his back under his jacket and produced a small, flat pistol. With Garrick gaping open-mouthed, he transferred the gun slowly from hand to hand several times as he thought something through. For whatever reason, he decided against using the weapon. A swift motion and it was returned to its hiding place.

His eyes fixed on Garrick, he danced forward, lithe and graceful. Garrick barely had time to assume a combat position when a foot lashed out, striking a precise area of his groin. He crumpled, waves of pain washing over him.

As easy and as quick as that the fight had ended, although more blows landed as he fell, punishing, perfectly delivered choppings to his kidneys and neck by the edges of Slade's stiffened hands.

A little, frightened, "Oh," halted the beating.

Roxana had materialized out of the gloom. Hand to mouth, she was poised like a bird set to fly. Her eyes, enormous with fright, darted between Garrick and the back of the cave, debating whether to flee into the darkness. Slade moved purposefully toward her. Those flowing, intent movements pinned her where she was, motionless and unable to move.

Garrick saw the scream in her green eyes and something heaved inside him. He wanted to shout: *Leave her alone, damn you! That's my woman! Don't touch her! Don't you dare touch her!* Numbed with pain, he could only lay on the floor and watch.

It was over quickly. Slade shot his hand out suddenly, gripping her lower lip and twisting it. The pain must have been intense, for she was forced to the cave floor in seconds. And there, in shock and fear, she lay still.

Moving in that deadly shuffle of his, Slade made for the entrance. The scaffold was tumbled loose and he was on the ladder in an instant, drawing it and the scaffold ropes up behind him.

He was gone, taking all means of escape with him.

Chapter Thirty
The Cliff Face

Titu danced with his shadow on the ground.

The sun had begun its downward arc, shadows were lengthening. Titu danced, and wherever he went, his shadow went with him.

He edged to the left. The black, misshapen creature flowed obligingly left. He stopped moving entirely and, stock still, studied his shadow intently. Slyly then, he skipped right. The big, black creature shot right.

Titu scratched his crotch, and gibbered happily away. "Huh-huh-huh."

Singly and in unison, Garrick and Roxana screamed at him from the cave. They might as well have been baying at the moon. They knew he heard them, because he looked up once to where they were waving frantically for attention. With the wretched fellow in his own world, however, he could not be reached.

Slumping to the floor, Garrick massaged his kidneys and neck, sore from Slade's pummelling.

"I'm sorry, Garry. I'm to blame for this. It was stupid of me to insist on coming back here."

"Forget it. It's more my fault for bringing Slade in the first place. I'm sure he's had something like this planned all along, anyways. It was going to happen...inside the cave or outside." He punched his leg in anger. "I must be the biggest fool on the planet not to have seen it coming."

"We'll just have to wait."

"Wait! Wait for what?"

She shrugged helplessly. "Well...for someone to come along."

Garrick snorted.

"Villagers from Pachac Puquio must pass by on the trail occasionally. We can shout to them for help."

"That could be months from now...or never."

"Cusi will come eventually looking for his mules."

"Mebbe," Garrick acknowledged slowly. "If Slade didn't take all the mules with him, Cusi would come eventually. He could have taken all of them, though. Or, Cusi, having found the missing mules, might just take them and go. There's no guarantee he'd try to get down here to check on us. He doesn't strike me as your average, friendly next door neighbor. Meantime, what do we do for food and water?" He punched his leg again. Perversely, the pain felt good. "And all the time, that scum-sucking bastard gets farther and farther away."

"We'll make it somehow," she said stoutly.

Good, brave girl! It came to him that they were probably going to die here, and the thought of this particular lady dying a lingering death in this terrible place was as horrifying for him as his own demise.

"Roxie," he invited softly.

She crept inside his arms and, huddled together for comfort and warmth, they watched the afternoon dwindle away.

Hours later, while looking out along the eastern rock face, a wild idea presented itself. The face on the eastern side was heavily broken with seams and holes. For an insane instant, he tried to visualize a man out there, moving from one precarious hold to another.

Impossible! It couldn't be done. But when the notion wouldn't leave him, he gradually began to consider it.

The eastern face, with its network of lines and cracks and ledges, offered the sole possibility. Forget about climbing up the cliff, gravity was against it and there was that bulge in the rock to go over. Down was just barely possible. An act of desperation certainly, but he could at least picture a man making it.

Just east of the entrance was an inches-wide ledge which led gently downward to an area much cut up by centuries of weather and volcanic action. The swallows lived there. White droppings stained the rock everywhere. If he could get that far, he could work his way lower using the same holes and ledges the swallows nested in.

With a critical eye, he worked systematically across the face and down, until he reached the area beneath the bird colony.

Big problem!

It was all smooth rock, slanting outward at a slight angle for a glassy slide of forty feet or so. At the end of the slide waited a drop of about fifteen feet which fell sheer to the ravine bottom near Titu's refuse pile.

A fall of fifteen feet was nothing, stay limber and loose and you'd make it okay. He'd have to think up a way to slow his slide on the smooth rock, though, or he'd wind up a broken heap at the bottom.

Pondering the descent, the craziness of it, a thought struck him. What would Harry Alexander and Aunt Diane think of this? For once, his motives were admirable. He was in love with a wonderful girl and wanted to save her every bit as much as himself. And while he lusted after Slade, it was as much to discharge a responsibility as to exact revenge.

And, not least, it would take a good deal of nerve to climb down that cliff–Harry would understand that part.

It had been days since he'd spared a moment for his aunt and her fiancé. It felt amazingly good to do so now. A little rush of warmth spread through him. Aunt Diane, Harry, and Roxana. At least there were three people who cared what happened to him.

His mind made up, he started mapping out the most feasible route across and down the face, choosing each handhold and toehold he would use. But, as before, the long, smooth slide posed the most serious difficulty. Dropping his head in thought, he spied two drill bits on the floor. Strong steel bits with sharp points. He picked them up.

"Baby, with these I can fly."

"What are you talking about?"

"Roxie, when I was in Afghanistan, I saw a guy piss his pants in fear once. He'd let the fear build in him until he couldn't control it. Sometimes you'd hear 'bout guys who'd actually shit themselves. Usually, it'd happen before the fighting started, or after the shooting was over. Too much thinking about things makes them seem even tougher than they really are." He forced out a weak grin. "Hell, climbing down that face out there probably isn't nearly as tough as it appears."

"What!" She was aghast. "It's not possible. This is one of your silly *he-man* notions. To prove something dumb. You bloody fool, you don't have to prove anything to me."

"Believe me when I say I'm not trying to be a hero. Frankly, the prospect scares the hell out of me."

"Well then, why do it? It's completely stupid! Why?"

"Because if I don't, we're going to die here."

She shook her head in a fierce unwillingness to accept this.

"It's true. It's best we faced up to it." He consulted his watch. "Less than two hours of daylight left. I'll have to get going."

"Wait 'till morning," she pleaded. "Maybe it won't be necessary. See what happens tomorrow."

Garrick gave his head a tight, little shake. "If I don't go now I never will. With all night to think about it, I wouldn't have the guts to try it in the morning. Like I said sweetheart, I'm no hero."

"Damn you! Why do you have to pick a time like this to call me sweetheart?"

He grinned crookedly at her. "Because, silly, I happen to have fallen in love with you."

"Stop that!" She was close to tears. "Go ahead and kill yourself then."

"I'd better get moving."

"Garry!"

Merely leaning out the entrance was scary, and for a moment his heart quailed. Recognizing that he must go this instant or not at all, he reached forward and wedged a steel bit into a crack. Then, tightening his hand on the bit, he slid the tip of his boot onto the tiny, sloping ledge.

For the initial twenty feet or so, everything went so smoothly, he nearly laughed in relief.

Never, ever, looking down, toe tips inching along the sliver of a ledge, right hand around the front bit in a death's grip, the left sliding behind ever so carefully from finger hold to finger hold, he strained toward the birds' colony. Already, he had picked out a horizontal crack, wider than the others, to use as a resting place.

Then, without warning, a wind rushed in, pushing its way between his belly and the wall. For a full ten minutes, with every muscle in his body screaming for relief, he clung to the face. And when the wind fell off, his muscles so jumped with tension it seemed he could not go on. His rear hand was locked in a pucker of rock and would not let go.

With a horrifying realization, he knew he was going to fall.

"Garry," a voice cried out.

Just one word, but it thrummed with despair. He heard her anguish and it aided him.

Easy, buddy. You're gonna be all right.

Rest your cheek against the rock while you find the next position.

Easy. Easy.

You're a damn good man! Don't forget that.

Get that rear hand moving! His hand slid forward, cactus spines biting into it from a small, green ball in the ledge.

Forget about the damn cactus!

Get that front bit going! He wiggled free the forward bit, and rammed it home farther on.

Slide your toes ahead.

Now, follow with your trailing hand.

Re-fix the forward bit.

Now, do it again.

Once more, he was crab-walking across the face of the cliff.

At the swallows' nests, he collapsed, chalky with fatigue, onto a bird shit-painted ledge. And he exulted at what he'd accomplished.

For a glorious, wonderful half-hour, he rested there. And when he continued his journey down the broken face, he gained confidence with each step. Yet, he still refused the temptation to look down. A few feet, yes, sufficient to locate a spot to put his foot. Never more than that.

Soon, he was at the top of the smooth, slanting rock.

Now for the beautiful slide.

Lowering himself as far as possible with his left hand, he set the points of the drill bits into the rock with his right as firmly as his waning strength would allow. In that position, he paused for a final second.

Take a last breath.

Remember, the instant you release the upper hand you must transfer it to the left bit.

Ready?

Close your eyes if you wish.

Let go!

In the distance, he heard Roxana scream. Her shriek, echoing off the walls, was his companion all the way.

The slide gathered speed at first, a sled on a snowy hill, then slowed as the bits dug in. Drill bits, elbows, knees, and toes were all brought into play to slow the descent. Forty feet down to the final drop.

When Garrick fell into space for the last fifteen feet, he knew he'd made it. He'd done it after all.

By Jesus Christ, he'd done it!

He dropped onto the ground near the refuse pile.

"Garry! Garry! Answer me. I can't see you. Where are you?"

He replied with an exhausted wave of the hand. Then he lay there, limbs sprawled, gulping air greedily, allowing the tension to seep out of his knotted muscles.

As he did so, the sun completed its arc to the west and the light winked out. Complete stillness settled in.

On the far side of the refuse pile, the piebald pig snuffled.

Time passed. Stones rattled off to his left. Something was coming.

"Huh-huh-huh."

Titu's gaunt form could be barely made out against the grey-black sky. Garrick heard rather than saw him settle by the pig. A lone star appeared in the sky, then several more. In that wan light, he observed two figures come together. The taller one coupled with the runty creature.

The pig's snuffle, louder now, mingled with Titu's idiot gabble: "Huh-huh-huh."

Locked in obscene embrace, both creatures seemed oblivious to Garrick's presence. Even as he heaved himself to his feet and stepped carefully around them.

Striking out along the mule path, shivering in the chill that darkness brings, he walked gingerly for a mile or two, obliged to feel his way along. Then the moon rose and the canyon was flooded with white light, as lovely as if all the silver of the Andes had been poured down its sides in molten form.

Garrick ignored the beauty, thinking only of Slade and his treachery, and of his own need to deal with him. He really must do something about that man. Lengthening his stride, he headed for the junction of mule path and rim.

Up on the rim, he found the place above the cave when a mule sounded off. The animal was tethered there by a rope. It was pleased to see him and nuzzled its nose against his belly. A second mule was nearby. The other two were missing.

He called down: "Roxana? Roxana?"

There was a moment of silence. Then: "Garry! Oh, Garry! Gracias a Dios!"

The rope ladder had been cast into the open grave, coiled on the ancient skeletons in the pearly moonlight. Flinging it over the side, he was down it and in the cave almost before the ropes stopped slapping against the rock.

She rushed against him, sobbing uncontrollably.

"Stop crying, sweetheart," he begged her. "It's all right now."

Fat, salty droplets ran runnels in the dust on her face. "Garry! Garry!" she sobbed, repeating his name over and over.

Putting warm, slender hands on either side of his face, she kissed him. Long, sweet kisses of gratitude that he had survived the descent of the cliff and was returned to her.

Chapter Thirty-one
A Question of Honor

The ravine cut into the hillside like a wound, a deep, lichen-covered cleft slanting down from the upper plateau.

Garrick stumbled out of the gloom at its mouth, and walked to the brow of a hill. Losing his footing in the scree there, he skidded down the hill to the side of a broad footpath. He sat there massaging an aching calf, but kept glancing over his shoulder to the ravine he'd just left.

Roxana limped out of the shadows. At the hill top she hesitated, flexing a sore leg while casting around for an easier route than the one Garrick had taken.

He shouted encouragement. "Get right down and slide. Go ahead, baby. Get right down on your backside."

She slid to the bottom in a shower of dust, and lay there on her back drawing in lungsful of air. Her face was drawn with fatigue, she was disheveled and dirty.

A night spent stumbling through cold mountains, falling often, becoming lost again and again, had drained them both. They had ended up striking across country, having to rely on instinct, when they missed several important landmarks in the dark.

The air was still, full of half-light. It was the hour of the small Andean dawn. Only minutes ago, the world had been inky black, now a scarlet penumbra en-flamed the eastern sky, joined by soft, yellow sunlight which grew stronger each second.

Around them the ground began to undulate, as jet-black frogs left hiding places in the grass to head for the nearby river, males riding the larger females in passionate embrace. In a clump of spear-shaped, wild lupins, a white-breasted Andean hillstar preened in the morning sun, stretching muscles cramped from the bitter night just ended.

A sense of urgency welled up in Garrick. Hurry! He scrutinized the trail trying to guess where they were.

"Recognize anything around here, Roxie? It's getting late. I'm gonna have to hustle."

"What makes you so sure Slade's at the mine, anyhow?"

"Like I said, he'll head for the plane. That's his way out of the country with the artifacts. You heard him talking about that plane the day we arrived at the mine. He was planning on stealing it even then."

"What're you going to do?"

"Stop him."

"The question I'm asking is how."

"I can't say. It'll depend, obviously."

"I want him stopped, too. I assumed the plan was to alert the mine. Get the security people to deal with him. That's what you have in mind, isn't it?"

"That'd be the easiest way," he hedged.

"You're not going to try anything stupid, are you? You can't have forgotten already what happened in the cave." Her voice brimmed with suspicion.

"Let me put it this way. I'm determined to stop that sonuvabitch...for what he did to you and me, and for all the unspeakable things he's undoubtedly done to other people in this world. For those reasons...and because it's simply the right thing to do, the proper, honorable thing, I'm gonna stop him. And yes, I'll try to get help at the mine. I'm not completely stupid."

"Quite a high-sounding speech. Now finish it. If you can't get help at the mine, or there's no time, then what?"

Garrick rose to his feet. "We're wasting time. There's enough light already for a plane to take off. Now, where are we? How much farther upstream is it to the mine?"

"Promise me you'll go straight to the mine and that's all. Otherwise, I'm not telling you."

"I can't promise. You know that."

"Then I'm not telling you anything."

"See you, then," he said curtly, and started off.

She attempted to follow, but quickly fell behind, hobbling painfully. Her final, shouted entreaty was lost when he turned a corner and she dropped from sight.

He had not been walking more than ten minutes when the town of Pinchollo appeared on the far side of the river. The Church of San Sebatian de Pinchollo was a landmark he recognized. Good! He was not far off after all. A short walk on, he came upon the Land Rover, canted to one side with the tires slashed.

A flock of sheep maneuvered around the vehicle–black, white, brown, and piebald–heading out to pasture. Herding them along was a short, stocky woman of indeterminate age, her hair in a long, braided loop down her back, and a young boy in sandals and ragged, brown trousers. Trailing the sheep were four black and white milk cows. A dog and a tiny pup trotted at the boy's heels.

Neither boy nor woman showed interest in Garrick, not bothering to look at him or offer greetings.

He struggled into a tired half-walk, half-run. The valley was springing into life. He must hurry. He couldn't let Slade get away. He really couldn't.

The hillside fell back, more open country appeared. He pushed himself into an unsteady trot. An ache entered his side and stayed there.

He passed a field in which three burros grazed, rounded a bend, and there, off in the distance, was a road and the complex of buildings which comprised Mina Madrugada.

He could see the plane, a mere dot from here, parked in front of the airfield shack. Thank God!

A few minutes later, a sound with a wicked ring to it reached him through the clean air. It was faint because of distance, but heard distinctly. He halted to listen, streaming perspiration, his breathing ragged. There was no follow up sound.

Had it been a shout? A short, sharp fart from a piece of unruly machinery?

No. Garrick knew that sound all too well. It was the vicious crack of a pistol shot.

He kicked back into a run.

~ * ~

A narrow field of alfalfa stretched between the airfield and a stone wall. Garrick crouched behind the wall, peering between the cactuses that grew on top. An access road cut through the lush, green field to the gate at the security fence. The two missing mules were tied to the gate. Across the landing strip, right outside the little shack, a man sprawled on the ground.

In the alfalfa field, a hummingbird hovered. Aside from it and the mules, nothing else moved or made a sound. Slade was nowhere to be seen.

Easing over the wall, Garrick slipped cautiously through the alfalfa. When he reached the security fence, he halted, mouth open, eyes alight in a search for Slade.

The front door on the plane's left side was ajar. Inside, a man was bent over working on something under the control panel. A half-minute went by and Slade's head bobbed up. His hands moved on the panel and the engine coughed into life.

He got out, went around to the right side and opened the cargo door at the back. Then, after a swift look around, he trotted over to the mules, passing behind the shack and momentarily disappearing. Garrick vaulted the fence and dropped to the far side. Flat on the ground, he waited for Slade to pass behind the shack again. When, with arms loaded, Slade passed from sight a second time, Garrick was across the airstrip and in the shack before he got turned around.

The man outside the shack was dead. As dead as a neat, round hole in the forehead could make him. The expression on his face was of stunned disbelief. A local villager from the looks of him, here simply to keep an eye on things.

After all, who would try to steal an airplane?

What to do next? Slade was a most formidable opponent. Even without a gun. With one, and a demonstrated willingness to use it, it was suicide to confront him head on. He'd have to delay his departure. Help was bound to come. Sooner or later, people at the mine would realize something unusual was going on here. Roxana would arrive soon and grab the first person she met to send for assistance. Perhaps he could damage the plane somehow, or block the airstrip?

His mind raced.

Poking quietly about the shack, he searched for a weapon of some kind. Nothing. Wait a minute! Maybe the dead guard carried a gun? He ducked outside to frisk the body. No, damn it! If the fellow had ever been armed, he wasn't now.

Slade crouched into view, bent under a load of gleaming artifacts. A large fuel drum stood upright by the door. Garrick leapt behind it. It was nearly empty and gave out a faint, hollow boom when his knee touched it.

Slade stopped in mid stride. His quick, grey eyes located the shadow behind the drum.

The artifacts hit the ground with a clatter. Sunlight glinted off metal as he whipped out his gun. Even as Garrick dove around the corner.

"Crack!"

Few things are less accurate than a light hand gun snapping a shot at a laterally moving target. The bullet pinged harmlessly into the dirt.

"Garrick, is that you, boy?"

A corner of the plywood siding had worked loose on the shack. Through the hole, Garrick watched his old friend glance anxiously toward the mine. That was the second shot. The plane's engine throbbed noisily. Too much noise. He had to get away.

"Better give it up, Slade."

Slade craned his head, trying to see around the shack. "You surprise me, Garry. I underestimated you." He edged toward the corner as he spoke. Garrick moved farther away. "How'd you ever get out of that cave?"

"You're not gonna make it. You'll never get that plane off the ground."

"Tell you what, soldier. There's a pile of money over there. Enough for us both. How's that sound? C'mon, buddy, let's haul ass outta here. You and me together."

Keep him talking. Stall him. "Where'd we go? It can't be easy to sell that kinda stuff. What've you got in mind?"

No answer. Garrick's eye darted back to the hole. Slade was gone.

Run for it! The alfalfa field! Too late!

"Well, well, soldier–now look at the mess you've gotten yourself into."

Lips white with rage, Slade swept in from the rear. His hands were empty, the gun out of sight. He came in swiftly, in that shuffle of his. Ready this time, Garrick took the kick on the outside of his thigh, protecting his groin. Pain shot up and down his leg, but he stayed on his feet.

Picking a spot behind Slade's head, he drove his fist at it. A smashing blow with everything he had behind it. It never landed.

He wound up in the dirt, humming between his ears and little sparkles before his eyes. Sensing rather than seeing the foot coming again, he bucked and heaved, dodging desperately. He got to his feet and stood there swaying, his nose at a peculiar angle, dripping blood.

Although an inch or two shorter than Slade, he was wider across the shoulders and a good twenty pounds heavier. Get in close, he told himself, wrestle him to the ground, then hang on until someone arrived.

Head lowered, hands hooked, he rushed in. Slade was sinewy, strong, slippery. They wrestled around to the front of the shack and fell over the drum.

A bomb went off inside Garrick's head!

When he awoke, the last of the treasure was going in through the cargo door of the plane. A mist hung before his eyes. He shook his head angrily to chase it away.

Slade was laughing. Shutting the cargo door, he ran around to the front of the plane. He'd beat them all. He was home free!

On hands and knees Garrick observed the plane swing around and taxi toward the end of the airstrip.

No! By God, no!

Stumbling, falling, he chased the plane, rolling the big drum in front of him.

When Slade got turned around and ready, the drum and Garrick were planted in his way.

In a fury, Slade leaped from the cockpit. He aimed the gun. "Get the fuck outta there or I'll kill you!"

With a stubborn, exhausted shake of his head, Garrick sank down by the drum.

"Move! Now! Or you're dead!" Slade's face looked wild. He shot a glance toward the mine, then back to Garrick.

But he still didn't pull the trigger.

Why doesn't he shoot? Why doesn't he just kill me and go? Slumped behind the barrel's flimsy protection, the answer came to Garrick in a rush.

"Your clip is empty," he said slowly, piecing things together. "That's why you don't shoot. And that's why you didn't use the gun in the cave. You didn't want to waste the few rounds you had." He forced out a laugh, spitting blood to do so. "An empty gun and a plane you can't get into the air."

Slade didn't need a gun. Garrick saw him shuffle gracefully forward, feet flashing, and knew what was coming. He struggled to his feet to take his beating.

After being knocked down a half-dozen times, he lost count. The blood in his eyes blinded him, and because of the humming in his ears, he couldn't hear very well. But he did hear Slade laugh one last time. He dug the blood from his eyes. The drum was above him, raised high in Slade's hands.

Garrick didn't plan it. It was a simple coiling and uncoiling of his body. The springlike reaction of a human body rebelling against further maltreatment. Legs curling into the tummy in a protective ball, then striking up and out against the tormentor.

The drum was crashing downwards when it met his feet whip-lashing up. It caught Slade under the chin. Arms wind-milling furiously, he lurched backwards.

The propeller caught his left arm first. Ruby droplets spattered the plane's windshield, quickly becoming a richer mix as his head was sliced into by the whirling blade.

There was a mangled sound from him, and it was all over. The breeze of the prop-wash, the hum of the engine, and his own tiredness, put Garrick to sleep.

~ * ~

Someone was tugging him awake. Slender hands cradled his battered head. He tried to sit up, but couldn't.

"Don't try to sit up. Just lay there." Roxana began to cry. "Oh, you fool. You bloody fool. Look at you. Oh, darling, just look at you. Wait. A car from the mine is heading this way. Lie here, darling. I'll go see."

He was able to hear now. "Roxie...."

"Don't you move," she sobbed. "Don't you dare try to move."

He clawed one eye open to watch her go. She had thrown aside her limp, was running as fast as she could, going with knees high. Running to get help for him. Good, brave girl! He would tell her how proud he was of her when she got back.

Her bad leg gave out on some loose gravel at the edge of the airstrip. She went sprawling, but got right back up again and kept on running, her long, black hair bouncing off her shoulders in the high, clean sunlight.

About the Author

The author, now retired, claims to have misspent his youthful years wandering the globe in vagabond, gypsy fashion. "I had a severe case of wanderlust," he says. This first hand knowledge of far off places and foreign cultures serves as material for the books he writes. His suspenseful adventure stories will have a special appeal to those readers, like himself, who prefer their escapism set in an exotic locale and back-grounded by an open sky. He enjoys the outdoors of Canada's Niagara region where he lives, and reads and writes.

Kindred Passage

In the 1960s while visiting central Africa, Ken Mallory uncovers intriguing information surrounding his great-grandfather, Lucas Lindsay, who fought in the Barotseland Civil War of a century earlier. Delving deeper into the puzzle, Ken begins to identify with Lucas, setting to rest agonizing problems from his own recent past. Through the eyes of these two young men, different generations of the same family, Kindred Passage views the native wars of the 1860s, along with Africa's post-colonial era. Although living one hundred years apart, the similar dilemmas the Zambezi River country and its people impose on both men underscore the basically changeless nature of Africa.